Pride

HILTON JONES

Copyright © 2025 Peter H Jones

All rights reserved.

The characters and events portrayed in this book are fictitious. Any similarity to real persons living or dead is coincidental and not intended by the author.

No part of this book may be reproduced, or stored in a retrieval system, or transmitted in any form or by any means, electronic, mechanical, photocopying, recording or otherwise, without express permission of the publisher.

ISBN: 9798264435355

Independently published.

ACKNOWLEDGMENTS

I am eternally grateful for the assistance and encouragement of my wife Rosemary when I am writing a story. She doesn't realise how much her interest helps the story along.

Assistance of a different kind comes from Rebecca Baskerville, who reads and comments from the point of view of a librarian.

I am indebted to both these ladies.

I am grateful also to my readers, many of whom I have met. Your interest and comments keep me going.

Thanks also to my son, Dale, whose expertise was invaluable.

Other books by Hilton Jones.

SCARLET FEATHER

Hugh Evans in his first adventure against an insurgent group in rural Wales.

LANDSLIDE

Hugh Evans meets a face from the past who needs some help. He becomes involved in a gang war as murders, money laundering and people smuggling are uncovered before he can return home to Wales.

TO WHOM IT MAY CONCERN

A whodunnit set in Cheshire in which DI Nick Price unravels a web of secrets to reveal the killer.

THE LOCK-UP

DI Nick Price is again facing a family mystery in which a suspect leaves the country and a smuggling ring is uncovered.

GREED

A murdered teacher in the woods leads DI Nick Price into the world of people smuggling and funeral directors in his attempts to find the killer.

Pride: The excessive love of one's own excellence; to take all the credit for one's accomplishments.

Pope Gregory I (540-604)

Pride goeth before a fall: A proverb meaning that excessive pride or arrogance will inevitably lead to a downfall or failure. From Proverbs 16:18 *Pride goeth before destruction and an haughty spirit before a fall.*

PROLOGUE

The humming filled the darkened room, echoing from the stone walls of the one-time chapel, now the shrine for the Odonian Church, whose devotees stood in rows with heads bowed. The humming changed imperceptibly to chanting, a haunting, mediæval sound which blended into the organ notes as the instrument's volume increased in a crashing crescendo. Then silence. Not a breath. Not a shuffle. It was as if the world had stopped turning. For the worshippers, it had. They waited for The Pastor to speak.

A spotlight suddenly cut through the gloom, illuminating The Pastor on the platform at the front, facing his congregation of followers.

'Cassie Morgan! Step forward into the light,'

A young girl, no more than fourteen years old, walked tearfully to where another spotlight had lit up a small dais at the side of the platform.

'Turn. Face your judges,' The Pastor commanded.

Reluctantly, she turned.

'Confess!'

'I…I…can't,' was her tearful response.

'Confess!' It was louder this time.

'N…no, I can't'

'Confess,' he shouted.

The congregation joined in.

'Confess. Confess. Confess,' they repeated, their chant starting quietly and rising as they went on until the room reverberated with the sound. Cassie was beaten. The Pastor raised his hands and the chanting ceased.

'Well, child?'

Cassie dried her wet cheeks with the sleeve of her cardigan.

'I…I…' She looked from side to side but no help was forthcoming, from her parents in the front row, from her siblings alongside them, no-one. She took a deep breath.

'I took some sweets.'

'Try again. Confess.'

She snuffled as she plucked up courage.

'I stole some sweets.'

'What does the Bible say about this?'

'Thou shalt not steal.'

'So should you be punished?'

'But I paid for them after.'

'Too late. It was only after you took them home. Should you be punished?'

'Yes.'

A disapproving moan filled the room as all present took in the serious event, followed by a communal chant of 'Thief, thief, thief, thief.,' her parents' voices clearly among the loudest in their condemnation.

Her impulsive snatch had been noticed by an eagle-eyed shopkeeper and had been reported to her parents. The shopkeeper had had no intention of taking matters any further, considering that the parents would deal with what he thought was a mild transgression. But the parents, as members of the Odonian Church, felt bound to report it to The Pastor. This was the result.

Cassie started to get off the dais, but The Pastor stopped her.

'Your punishment will be as follows. You will stand there where everyone can see you, for the rest of the convocations in this month, so that we can all be reminded of what a thief looks like. No member of this faith will speak to you for the next four weeks, and your parents will restrict their words to instructions only.'

Cassie knew that rules were meant to be obeyed and

that The Pastor was merciless in his punishments. Not physically, but ridicule and isolation were effective punishments. Some adults had paid large amounts of money for their misdemeanours, in addition to the regular donation of a percentage of their income for the upkeep of the church.

The Pastor then continued, 'We now have a pleasant duty. Two new members are with us today. We will welcome them in the usual way. Step forward, Toby and Hannah, and stand at the front.'

A middle-aged couple moved forward and The Pastor came down and hugged them both, uttering words of welcome. The congregation followed suit, making a big fuss of welcoming the newcomers, with much laughter and jollification, hugging and hand-shaking, all of which added to Cassie's feelings of isolation, standing alone on the dais, completely disengaged from the proceedings. In a crowd but ignored by its members. The loneliest place in the world. She would never steal again.

ONE

Crisp autumn leaves crunched under DI Nick Price's feet as he walked across the pavement in the city of Chester. The gusty wind tugged at his hair as he pulled his coat tighter around him. Impatient drivers honked their horns, the cacophony echoing in the cavern of tall buildings. The source of their frustration was a police car parked at right angles across their usual lane, forcing them to take an impromptu detour to find another route into the city. A constable waved his arms urgently to move on those who slowed down to see what was the cause of the redirection. The wind plucked at the pages of DS Dave Martin's notebook as he attempted to make notes of the situation before him.

Nick turned and looked up at the building behind them, its glass front rearing up to four floors, reflecting the buildings and traffic opposite. Inside the door he could make out people gazing through the glass, some hugging, some weeping, all being shepherded by a yellow-coated constable. Other constables were already approaching the nearby bystanders on the pavement, taking witness statements from those who had seen it happen. Many had, of course, come to look purely out of a ghoulish curiosity. The blue-and-white police tape and a couple of constables held back the crowd of gawpers, some of whom were busy with their mobile phones, recording the grisly scene.

The tape was lifted for one person to come through in her white coveralls.

'Morning, Anu,' Nick said.

Anuradha Rintoul was the Forensic Pathologist, best in the country Nick reckoned, who had arrived very swiftly from her office at Thornhill Hospital, ten miles away.

'Morning Nick, Dave.' she greeted them, keen to get to work.

Nick looked up at the building again

'That's where he came from, up there. I can't see any broken windows but we haven't been up there yet,' he said.

'I don't think I'll be long here,' Anu said. She looked down at the young man lying face down in a pool of blood on the pavement, his smart business suit ruined by the blood which had spattered out as he hit the flagstones.

'Cause of death is fairly obvious,' she said, 'unless he was dead before he fell. My examination should tell us that. Why he fell is another question. That will be up to you to find out. I'll examine the body at the morgue, looking for signs of a fight, perhaps. Was he pushed? Drugs or alcohol might indicate suicide, or not. So there's work to do. I'll let you know what I find.'

'We'll leave you in peace then. Thanks Anu,' Nick said and led the way into the building.

The crowd of onlookers within parted as Nick and Dave approached.

'Does any of you know who he is?' he asked the crowd in general.

'We all do. He worked with us.' A tall young man, neatly dressed, spoke up.

'And you are?'

'Stuart Reid. Office manager.'

'Well, Mr Reid, I'm Detective Inspector Nick Price and this is Detective Sergeant Dave Martin. We're from Cheshire Constabulary and we'll be conducting enquiries into this incident. It would be helpful if you could take your staff away from the front door now. I shall need to speak to everyone to establish what has happened here and why.'

'Very well, Inspector. Our offices are situated on the top floor' Reid explained, then turned to the group 'Right, everyone. You heard what the Inspector said. Back to the office and please, nobody leaves the building.' The group slowly turned and some made for the lift, some for the stairs.

One young lady seemed reluctant to leave. She looked continually at the prostrate man on the pavement outside, twisting her handkerchief in her hands, on the verge of tears. Finally, the flood-gates opened and an older lady placed a comforting arm around her shoulders and guided her away, following the other staff members.

'Come along, Ellie. Let's get you back to the office. We all need some strong tea, at least,' she said and steered Ellie towards the lift.

Nick and Dave waited until the lift was free and rode up to the fourth floor, to be met, almost before they had come out of the lift, by a man who introduced himself as Neville Formstone. Nick introduced themselves.

'I'm Managing Director of Bertrand's. We're a Motor Dealership with outlets all over the country. You may have seen our adverts on television. Our Head Office is here in Chester. We have the whole of the top floor of this building. Staff of about forty. We're very busy preparing for a car show in Brussels in December so I hope you won't need to delay my team for long,'

'A lot depends on what I find, but rest assured, I won't delay them any longer than is necessary,' Nick said, as diplomatically as he could.

Neville glared. 'Very well, then. I'll leave you to it. I'm due at a presentation in ten minutes,' he said, consulting his wrist watch, and turned away to return to his office.

The reception office was next to Formstone's, set back in a small glass-fronted bay, halfway along a long corridor. A pot plant on a small table and a pair of small but comfortable chairs completed the furnishings and a press button on the counter invited callers to ring for attention. As they came out of the lift, Nick and Dave could see, to their left, that the corridor led to a small flight of stairs, with a range of office doors marked ACCOUNTS, SALES, HUMAN RESOURCES down one side with BOARDROOM, STORES and TOILETS on the other, plus two others marked PRIVATE. To their right, they had seen the two ladies from downstairs entering a door at the end, marked SHOW TEAM and followed them in.

They walked into a large room with half a dozen desks separated by low screens, forming a private area for each worker while still maintaining the team atmosphere. At the end of the room was a glass-fronted office, through the sides of which, Nick could see Stuart Reid, who looked up and beckoned the detectives into the room.

'Sorry I couldn't wait to bring you up,' he said. 'I've been inundated by phone calls since this happened, mostly from across the road, just nosiness. Added to which, we were doing interviews for an upcoming vacancy this morning. Ryan, the young man who fell, was one of the candidates. The other one was in the waiting room. I sent one of my staff to explain to him what had happened. Fortunately, he's quite happy to wait until we are ready to see him. Please, take a seat. We need to get on.'

Nick and Dave sat facing Stuart Reid across the desk. Dave already had his notebook out.

'First of all, I'd like you to tell me about your offices and the staff set-up here.' Nick began.

'In this office we have the Special Shows Team, a select group with marketing and organisational skills. The team leader is Caroline Paterson. She's been with the company from day one, when Mr Bertrand sold used cars from a small village filling station. There is nothing she doesn't know about the company. She is about to retire, hence the interviews this morning to appoint a replacement. The young man downstairs, Ryan Palmer, and Ellie Mason were our stand reps.'

'Stand reps?' Dave required an explanation.

'Yes, they represented the company at all the prestigious shows in this country and abroad. They manned our stand.'

'Abroad?' Dave was surprised.

'Yes. The motor show at Brussels in Belgium is our next target. It's in December. Dubai is another of our targets. And the Geneva Motor Show, of course. The biggest is in Los Angeles. We have that in mind for next year.'

'Impressive,' Dave said.

'We have to go where the money is. We sell expensive cars. But back to the staff. Ryan and Ellie were our most experienced and knowledgeable members. Also there's John Cooke, who organises all the transport for each show and Susan Taylor who organises the accommodation for reps and drivers.'

'A happy team, are they?' Nick asked.

'Yes, they work well together. In fact, the young lady who was so upset is…was…Ryan's girlfriend, Ellie. It was going to be difficult enough to re-arrange the team…'

'How so?'

'With Caroline about to retire, Ryan would have been a perfect replacement, but we have to advertise these vacancies. And we would need to replace Ryan on the stand. Hopefully, the other candidate would be able to fill that role. But Ellie might not fancy a change of partner, especially for the foreign travel involved, so we could lose her as well.'

'Has Ryan upset anyone in the other departments of the company?'

'I wouldn't have thought so. He was highly popular. Everyone could see that he was destined for bigger things. He will be, as they say, greatly missed.'

'How would he have gained access to the outside world? I didn't see any doors or windows in the front of the building.'

'There aren't any. There is the roof, of course. That's the only place he could have jumped from.'

'Or been pushed,' Nick added. 'We have to consider all possibilities.'

'I can't think of anyone who would want to push

Ryan off a roof. And I can't think of any reason why he would want to jump. Could it have been an accident?'

'That's what we're here to find out, so can you take us up to the roof now?'

'Certainly'

'And is there a room which we could use to talk to the staff?'

'Yes. Follow me.'

He showed them to one of the unmarked rooms down the corridor, explaining to the staff as they passed through the outer office that the police would be wanting to speak to them all in turn. He asked Nick if they required anything, which they didn't.

Stuart Reid led the way along the corridor to the short flight of stairs, at the top of which stood a door with a 'Push to open' sign on it. As Reid raised his hand to open the door, Nick snapped 'Don't touch it!'. Reid lowered his hand and said 'Fingerprints. Of course. Didn't think. Is it OK for me to go back to the office now? I could be needed there.'

'Of course. We'll know where to find you if we need you.'

Dave pulled on his latex gloves and opened the door and stepped out into the wind. They walked around the roof, closely inspecting the surface, especially above the point where they worked out had been Ryan's point of departure.

'There's no scuff marks of any sort,' Nick said.

'So no signs of a struggle.' Dave said, 'and the handrail is intact, not bent in any way.'

'Perhaps it was accidental.' Nick thought aloud.

'Why on earth would he come out here?'

'Pressure of the interview, perhaps. Needed a breath of fresh air to calm his nerves. Wandered about. Got too close to the side. Sudden gust of wind caught him off balance? Is that possible, Dave?'

'Perhaps the fingerprints on the door will give us more to go on.'

They left the roof and Nick texted DC Rob Davidson, Scene of Crime Officer, to include the roof in his areas of interest and to have blue and white tape put across the corridor leading to the roof door.

Back in the warmth indoors, Nick and Dave checked out the room they had been allocated. There was a hurriedly-prepared notice indicating POLICE INTERVIEWS already sellotaped to the door. Four chairs stood around a table in the centre of the room. Four glasses and a carafe of water completed the furnishings. They prepared to question the staff.

TWO

'Let's start with Caroline Paterson,' Nick said.

Dave collected her from the office.

She wore a navy-blue trouser suit with a white blouse and a minimum of make-up tastefully applied. Her nails, polished red, were professionally manicured. Her hands showed no sign of wrinkles, the result of hand care over the years, in fact, the only concession to age was her hair, which was wavy, short and grey. Her slim figure was that of a younger woman. She presented herself in what she felt was the image of the company.

'Hello. Caroline Paterson?'

'Yes, but please call me Caroline,' she said.

'Please take a seat. I'm Detective Inspector Nick Price and this is Detective Sergeant Dave Martin of Cheshire Constabulary. What can you tell us about what was happening here this morning, please?'

'Before the … er…?' She wafted a hand to indicate her inability to find a term which, at this early stage, was honest without being either brutal or casual.

'Yes, please.'

'Everyone was in on time.'

'Which was?'

'Eight thirty.'

'We had a meeting in Mr Reid's office at nine fifteen. We were all involved, except Ryan. He was due to be interviewed at ten o'clock…'

'For your job, I heard.'

'Yes. It's such a tragedy. None of us can believe it.'

'So did he stay in the office until called for interview?'

'Yes, although he left the office just before nine thirty. I saw him through the glass. I even gave him a thumbs up as he left.'

'How did he seem this morning?'

'His usual self. Serious, yes, but I put that down to the impending interview. Otherwise, quite normal.'

'Not nervous? Confident?'

'Now you mention it, he may have felt the weight of the promise of a new job.'

'How do you mean, promise?'

'You know what they say, 'It's always the insider who gets the job'. He may have thought it might not happen. If the outside candidate was successful, for instance, he'd be letting us down in his eyes. There's been a lot of assumption in the office about this interview since the job was advertised.'

'Did he get on well with the team?'

'Yes, perfectly well. He was showing up well as a leader, which is why he was the prime candidate for my job.'

'What about his relationships with staff in other departments?'

'There was never any trouble. No complaints. Nothing untoward. He just got on with everybody.'

Caroline's description of Ryan was repeated by John and Susan in their written statements, which Nick skimmed through before handing the sheets to Dave.

'Too good to be true, would you say?' Nick commented, followed by 'Let's have Ellie in next, please, Dave.'

Ellie, red-eyed from crying, sat demurely with a fresh, dry, handkerchief screwed up in her hand. She was a pretty young lady, mid-twenties, with long brown hair neatly tied in a ponytail. Its length surprised Nick, as it reached down to her waist. Dressed in a business suit of grey with a red blouse she was normally stunning to look at, but today she had, understandably, lost her sparkle.

Nick was sympathetic.

'It's a terrible thing that's happened today,' he began, 'Have you any thoughts about what might have caused it?'

'No,' she whispered, fighting back the tears.

'He was your boyfriend, wasn't he?'

'Yes. We were going to be married next year.'

'Was there anything that he was worried about?'

'Such as?'

'Money? Work? The interview? Getting married?'

Ellie took a deep breath. Thinking about their now non-existent wedding took some courage on her part.

'None of those things. We're both well-paid here. If there was anything at work I would know. We worked closely together. He wasn't worried about the interview, he looked forward to it. It would mean promotion. And we were…we…' Nick could see that she was wanting to say that they were in love, but realised that that dream was now impossible, so he pressed on.

'So then is there anyone you can think of who would want to do him harm?' he asked.

'No!' Such an unlikely thought had never entered her mind.

Nick sympathised with her as the interview concluded and let her go back to the office. He turned to Dave.

'No progress so far, Dave. Nobody has mentioned any problems with other departments. Perhaps we'll need to interview others as time goes on, but nothing is pointing us in any direction at the moment.'

'What about the other interviewee?' Dave asked. 'He must be still here, and he was in the building when it happened.'

'Good point. Go and ask Stuart Reid if he's still about.'

Dave left and Nick mulled over what he knew so far. All he knew was that a man with no enemies, or money worries, or relationship worries, suddenly hit the pavement. Mental health was a minefield. What goes on in people's minds to lead them to such tragic results is a mystery that no-one could fathom. Even those close to them have no clue as to the thought processes which led to them doing awful things. Nick was coming down in favour of suicide as a reason for Ryan's death.

The door opened and Dave returned, in the company of a young man.

'This is Daniel Thompson. He's just finished his interview, which went on despite the tragic circumstances. I managed to find him before he left.

Daniel stepped forward, hand outstretched, to shake hands with Nick.

'Call me Daniel,' he said. 'And you are?'

'Detective Inspector Price of Cheshire Constabulary. Have a seat, Mr Thompson.' Nick was wary of anyone who feigned this hail-fellow-well-met approach to give the impression of presumed innocence.

They sat and Dave took out his notebook.

'What can you tell me about this morning's events, Mr Thompson.'

Daniel smoothed his hands on his light grey business suit and straightened his red tie, which contrasted nicely with his pink shirt. He looked Nick in the eye.

'Well, Inspector Price,' he failed to keep the sarcasm out of his voice, 'I arrived here at nine o'clock and they put me in the waiting room where your colleague found me. And I waited there until they were ready for the interview. There was no offer of tea or coffee; there was a couple of last month's magazines to read. Pretty shabby treatment, I thought. Perhaps the job was not for me after all, but when the office manager came in and told me what had happened, I could see why, so I could understand. Now I've been interviewed it seems as though I'll get the job.'

'Congratulations,' Nick said. 'So you didn't come out

of the room at all until called for?'

'Exactly. Not at all. Not even a comfort break. I was glad to get it all over, though.'

'Why? Was there any doubt?'

'Not really. I was looking forward to the managerial post. I knew they had a good team here and I thought that the internal candidate was likely to get it. If he had, then I might have been offered his job as he moved up. I am a salesman in a Mercedes dealership in Liverpool, Burke's of Anfield, so it would have been demotion to be a stand rep. This will be my dream job. Team manager, then office manager then on to bigger things.'

'Good salesman, are you?' Dave asked.

'The best. Top salesman in the company for six months running. Team of ten. Special Award certificate from Mercedes last year.'

'Impressive,' said Dave.

'Nobody else in the North West region has done any better. Something to be proud of. On top of which, I devised the slogan which is on the sticker in the rear window of every car that goes out.'

'What's that?' Dave asked.

'Burke's for Mercs. Sometimes these advertising people have no idea what sells a car. Catchy slogan, I said. Jonathan Burke, the previous owner, loved it, so they had to use it, and the new owner kept it on. On the cars. On the TV advert. In the papers. It takes a salesman to sell cars.' His triumphant smile showed how proud he was of his achievements.

'Indeed,' Nick said. intent on bringing the conversation back to the matter in hand, 'But you stayed in the waiting room all the time?'

'Yes, and I didn't know what had happened until they apologised for the delay when they called me in for the interview.'

'I think we can let you go, now, Mr Thompson. I have

no more questions.' Nick said.

'Thank you. Goodbye to you both. I hope you get to the bottom of this one,' and he was gone.

'He was keen to get out, wasn't he?' Dave said, noting the speed of Daniel's departure.

'So will I be,' Nick said. 'Come on, Dave. It's been a long, unproductive day. I think we can write this one off as suicide. Traffic's building up already.'

They left, joining the queue of office workers waiting for the lift.

'I'm glad I don't have to do this every day,' Dave said.

'What?'

'Sitting in an office and joining the rush hour. Lemmings come to mind.'

'Me too. Ah, here's the lift. Ground floor for us.'

Meanwhile, Daniel Thompson was on his way home, quietly patting himself on the back for a job well done. A few lies here and there had always got him out of trouble. Even in Primary School. 'It wasn't me, miss,' together with a pleading look from his blue eyes had been enough to confirm his innocence of whatever misdemeanour had taken place.

His agile mind had come up with excuses which always favoured Daniel Thompson. At his mother's funeral, he had arrived at the graveside with an ornate urn to hold the flowers he had brought. There was universal approval from the family, but the other mourners did not recognise the urn, which had found its way across the graveyard from another grave.

At work, his skill in shifting the blame resulted in others being dismissed, though it had been Daniel who had phoned customers of rival firms to cancel appointments. His sales patter invariably rubbished those rival firms with phrases such as 'Are they still in business?' and 'I think they've recovered from their financial troubles by now.'

He was very proud of the parting shot from his

previous employer when he left to join Burkes Mercedes dealership. 'So it'll be Burkes for Mercs from now on then?' his boss had said. Daniel smiled.

'I can use that,' he thought, as he closed the door behind him.

Now he had a foot in the door at Bertrands. 'What havoc can I wreak here?' he asked himself, as he looked forward to his smart, business-like appearance and his blue eyed innocence working in his favour. He was particularly proud of his performance in his first police interview.

So far, so good.

THREE

Ellie Mason had been looking forward to marriage. The last she had seen of her fiancé was when he left the office to go up to the roof to calm himself for the interview. He looked cheerful, returning Caroline's thumbs-up with one of his own and a smile and a wink towards Ellie through the glass as he made his way out of the office.

Theirs had been something of a whirlwind relationship. Ryan had arrived about twelve months previously to take over when his predecessor, Stuart Reid, had been promoted to Office Manager. Ellie and Stuart had been the company's stand reps for a couple of years, travelling at home and abroad to prestigious motor shows. The job was not the only thing which Ryan took over from Stuart. Until his promotion, Stuart had been romantically close to Ellie. Everyone thought it was a match made in heaven, but Ryan's charm and good looks prised Ellie away from Stuart. It must have hurt Stuart deeply to see his ex-girlfriend working so closely with his successor. However, he managed to hide his disappointment and carried out his duties as Office Manager without any sign of rancour towards the couple. There had been hope of reconciliation a couple of months previously when he met Ellie in the city centre. It was a chance meeting one evening which had developed into a chat over a drink. One drink led to another, culminating in a visit to Stuart's flat overlooking the canal for a night-cap. Their relationship had not, however, been rekindled.

Now, in the light of Ryan's fall, Ellie felt empty. Her enthusiasm for the job had gone. While she attempted to soldier on, she wondered whether Stuart would come to Belgium with her. Caroline was capable of looking after the office while Stuart was away.

The CEO had had a word with Ellie earlier in the afternoon. He said that he was interested in her well-being. She was looking 'peaky' today he said. Understandably so.

She had been ill, too. Was she able to carry on today after this tragic incident? She must take time off if she needed it. He would quite understand. She had told him that time would put her right. She was shaken, of course, but there was too much work to do, especially now Ryan would not be there to help her. At this point she had burst into tears once more and Mr Formstone had let her return to the office.

Ellie had told Caroline Paterson that she would work late that night, despite Caroline's insistence that she should go home and rest. The work needed to be done, the visit to the Brussels Motor Show was looming large on the calendar and she had lost a lot of time, what with the morning meeting and then the aftermath of Ryan's fall.

Long telephone conversations with her mother and Ryan's parents had also eaten into her time, then there was that long interview with Mr Formstone, so it had been late afternoon when she had finally found a chance to check her phone for texts and emails. The phone had been on 'Silent' during the meeting, Stuart always insisted on no interruptions, and she had no reason to check it during the day afterwards.

It was five-thirty before Ellie finally had the office to herself. She released her hair from the confines of the ponytail, letting it hang down on either side of her face. She checked her phone for texts and emails. Then, as she read, she let out a loud cry of 'Oh! No!'. She flung her mobile into her drawer in frustration, slamming the drawer shut as tears flowed down her face. The knowledge her phone contained would not bring Ryan back, but it would be important in helping the police in their investigations. She now knew that Ryan had not jumped from the roof and there was only one person who could have pushed him.

That idle moment, late in the day, had produced the shocking news.

She worked on quietly for a couple of hours, her mind not entirely on the work. Missing Ryan's presence, his jokes, his infectious laugh. Then the door creaked slightly.

FOUR

Next morning, Nick and Dave were seated once more in Stuart Reid's office. They had responded to Caroline's urgent call telling them that Ellie had been found dead when they arrived at the office earlier.

There was an atmosphere of shock in the office as the other staff had been removed, away from the crime scene, and were working in another room, though very little work would be done today, Nick thought as he watched the Scene of Crime team examining the area around the desk and the slumped body of the young lady. Anu and her forensic team had examined Ellie's body, had taken their photographs and would supervise the removal to the mortuary at Thornhill.

Stuart seemed relaxed as Nick began the questioning.

'Who knew that Ellie was working late last evening?'

'Just the staff in this department, I should think. She told Caroline, but we all heard her.'

'Is it normal for staff to work late?'

'It happens from time to time, as the work demands. It doesn't happen very often, though.'

'Who found the body this morning?'

'Caroline was in first, I followed her up from the car park. She came up in the lift, I walked up the stairs.'

'Any reason?'

'I try to keep fit. The exercise is good for me, or so my doctor says. Caroline met me with the news as I reached the top of the stairs. We came in, saw what had happened and phoned 999 right away.'

'And what had happened did you think?'

'We didn't know. We thought she might have come in early and had a heart attack or something. Young people do have heart attacks, don't they?'

'Did you touch her?'

'Yes. Just her arm. It was so cold. As though she'd

been dead a long time. Not consistent with coming in early we thought.'

'We?'

'Caroline and me. We set about moving John and Susan to another room. Most of their work is on-line, so there was no need for them to come into this office. They are in the other room temporarily. So is Caroline, as it happens.'

There was a tap on the door, followed by a constable putting his head into the room.

'Excuse me, Inspector. There's a Mr Formstone wanting to come in...'

Formstone pushed past him.

'Of course I'm wanting to come in. It's my office, after all. What's all this blue and white tape around the place, anyway? I thought you'd finished with that nonsense yesterday.'

Nick stood up and faced the CEO.

'It's because we have another crime scene to be protected until we finish our investigations.'

'The crime scene was on the roof, not in this office.'

'I'm afraid it is, sir. One of your staff, Ellie Mason, was found dead here this morning. In the absence of any knowledge of how she died, it is being treated as a crime scene until we can prove otherwise. The constable will escort you out again. Please do not touch anything in the office as you leave. I promise to come and advise you of progress as soon as I have anything to report.'

'But...'

'Constable.' Nick nodded his head to indicate the door.

'This way, sir.' The constable was at pains to keep the smile off his face. He doubted whether Formstone had been ejected like that before.

Nick tuned back to Stuart.

'So, Mr Reid, from what you described yesterday as a happy team, we now have two of them dead in suspicious circumstances. It's hard to believe that a suicide and a heart attack could happen so close together, especially to a couple who were engaged to be married. There must be a connection. I don't believe in coincidence. Do you think there could be a connection?'

'I must say I'm mystified,' Stuart Reid said. 'They seemed to be so much in love – with each other and, in a different way, with the job. I can't imagine what has happened in their lives to cause this train of events.'

'Let's look at Ellie first. How could someone enter the building after hours? I take it that it's locked at night.'

'Yes. And there's a night janitor in the reception area downstairs. George is an ex-policeman. Very thorough. Nobody gets past him.'

Dave made a note to talk to George. No doubt later in the day. He'd surely be at home and fast asleep this morning.

'What about CCTV?' Nick went on.

'There isn't any. When Mr Bertrand took on the lease of the whole building, he insisted on no CCTV. He reckoned it was not necessary. The only way in is through the front door and reception is manned twenty-four hours a day. There are no opening windows. We have air-conditioning. There are a couple of exit doors at the back of the building, but they are opened from inside with a push bar. There are no handles on the outside.'

'You and Caroline were in first, you said.'

'Yes.'

'And she found Ellie's body?'

'Yes. Just before I arrived at the top of the stairs.'

'Did either of you touch Ellie?'

'I told you, I touched her arm. It was cold. Very cold.' He shuddered slightly at the memory. 'But we didn't attempt to move her in any way.'

'Who was last out yesterday evening?'

'That would be me. I'm usually last out. First in, last out. Sets a good example for staff punctuality. But last night,

Ellie was at her desk when I left, so I suppose I was last but one. You get the picture.'

'Did Ellie seem all right when you left?'

'Yes, allowing for the kind of day she'd had. Refused to go home and rest. She said she would be better working. Brave girl. She and Ryan worked on things together and she would be looking at emails and letters that he had written, dealing with phone calls from people he had spoken to, explaining time and again what had happened. I don't think I could have done it like she did. Perhaps it all got too much for her. Perhaps it was a heart attack, after all.'

'We'll see.' Nick said. 'Let's go on to Ryan. Where were you when he fell?'

'I was in our morning briefing.'

'In this office?'

'Yes.'

'Did you see Ryan leaving at any time?'

'Yes. I thought he was going either to the toilet to get comfortable before his interview or out to the roof for a breath of fresh air.'

'Was that normal?'

'Yes. As I explained, we have no opening windows and air-conditioning can get oppressive. We often popped out there to get a change of air, even on a cold day.'

'So you didn't think it was odd in any way?'

'Not at all. I noticed that Caroline gave him a thumbs-up as he went.'

'That will be enough for now. I may need to see you again. We'll go to see Mrs Paterson. Our room is still available, I take it?'

'Yes. The other staff are sharing the accounts office at the far end of the corridor.'

'Thank you,' Nick said and he and Dave left. Nick entered their allocated room and dispatched Dave to the accounts office to collect Caroline Paterson.

'Good morning, Caroline. A sad morning indeed.

This must have been a shock for you.' Nick said as Caroline entered.

'Yes,' she said, dabbing a tear without ruining her make-up, which was as immaculate as the day before.

'I'd like you to help me get the picture of what happens here. Who would have been last out of the office yesterday?'

'Normally it's Mr Reid, but last night it would have been Ellie. She was busy at her desk when I left. She said she needed to work late after all the delays yesterday. It was a way to keep busy'

'And what about this morning? Who was first in?'

'That was me, today. Normally it's Mr Reid. He likes to think his punctuality sets a good example for the staff, but I'm not so sure.'

'So it wasn't Mr Reid today?'

'No. It would have been. But as I drove in, I could see him across the car park. He seemed to be waiting for someone or something, because as soon as he saw me, he walked across and we entered the building together. I came up in the lift and he walked up as usual. Keeping fit, he likes to think. By the time he reached the top of the stairs, I had been into the office and found poor Ellie. I rushed out to tell him.'

'How did he seem when you found the body?'

'Upset, I would say. He had his handkerchief out, blowing his nose etcetera. Why men can't have a good weep and get done with it, I don't know.'

'He didn't seem as upset as that when Ryan was on the pavement.'

'No. But then he wasn't that fond of Ryan.'

'Fond?'

'Yes. He was certainly fond of Ellie. They were an item until Ryan came to work with us last year. Stuart took it very hard when Ellie dropped him and took up with Ryan. I think he still had hopes that they might break up, but they were dashed by talk of the wedding next year.'

'How was Ellie during the meeting? Nervous on Ryan's behalf?'

Caroline thought for a moment.

'She seemed subdued. I mentioned it and she told me that she had mixed feelings about the interview. Of course she would be pleased for Ryan if he was promoted, but that would mean that she would end up with a new partner on the stand. That was her worry.'

'This was during the meeting?' Nick asked. 'Ellie told me that Stuart didn't like interruptions in his meetings.'

'He doesn't. This was when he went out to the accounts department to check some figures. He was away for ten minutes. He was a little breathless when he came back, So much for your keep fit regime I thought.'

Dave looked up at Nick. He didn't have to speak. They both realised that Stuart had not mentioned this departure from his normal routine. He would need a good reason to explain the omission.

FIVE

Anuradha Rintoul inherited her looks from her Indian mother, an attractive combination of jet black hair and flashing eyes which would have brightened any Bollywood film. Her analytical brain came from her Scottish father, an eminent Edinburgh cardiologist. She had grown up wanting to follow him into surgery but had developed into one of the finest pathologists in the country. The fact that she had settled in Cheshire was a boon to Cheshire Constabulary as she consistently and promptly communicated her conclusions to investigators, added to which she discovered the tiniest, seemingly insignificant, features of the bodies that she examined.

Such was the case with Ellie Mason's body, as she explained to Nick Price, who had driven over to Thornhill to visit her mortuary.

'Well, Anu, any idea of the cause of death?'

'Strangulation.' Anu began, as Nick viewed the body.

Nick was puzzled. His experience of looking at corpses, while not as clinical as Anu's was still extensive, and he saw no signs of strangulation.

'I don't see any ligature marks. Surely a cord or rope would leave a mark?'

'True.' Anu was happy to let him struggle for an explanation.

'There are no finger or thumb bruises on the windpipe either, so it was not manual.'

'Also true.'

'So how can you conclude that she was strangled?'

'Petechiae.'

'What are petechiae? That's a new name for me.'

'Pinpoint haemorrhages in the skin. They are like tiny bruises that are around the neck, as you can see, caused by pressure on the skin.'

'Does that give us a clue as to the method used in the attack? If not a cord or hands, what?' Nick asked.

'Not entirely. But the petechiae are only on the front of the throat. A ligature would leave them all around. They would appear where the hand would have been in the case of manual strangulation. So we have to look for other signs. For instance, there are bruises caused by fingers and thumbs here…' She pointed out finger marks on the front of the shoulders and turned the body to reveal the single thumb marks on the back. '…and there.'

'That suggests that she was held from behind,' Nick said.

'Yes. And she was sitting in her chair when we found her, so whoever did this was standing behind her. These bruises are quite deep, suggesting that she was held forcibly, possibly trying to break loose from the grip.'

'But that doesn't help us to work out how she was strangled.' Nick tried to picture the scene of Ellie, seated in her chair, with her killer behind the chair, holding her by the shoulders. His imagination stopped at that point.

'We also found a number of broken long hairs in her lap and a couple of single hairs across her throat, under her chin. I think that the killer used her long hair to strangle her, then placed it to hang back in its usual place.' Anu smiled as she finished.

'So,' Nick was thinking aloud, 'it sounds that the killer didn't come with the intention of killing her. He brought no weapons or tools. Were they discussing something which developed into an argument, he held her in the seat until the argument came to a climax. In temper or desperation or both, he grabbed the first thing that came to hand - her long hair - and pulled it across her throat.'

'That sounds extremely plausible. Certainly, you can work on that basis.'

'All we have to find out is what anybody would get into an argument about with Ellie' Nick concluded.

'Perhaps they were talking about her pregnancy,' Anu said with an impish smile on her face.

'Pregnancy?'

'Yes. Three months.'

'So Ryan would have been a daddy?'

'No. I've checked the DNA. It's not his.'

'I wonder whose, then?'

'I can't help you with that. I've nothing to compare it with. That's down to you. Perhaps one of your other suspects may be to blame.'

'It certainly gives me something to work on. Thanks, Anu.'

As Nick drove back into Chester, his thoughts led him to Stuart Reid. He'd been close to Ellie before Ryan arrived. Had he and Ellie had a fling three months ago? Did he kill Ryan out of jealousy and hoped that Ellie would come back to him? Did he go on to kill Ellie when she refused? Stuart would know how to get into the building after hours. Could George at the door be bribed? Did he ever leave reception? Nick was full of ideas when he reached the office. Of course, if Stuart were not the father, all this conjecture would be meaningless. A DNA swab from Stuart was necessary.

He walked into the office to find it a hive of activity and called everyone to a brief meeting to update them on his news.

'I've spoken to forensics this morning and it seems that Ellie Mason was strangled with her own hair. Those of you who have seen her will know that she had a waist-length pony-tail. It also appears that she was three months pregnant and, according to DNA, Ryan was not the father. That suggests to me that Stuart Reid is a prime suspect. He and Ellie were close at one time and there may have been some re-kindling of their relationship. Therefore, he is also now a suspect for Ryan's death on the grounds of jealousy. Obviously, we'll need more evidence, but we'll have him in for an interview. Does anyone else have anything to report?'

DC Rob Davidson got to his feet. He had been the Scene of Crime Officer at both incidents.

'Yes, I do.' he said.'

'Go ahead, Rob.'

'We have the mobile phones of both Ryan and Ellie. The digital team have opened them and they make interesting reading. On the morning of his death, Ryan texted Ellie to say that he had gone out to the roof for some fresh air and he had taken Daniel with him, to show him round. That was his last message. It was timed at about five minutes before he fell.'

'How do you know that?' Eamonn asked.

'The time of the text is in the phone, and fortunately, the overnight receptionist, night-watchman or whatever, George Smith, was leaving the building on his way home just as the body fell. As an ex-policeman, he noted the time. He knew it would be useful, important even.'

'Well done him,' Nick said. 'So this puts Daniel in the frame. He told me he hadn't left the waiting room. Obviously, he had. He *was* on the roof with Ryan and he lied to us. There must be a reason for that.'

'The time of the text is confirmed by Ellie's phone,' Rob went on. This also revealed a succession of texts in the past to Ellie from Stuart Reid. They seem to have been close at that time. He sounded desperate to get Ellie back. I'll put the detailed conversations in my report, but suffice it to say, it looks like they had one or two steamy encounters since they split up. He was begging her to dump Ryan and go back to him.'

'What was her reaction?' Dave asked.

'She kept him dangling, raising hopes then playing hard to get. It must have been frustrating for him. Some of his responses hinted at violence, both to Ryan and Ellie herself.'

'Such as?'

'I made a note of one or two. A mild one was *'When you go to Belgium, I'll book a one-way ticket for Ryan and you can leave him there.'* The worst one was last Friday. It read *'I feel like pushing Ryan under a bus. It would be easy in Chester.'*

'That certainly sounds as though he's getting desperate,' Dave observed.

I also fingerprinted the staff in Stuart Reid's team and the stairs and roof area. Stuart's prints were not on the door to the roof, just Ryan's and one other. No doubt, other staff used the roof from time to time, but with a staff of forty, I thought it best to wait until you had an opportunity to take Daniel Thompson's prints before checking the whole staff. But I did find Stuart's on the door-stop that they used to keep the door open while they were on the roof.'

'Good work, Rob. So we have two murders and two suspects to interview. Stuart Reid in respect of Ellie's death and Daniel Thompson in respect of Ryan's death. We'll need to go up to Liverpool to interview Daniel. I'll set up an interview room at Rose Hill. We also need a word with George Smith, we can do that tomorrow afternoon after seeing Stuart Reid. Liz, will you dig out what you can on either of the suspects, please. He closed the meeting and returned to his office.

He picked up the phone and rang DI Diane Coleman, his opposite number in Merseyside Police. Each police force had its geographical limits, but criminals did not, and there were many times when neighbouring forces needed to co-operate. This was one of those occasions.

'Hello, Diane. It's Nick Price.'

'Hi, Nick. Long time...'

'Yes. Too long, Diane. I'm looking for a favour.

'Go on.'

'We've had a couple of deaths in odd circumstances in Chester...'

'Is it the one I saw on the news last evening? Young man went off a roof.

'That's the one, then his girlfriend was found dead in her office this morning. so I need to interview a witness who lives in Liverpool and works at Burke's Car Dealership at Anfield. Do you have an interview room that I could borrow for an hour one day this week?'

'I'm sure we can find a corner here at Rose Hill for you. Do you have date and time?'

'Not yet. I'll text you when I know.'

'That'll be fine. See you soon.'

'Thanks. Bye.'

They were both busy people without time for small talk. Nick turned to Dave.

'Did you get Daniel's details while we were at Bertrands?'

'Of course.'

'Let's give him a ring and set it up.'

'Voluntary?'

'At this stage. I'm sure there's more he can tell us.'

SIX

'You know, Dave, we could have easily been fooled into writing Ryan's death off, either as suicide or an unfortunate accident. No witnesses, no marks of a fight on his body, no scuff marks on the roof. But there have been so many lies and omissions, that tells me that there is something to hide. Add in that Ellie was murdered within twenty four hours, it looks like we've got a big case on our hands.'

'Yes, we have,' Dave agreed They were driving to Liverpool to interview Daniel Thompson and a car journey was their ideal opportunity for a review of the progress of the case.

'Basically, Stuart didn't tell us that he left the meeting but Caroline said he did.' Nick began.

'Liz looked through the written statements from John and Susan and they also confirmed it,' Dave added.

'Then Daniel said he never left the waiting room but Ryan's phone contradicts that.'

'The answers to these two questions will be interesting. They could alter the whole course of the investigation.'

It wasn't long before they were seated in a small interview room at Rose Hill, Liverpool's headquarters for Merseyside Police. Diane Coleman had welcomed them at reception and issued ID lanyards. Daniel Thompson sat opposite. He had declined the offer of having a legal representative with him, so confident was he that he could outwit these country bobbies. Cheshire was country, wasn't it? He remembered field after field after field when he travelled there for the job interview. For his part, Nick had emphasised the help a solicitor could give, but his suggestions were spurned. This was recorded along with the names of those present, a caution and that he could end the interview at any time.

Nick began. 'Looking at my notes of our last interview, you said that you were in the waiting room from the time you arrived until you were called for interview. Is that correct?

'Well, not quite. I didn't say anything at the time. I mean, nothing happened that would affect your investigation.'

'You'd have to let me be the judge of that. So what did happen?'

'Ryan – that was his name, wasn't it? – came into the waiting room and introduced himself. He seemed a nice enough fellow. Offered to show me round before the interview as, whatever happened, we would be working together. We walked up the corridor. He pointed out the different offices; just popped our heads round a couple of doors, then he said he wanted to show me the roof. He said it was the only source of fresh air and they often went up there for a break from the air conditioning. I'm not too good with heights and the wind was cold, so, after a few minutes, I said I'd prefer to go back in. I also got the impression that he was expecting to meet someone up there; he texted someone while we were up there, which I thought was odd, so I left. As I walked back along the corridor, another guy passed me, running towards the stairs, so I thought he was the one who Ryan was expecting. I mean, two men together, you don't ask these days, do you? I didn't recognise him at the time. It was only later when I was introduced that I realised he was the office manager. And that was it. As you see, nothing happened to affect your investigation.'

Daniel spoke confidently, without hesitation or mumbling. Almost as if he had rehearsed his speech. Which he had, when he assumed that the police knew he had actually left the room.

Nick said, 'You must know, though, that as the last person to see Ryan alive, you would be in the frame for being involved in his death.'

Daniel seemed contrite. 'I hadn't thought of it that way. I'm sorry. I should have told you sooner. It would have saved you the journey up here if you had known this before. I've never been involved with an investigation. I didn't know. I am sorry'

'Very true, Mr Thompson. We could have avoided the trip. I think we can leave it there. We do need to take your fingerprints, though. Just for elimination purposes, as you might understand, having been in the building. And we may need to see you again. Thank you for coming in.'

Nick led the way down to the reception desk, where the duty sergeant was able to take Daniel's prints.

Daniel breathed a sigh of relief as he walked to the car park. Kieran's advice had been good. Who needs a solicitor when you have a hardened criminal to prepare you for a police interview?

SEVEN

Back in Chester, Nick and Dave called into the Bertrand building, where George Smith was seated at Reception. Introductions over, Nick asked why George needed a part-time job. Surely his police pension would be sufficient to see him through, Nick suggested.

'Yes, it would. We had such plans for my retirement, then I lost Doreen, my wife, to covid. I didn't fancy foreign travel without her. I needed to do something. I've never been much of a gardener, Doreen saw to the garden. I don't mind pottering with a few pots, but they only take an hour or so once a week, so I turned my day around. I work here all night, sleep until mid-afternoon, have a good meal and come to work. It's worked so far. Anyway, what can I do for you?'

'I need to visit Bertrand's accounts department, then I'd like to have a word with you.'

'You'll have to be quick. The offices close in ten minutes. I'll be here all night, so you'd better get upstairs as quickly as you can.'

'Thanks. We'll be back.'

The lift took them up to the fourth floor and Nick strode up to the accounts department. There, the Accounts Manager, a young woman with long black hair, centre parting, and black-rimmed spectacles to match her hair, asked whether she could help. Her name badge told Nick that she was Roberta Nicholls. Nick introduced himself and Dave, but not before she had explained that visitors should go to Bertrand's reception office next door.

'I believe you are finishing soon, so I' only have a

couple of questions. Perhaps you would be good enough…?'

She sighed,

'Go ahead. If you must.'

'On the morning of Ryan's incident, did anyone come to this office just after nine-thirty?'

'I don't know. I wasn't here.'

'Could any of the staff answer that question?'

'No.'

This was going to be a struggle, Nick thought.

'Any reason why not?'

'At that time, we were all in the boardroom. Mr Formstone had arranged for a presentation by one of our suppliers at nine-fifteen. As the boardroom is the only room with a big screen, all the accounts staff were in there. Until ten o'clock, before you ask. None of us knew anything about Ryan's …incident, as you call it, until we came out. If there's nothing else, …we're ready to close the office.'

Nick and Dave took the hint and left.

'Do you get the feeling we've been dismissed?' Dave asked as they made their way to the lift. They received a better reception from George Smith, who had, in their absence, arranged two chairs, three cups and saucers and a pot of tea at his desk. Nick expressed his surprise. George smiled.

'I've never met a copper yet who refused a cup of tea. Sit down and pull up a chair. Much more civilised this way.'

As George poured the tea, Nick started the conversation.

'Let's start with your job here. What does that entail?'

'Not a lot. It's much easier than being desk sergeant at the police station..'

'That was what you did before you retired, I take it.'

'Yes. In Ellesmere Port. Never a dull moment there. We have six companies occupying this building and the job is to direct people to the right one. The travel agent on the ground floor is easy enough. Their sign board with special offers is just on the side here; it's self-explanatory. Two accountancy firms on the second floor cause a bit of confusion sometimes. People get confused between left and right when they step out of the lift and go to the wrong place. It doesn't help that their names are Roger Hanbury to the left and Rogers Davies and Co on the right. The third floor is where you'll find a head office branch of HSBC. Very few visitors go there. Then Old Man Bertrand, who owned the whole building, kept the top floor for his own company. There's also toilets and a small kitchen over there.' He pointed to the wall behind him.

'So what time do you hand over to the day staff?'

'It's supposed to be nine, but Jess comes in from Wrexham and doesn't always make it on time, what with taking her two kids to school and hitting the rush-hour traffic, so I stay on until she gets here. That's why I was late finishing on the day the young man fell. Gone half past nine.' He opened his desk drawer and brought out a slip of paper. 'Nine thirty six that day,' he said. 'And that was the time he fell.

'Did you know him?'

'I usually saw him for a short period before I went home. He was always in before 8.30. They all were on that floor. He was always cheerful. 'Morning, George!' he said. Occasional comment about the weather, or told me a joke he had heard in the pub the night before. He certainly enjoyed his job.

'What can you tell me about that morning?'

'Not much, I'm afraid. I was about to leave after doing the night shift, as usual. As I got to the door on my way home, he fell on to the pavement in front of me. It was a shock, I can tell you. I've seen dead bodies in various places, RTA's, fires etcetera, but never actually seen anyone being killed.'

'What did you do?'

'I ran outside and looked up to where he must have come from. There are no opening windows, but I couldn't see anyone else up on the roof. I think you would look over the side if you had seen someone falling off, wouldn't you? Then

I ran back in and dialled 999. I went outside again and helped a constable who had already started some crowd control. Then his colleagues arrived and I left them to it.'

'What time was that?'

George opened the drawer again and consulted his paper.

'Nine fifty. I was late getting to bed, that morning.'

Dave was busy making notes.

''What about the evenings? It's quiet, I suppose.'

'Yes. The travel agent stays open until seven to catch customers who work in the city and can't get here during the day. Everyone else works normal office hours. Occasionally, someone works late, but that's no problem.'

'And are you here all the time?'

'Yes. After seven, I lock the doors.'

'What about a break, toilets or making coffee? Could someone get in without you knowing?'

'The doors are locked. If anyone needs to speak to me or to come in, I see them through the glass. They would have to ring the bell. I do a round of the building at seven-thirty and again at midnight. Just to make sure all is well'

Nick needed further explanation as George seemed to have it all covered.

'So how do you suggest someone came in to kill Ellie that evening? Are there any other doors to the building?'

'Yes. There are two doors at the back, but they are opened with push-bars from the inside. They were both shut when I came in. It's the first job, to go round and make sure the back of the building is secure. Just a visual check.'

'Could someone have hidden inside at the end of the day, killed Ellie, then exited through one of the back doors?' Dave asked.

'Good thought, Dave,' Nick said.

George shook his head.

'Wouldn't have thought so. I'd have heard the push-bar being operated when they left. Noisy things, they are. You have to give them a hefty push to get them to work.'

Dave looked up. 'What if George and I go down there and try to open the door as quietly as we can? You stay in here and see if you can hear us.'

'OK. Let's try it,' Nick said. 'Off you go. Try both doors.'

Dave and George made their way to the rear of the building and tried to open both doors in turn. On both occasions, the effort to use the push-bar quietly generated a noise loud enough to be heard at Reception.

'What did you think of Ellie, George?' Nick asked, as the two men returned to their seats.

'Pretty girl. Lively. Rather proud of her long hair. Could be a bit flirty if Ryan wasn't with her. Use to call me Uncle George. She was well matched with Ryan. They were going to be married, weren't they?'

'So I believe. Now they're both dead. We have to find out why.'

On that sombre note, Nick and Dave left George to his lonely vigil.

'We now have three suspects,' Nick said, as they drove away.

'Three?' Dave sounded surprised.

'Yes. Daniel is not in the clear yet. We'll have to find out what time he left the building. Then there's Stuart. Did he hide in the building until they had all left? And if everyone had left, the only one left in the building with Ellie was George.'

'George? But he's an ex-policeman.'

'Exactly. Widowed for a couple of years. No doubt missing his wife. Knowledgeable about crime, so no clues. He would know exactly what we would be looking for. Keeping those times on a slip of paper, for instance. He was the only person in the building. With Ryan out of the way, did he fancy his chance with Ellie, went up and tried his luck, got rebuffed and in his temper, killed her?'

'I see what you mean. Motive - failed approach for sex. Method – strangled with her own hair. No weapons. No clues. Opportunity – they were the only people in the building. No witnesses.'

'But that means no alibi, either. He's got no hiding place. We'll add him to our list.'

'There's one other thing that may or not be relevant.'

'Oh, yes. What?'

'When I opened the back door, I found it sticky, inside and out.'

'All over?'

'No, just around the lock. But I've no idea what caused it.'

'I can't think either. We'll have to bear it in mind.'

EIGHT

'I think they believed me. I did as you said. Apologise. Come up with a plausible story....'

'And what's the important bit?'

'Remember it!'

Daniel was sitting in Kieran Donovan's sumptuous office. Kieran had tutored him about police interviews. 'Tell them a story. Make it believable. A string of 'No comments' makes them suspicious, as though you've got something to hide, so they keep digging until they find it. Put them off the scent with a good story. But it's important to remember it. To be a good liar you have to have a good memory. They'll keep asking you the same question until you contradict yourself. Then you're sunk.'

Kieran was giving Daniel the benefit of his own experience of a life of crime, which had been extremely successful. Not only had he stayed out of jail, he had also amassed a vast fortune, though that was never going to be big enough.

One of his successes was the acquisition of Burke's Mercedes dealership. He needed a business with a big-ticket product. While Bingo halls and casinos brought in the money and provided an outlet for his drugs dealing, a business with a high turnover would provide a respectable front for his criminal activities. Now he was in the motor trade, he discovered that Bertrand's of Chester were the leading distributor of top-of-the-range cars. He wanted them under his belt, but at his price. If he could tarnish their reputation, there would be an opportunity to purchase the company at his price.

Added to which, a lead into Cheshire would provide a new route for his drug dealing. At Burke's, he had found a young man who was an excellent salesman with ambitions to go higher and the ability to back up those ambitions. He therefore groomed this young man and rubbed his hands together when the Team Manager's job at Bertrand's was advertised. Daniel Thompson needed no encouragement to apply for the job.

Daniel had come in to work on the day following the interview with good news for Kieran. He had got the job that he wanted, the manager's job, probably due to the fact that the internal candidate had sadly fallen off the roof just before the interview.

'Tell me about that,' Kieran said.

'First of all, there was Ryan, the internal candidate. He was a fool to think he could tell me anything about selling cars. I'm the top salesman in the North West, as you know. I could run rings round him. As the internal candidate, it was pretty sure that he would get the manager's job and I would be stuck with doing shows. What a shambles that would be. Going to Belgium or wherever with Ryan's girlfriend.'

'How come?'

'She and Ryan were on the stand at shows. He'd be office manager, so I'd be on the show team.'

'Not like you to turn down a few nights away with a girl.'

'She was pretty enough, but Ryan would always be in the background. Anyway, I operate better on my own. And office relationships often end in disaster.

'So what happened?'

'Ryan tried showing me round. He pointed out that there was no CCTV in the building. He even took me on to the roof. What a blessing that was. He was a bit nervous, but as we strolled along, a quick push and it was all over. Then, it was back to the waiting room and wait to be called.'

'Neat,' Kieran smiled. The training was paying off

'I then spent some time concocting a plausible story

to explain my movements to the police. I think they believed me. All in all, a successful day's work.'

Kieran was impressed with his prodigy's progress. He was indeed a cool. opportunistic operator, to have seized the chance to dispose of a rival on the spur of the moment. He would be an important addition to his team. Not only that, but Kieran also now had a hold over Daniel.

He reached under his desk and switched off his recorder. Daniel would do his bidding for ever more, or a copy would go to the police.

NINE

Detective Chief Inspector Tom Cameron invited Nick to take a seat opposite to his as he sat at his desk. Surprised at the unaccustomed courtesy, Nick sat. He was rarely offered a seat; usually he was left to stand while Cameron analysed the progress of his cases or lack of it, the performance of his staff, and listed their shortcomings. This was a new experience for Nick.

'I'm looking at staffing this morning. Promotions and transfers,' Cameron began.

This was a subject that Nick tried to avoid. He had a happy team. They worked well together. Promotions would mean transfers. Transfers out meant transfers in. Transfers in meant new staff to train into his way of working. The existing team had gelled and he didn't want to lose any of them. Nor did he want to leave the team if he was to be the subject of a transfer. Promotion would be nice but he was settled in his job and wasn't ready to move elsewhere yet.

'What had you in mind, sir?' he asked.

'I'd like to have your honest appraisal of your team, informally at the moment. Nothing in writing. Formal appraisal forms will come later. So, what are they like? What are their prospects?'

'DS Martin is excellent at his job. Keen eye, sharp intellect. I'd hate to lose him, but I'm sure he would appreciate promotion if it was offered.' Nick was trying to be fair to Dave. Secretly he would be mortified to lose him. On one hand, Dave deserved promotion. On the other, his would be big boots to fill.

'DC Liz Marston is a real worker. She is good at research and is well organised. I don't know how she coaxes information from her computer, but she does it consistently.

She is invaluable in the office.' Tom Cameron was making notes as Nick spoke and nodding approvingly as he did so. Nick continued.

'DC's Davidson and Carr are a reliable pairing. Davidson is serious, Carr has a cheerful view of life, but both are knowledgeable. A solid pair. All four that I have mentioned are promotable. I would hate to lose any one of them, but I suppose it's inevitable. It would be selfish for me to stand in anyone's way.'

'What about the other two?'

'DC's Roberts and Irvine are settling in nicely. I have no complaints about either of them, but they'll benefit from more experience before considering promotion.'

'Thank you for that,' Cameron said. 'Now, your present case. What's the state of play at Bertrand's?'

'I'm still unhappy about the three suspects. In recent months, Stuart Reid had had a fling with Ellie, Ryan's fiancée. Anu said she was carrying a child when she died, but Ryan was not the father. We'll need to get a swab from Stuart and take it across to Anu Rintoul for a DNA test. Stuart and Ellie had also been an item before Ryan arrived on the scene last year. No-one in the office has mentioned any difficulty between Stuart and Ryan in the meantime, so it's hard to decide whether Stuart could have pushed Ryan off the roof out of jealousy following a dispute or not.'

'I thought Stuart Reid was in a meeting in his office at the time,' the Chief said.

'He was, but he left for a short period. He said he went to the accounts department but there was nobody in the accounts department that morning, they were all in the boardroom, so there was no-one who could verify that story. Thompson, our first suspect, saw him running along the corridor. Whether that was to go to the roof or to the accounts department we don't know. Thompson admitted that he was on the roof with Ryan, but Ryan remained up there when he left. He said it was too cold to hang about on the roof.

Apparently, he saw Ryan texting a message which we found on Ellie's phone. Ellie was therefore the only person who knew that Thompson was on the roof. Could he have murdered Ellie to silence her? But that pre-supposes that he got into the building that evening. It's like Fort Knox, with one entrance at the front, locked and supervised at night, two emergency exits at the rear, only operated from inside, with push-bars. Finally, there's George Smith, night supervisor. He was normally the only person in the building at night. We are suspicious about him. He has motive, method and opportunity to have killed Ellie, and as an ex-copper, he would know enough to have covered his tracks well. There are certainly no clues, and with the absence of CCTV, we're stumped.'

'So you have three suspects, and you can make a case against each of them. Crown Prosecution Service will make mincemeat of us if we don't get it right. Keep digging. One of them will make a mistake soon if you keep the pressure on them. So get to it. Remember, results, not excuses. I'm looking at your appraisals this afternoon. Transfers may be in the offing.'

With that stark warning, Nick left the room.

TEN

Nick was looking forward to the weekend. There was a busy week behind him. A couple of unsolved murders and his boss thinking about transfers had been enough to set him off worrying about his future. He was determined to give his girlfriend Helen his full attention this weekend. Living together had been one of their more successful ideas, and he looked forward to a couple of days relaxation with her. Forget Bertrand's; forget appraisals. They can wait until Monday. They wouldn't, of course. They would be a constant undercurrent in his brain, regardless of whatever else he was doing, but if he could keep them as an undercurrent, he would be happy. At least, spending the time in Helen's world of horses would occupy his mind for much of the time as he learned the strange terms for the tack and equipment that went with owning a horse. Curry comb and dandy brush were self-explanatory. Martingales and snaffles were, however, just two of the new words in his vocabulary.

He had even spent time in the saddle. Riding along country lanes with Helen alongside on one of her horses, they had trotted until his back ached, but at the end of a long ride he had mastered the rising trot and reached the end of the back-ache. He started to enjoy riding. Helen was pleased with his progress, as they exercised her horses together. It also meant that they spent time together grooming the horses, cleaning tack and travelling to shows for Helen to compete.

In the heat of competition, even Bertrand's and Tom Cameron seemed a long way away.

Helen had given her horses a wide experience, from

the controlled discipline of dressage to the stamina-draining efforts of a two-mile cross country course. This improved their natural agility and their obedience so that they excelled at show jumping. Helen was known for the cheeky tight turns when competing against the clock, where seconds really counted. This suited her tigerish will to win. Consequently, show jumping was her favourite discipline, evidenced by the rows of rosettes in her tack room and the silverware displayed at the family home.

Helen could not recall any time in her childhood when she could not ride. Before she could walk, she had been placed on a pony, her father walking alongside, his hand supporting the toddler's back in case she slipped off. Her adventurous spirit showed even at that tender age as it was not long before she cried 'Let me go, Daddy. I want to trot!' The determination in those sparkling blue eyes shone through, confirming to the parents that they had a winner here.

A winner indeed.

As she grew through the age groups, competing at local shows and gymkhanas, she displayed that same grit and determination.

Her father, Ross Fletcher, recognised this and ensured that she always had a safe, sensible ride on ponies with bags of ability. The result was a continued rise through the grades into adult competition. Never content with second best, she had been selected for the equestrian team for the Olympic Games. Ross and Ruth were thrilled to see their daughter jump the only clear round in the Show Jumping Final.

Her life had not been exclusively bound up with horses, however. Ross had always recommended having a second string to her bow. 'You never know what's round the corner,' he said.

Academically above average, she had gained a degree in Business Studies and followed it by taking employment at

Thornhill Hospital as the CEO's Personal Assisitant. Which was fortunate. Ross's advice proved to be sound when she suffered a fall while exercising a horse in Bickerton Hills. Severe back injuries resulted in six months immobilised in hospital, followed by over twelve months in a wheelchair, the first period in her life when she had been unable to ride. It was in this dark period of her life that a certain detective inspector had entered her life.

Nick had found it easy to immerse himself in Helen's horsey world and he became her part-time groom and horse-box driver at weekends, when he was available, helping her to manage the horses at the indoor shows around the country. Working together as a team brought them closer together, both physically and emotionally.

In addition, they had found living together to be equally agreeable. Life together was sweet. Nick wished the sweetness would translate to his work as well.

ELEVEN

In the weeks following the double murders, Daniel worked hard, impressing everyone at Bertrand's with his keenness to learn. During the spell with John Cooke he had spent time on the computer, working out routes and timings to the various shows where they intended to take their cars. Hiring transporters for car deliveries from the sales department as well as the show cars were something else of which he had no experience as a salesman at Burke's, but he found it interesting. John gave him theoretical tasks as exercises to test his ability, some of them to do with shows that they had attended in the past. Daniel showed that not only was he able to plan routes and stops *en route* but also what vehicles would be required, which needed to be hired and which were available from their own car pool. When John compared the results with what he had planned in the past, he found that they were identical, in one case an improvement. Daniel was a quick learner and moved on to work with Susan Taylor, the accommodation expert.

This was way outside his experience, but having worked on the transport side, he quickly caught on to their accommodation requirements.

'Just like booking a holiday,' he joked.

'More or less,' Susan said. But you are booking for other people, and you have to take their preferences into account as well. For instance, when we go to the Brussels show, you'll have to liaise with John to find out where the stops are, what time the ferries go. Are you crossing from Hull to Rotterdam, Harwich to the Hook of Holland or Dover to

Calais? All with different journey times, different distances from Chester. A night ferry might save the cost of an hotel. You need to balance time to reach the port with the cost of ferry fares.'

'You make it sound complicated,' Daniel said.

'It is complicated, but as long as you bear all these things in mind, it's possible. It's also very satisfying when they come back and report that it all went like clockwork.' Not surprisingly, Daniel applied himself to the task and finally understood all that was required. He was ready to move on to Caroline's job.

'I started with Mr Bertrand when he had a small filling station at Cottage Green, just outside Chester,' Caroline explained. 'I could type and I was a bookkeeper. He was selling second-hand cars, but that soon outgrew the filling station and we moved into Chester. Mr Bertrand was very astute. He became known for expensive cars. The wealthy people of Cheshire flocked to his door and he was happy to relieve them of their money by supplying what they wanted. We now have three outlets, Chester, Liverpool and Crewe. There are plans for a new one in North Wales soon, Llandudno, probably. I'm very proud to have been a part of this progress and it will be a pity to leave the company, but hey-ho, life moves on.'

She proceeded to tell him of his duties, largely supervisory, but also cultivating the many contacts she had made over the years. Efficient as always, she had prepared a folder with notes on all the contacts. They were not just numbers on her phone. Details of families, likes and dislikes, usefulness in an emergency. 'Finally, please remember that you are representing Bertrand's. Always be smartly dressed, well-mannered and well-spoken. It sounds a bit old-fashioned, I know, but it goes a long way in business. I don't have to tell you that, though. You were a smart salesman at Burke's. You wouldn't have sold many cars if you hadn't been.'

Daniel agreed and thanked her for the compliment. He wondered if she had spoken to Kieran to get that glowing report, or had it just come from his reference when he applied for the job?

Daniel smiled. He felt great. From top salesman at Burke's, he now had a satisfying and interesting job at Bertrand's. He was enjoying his job. He was also looking forward to the task that Kieran had given him, to ruin Bertrand's name, but that was for the future. He was popular here in Chester. The police seemed to be off his back at last – he hadn't heard from them in a couple of weeks. It was win-win all round.

TWELVE

Nick Price faced his team at their morning briefing.

'First of all, this morning, I want to welcome a new member on the team. DC Bridget Carson, transferred in from Ellesmere Port. Over to you, Bridget.'

She stood up, about five foot seven or eight, athletic frame with a blonde ponytail.

'Good morning everybody. As DI Price said, I'm Bridget. I've done a couple of years at Ellesmere Port while on the National Detective Scheme. I've got my PIP2 certificate and I'm looking forward to working with you all in Chester.' There were smiles and welcoming words all round.

Nick took over.

'Thank you, Bridget. Now, down to business. 'I appreciate that you've all been engaged on other enquiries, but we mustn't lose sight of the double murder at Bertrand's a month ago. We don't want it to become a cold case.'

'Are we looking for one killer or two?' Eamonn asked.

'Good point, there seemed to be a connection between the two, especially as they both happened on the same day, but no clear link has presented itself.'

Liz joined in.

'I've been looking at Daniel Thompson. He seems to have settled in at Bertrand's but...'

'They used to say the murderer always returns to the scene of the crime,' Eamonn put in. 'Perhaps it's true in this case.'

'Old wives' tale,' muttered Rob Davidson.

'OK You two. Can I carry on?' Liz tried to keep to the subject. 'As I was saying, he's settled in at Bertrand's but I've been on the phone to Mercedes in Germany...'

'Ordering a new car, Liz?'

She withered Eamonn with a glare.

'… and they told me that they only send out certificates if people have successfully attended courses at the factory. Dealership sales are not their concern directly.'

'So Daniel lied about his certificate. I wonder what else he's lied about,' Nick mused.

'He came up with a plausible story about going on the roof with Ryan. Perhaps that was all lies as well,' Dave Martin said.

Nick agreed.

'He seems cocky. Big-headed for sure. Top salesman so he reckoned. Perhaps that's a lie as well. We ought to have a word with his previous boss. I'll get Diane Coleman to do it. He's on her patch.'

'What about the other suspects?' Dave asked.

'Stuart Reid, the office manager. Ex-boyfriend of Ellie - , the murdered girl' he added for Bridget's benefit. 'Could be the father of her unborn child. He was jealous of Ryan, her new boyfriend and later fiancé. He left a meeting for a short time, but lied about it. He was seen running towards the stairs to the roof, but said he was only going as far as the accounts office. No witnesses, of course. And finally we have George Smith, ex-police sergeant. He might have had some kind of a crush on Ellie and was alone in the building with her that evening…'

Bridget spoke up.

'Excuse me. Did you say George Smith. Not W H Smith?

Nick looked puzzled. 'I only know him as George.'

'Was he at Ellesmere Port?' she asked.

'Yes, so he said. Why W H Smith?'

'It was a nickname we gave him between ourselves. The female staff there. W H stands for Wandering Hands. He always needed to touch us. If we handed him a file or a cup of tea, he always managed to touch our hands. If we met in the corridor, he would put a hand on our shoulder as we passed.'

'He was probably like that with everybody,' Eamonn suggested.'

'Not the men. We started to take special notice. It was just the female staff. It was nothing that we could complain about. Nothing sexual, you understand. We'd be laughed at if we complained, but it really was noticeable. He liked touching women.' She was emphatic.

'That's good to know. Thank you, Bridget. So he might well have been sweet on Ellie.'

'Plan of action?' Dave asked.

'I'll contact Diane Coleman at Merseyside and ask her to interview Daniel's old boss. Rob and Eamonn can take a DNA swab from Stuart and get it over to Anu Rintoul. I'll take Bridget to see George last thing this evening, 4.30ish, he should be in by then, to test this touching idea. Then we can compare handshakes.'

'Wouldn't it be better if someone else who he hasn't met before goes with you? He could put an over-enthusiastic handshake down to the pleasure of meeting an ex-colleague.' Eamonn put in.

Liz replied 'Very true. I'll come with you, boss. He doesn't know me.'

'That's the plan, then. Let's hope it produces results.

THIRTEEN

DI Diane Coleman of Merseyside Police drew into the forecourt of Burke's Mercedes Dealership in her blue and yellow chequered BMW.

'Come to swap it for a proper car?' grinned a young man who was polishing a silver Mercedes.

'Ho, ho,' she said in mock amusement. 'Where will I find your boss?'

'He's inside This way.' He led Diane through the swing doors into the showroom, where Kieran was standing talking to one of his salesmen.'

'Visitor for you, Mr Donovan,' the young man said.

Kieran looked up and saw the police BMW outside.

'Wanting a part-exchange price are we?' he said.

'Is that joke of the week round here? What has happened to Scouse humour?' she said. 'Can we have a word? In your office. Please.' She showed him her ID. 'DI Diane Coleman. Merseyside Police.'

Kieran led the way into his office, a tidy, modern office with very little paperwork on view, modern furniture, a couple of computer monitors and a silver model Mercedes sports car on his desk. He invited Diane to sit as he sat behind the desk.

'What can I do for you today?' he asked. 'One of my boys been speeding?'

'Nothing like that. I'm here on behalf of Cheshire Police. They have a murder enquiry ongoing and I have some questions.

Kieran thought hard. Surely Daniel hasn't done

something silly already.

'Sounds serious. Fire away.' he said.

'It's about a man named Daniel Thompson. I believe he used to work for you.'

'Yes.' He decided to keep his answers brief until he could see where they were going.

'Good worker, was he?'

'Yes.'

'What were his strong points?'

'He was young, keen on his job. Good product knowledge. Tendency to exaggerate, but that's part of being a salesman, isn't it?'

'You would have been sorry to lose him, then?'

'Yes. He was our best salesman.'

'Do they have awards for this kind of thing in your trade?'

'Like the Oscars, you mean? Yes. Retailer of the Year is the one we would like.'

'Have you ever won it?'

'No, Top ten in UK is our best, in 2023.'

'Was Mr Thompson here then?'

'Yes.'

'What about awards for your employees?'

'The Best Sales Team Award is for the team that sells the most cars. Obviously, the big dealers are in for that award. We do pretty well, but not well enough for that one.'

'So Mr Thompson doesn't have a certificate from Mercedes.'

'No'

'What about your slogan, Burke's for Mercs. Who thought of that?'

'He did. He's quite proud of it when it appears on TV.'

'Was he a good salesman?'

'As I said, the best we had.'

'So you were sorry to lose him?'

'Of course. He could sell sand to the Arabs. He's destined for bigger things. It would have been wrong to stand in his way. That's why I gave him a glowing reference when he applied for this job in Chester.'

Diane closed her book and clipped her pen to it.

'Well, thank you, Mr Donovan. You've been very helpful.

'What's it all about, anyway?' he asked, hoping he would learn more.

'They haven't told me much, so I can't really answer that. Goodbye, Mr Donovan.'

FOURTEEN

DCI Tom Cameron looked over his spectacles at Nick Price across his desk. This was his intelligent look, reserved for occasions when serious, potentially bad, news was to be dispensed. Nick wondered what it was this time. Since his last meeting with the Chief, when staff changes were mentioned, he had spent those sleepless hours in the middle of the night wondering whether he was about to be transferred out, away from Chester to parts of the county which were strange to him. It was the look on the face of the Chancellor of the Exchequer trying to put a positive gloss on a tax rise or a vet who has bad news about your sick cat. Nick awaited the opening words with trepidation.

'Well, Nick…'

That was a bad omen to Nick.

'…as I said the other day, I've been looking at appraisals. So have Head Office, and they have decided that we are overstaffed. I did my best to keep your team together, but, as in life, so in staffing, we have to make compromises. We therefore need to reduce your team by one member.'

'Here it comes,' Nick thought..

'As you have just received a new member, the young lady from Ellesmere Port, I thought that… no, I have decided… that DC's Roberts and Irvine will benefit from a different experience in another area. They are excellent officers and I have recommended that they stay together, though whether that will be possible is up to Head Office. What do you think of that?'

'It sounds an excellent compromise, sir. DC Carson seems keen and capable. I'm sure she will fit into the team very well. Whoever gets Roberts and Irvine will be grateful to receive two superb officers who work well together.'

'Good. If you would like to send them in, I'll give them the good news. Transfers will be effective from the end of the month.'

A relieved Nick left the room. He'd be staying here with the bulk of his team. With three weeks to go until the end of the month, he would take full advantage of the extra team member.

Rob and Eamonn were writing up their report on their visit to Stuart Reid.

'How did it go?' Nick asked.

They said that Stuart was reluctant to co-operate at first, but after Eamonn had explained that, as he was one of the 'persons of interest' in enquiries about two deaths, we needed samples for elimination purposes, he agreed. Rob then took a swab from inside his cheek. They had delivered it to the path lab, as instructed.

'Let's hope it bears fruit,' Nick said, then turned to DC Liz Marston, who was showing Bridget Carson how to get the best out of the computer.

'Get your coat, Liz. It's cold out,' he said, as he wrapped his scarf around his neck. As they left the office Nick said, 'Remember, we're testing this handshaking theory, so if he does shake your hand or holds on a bit longer, don't resist. Go with it, unless he goes too far, of course., but that's unlikely in public, I should think.'

They walked down to Bertrand's offices. Christmas lights in shop windows lit their way and the cheerful sound of seasonal songs from open doorways made for a happy atmosphere in the city streets. The evening rush-hour was building up and a few dead leaves still blew around the pavement. A tall Christmas tree with colourful flashing lights standing outside Bertrand's building illuminated the pavement nearby. That a young man had met his bloody and shocking end just yards away, not a month before, had almost been forgotten.

George Smith smiled and got to his feet as they

entered the foyer. Nick approached him and offered a handshake to which George responded with just a perfunctory contact.

'Nice tree you have outside, George.'

'Yes, it's a beauty. From the Duke's woods. We have one every year. I believe the Duke always gets his cars from Bertrand's as well. Old man Bertrand must have done a good deal there years ago.'

'We were passing this way and I thought I would say hello.' He laughed. 'Bit early for Merry Christmas, though. This is DC Liz Marston, one of my team, by the way.'

George came round the desk to Liz and offered a handshake. She responded, but George continued to hold her hand.

'A pleasure to meet you,' he said.

'Nice to meet you. Mr Smith, is it?'

'George, please.' He stroked her hand.

'Er…it's a bit of a cheek, but do you have a Ladies here. This cold weather, you know.'

'Of course. Come this way.' He led her, still holding her hand, to the door to the back corridor. 'Just down there, on the right,' and steered her with a hand on her shoulder.

'Nice young lady. Been on your team long?'

'A couple of years.'

They fell into small talk while waiting for Liz to return. Nick was certain that George was as tactile with women as Bridget had made out. Nick noticed that he certainly held Nick's hand for as short a contact as possible, in contrast with the length of time he held on to Liz's hand. This didn't make him a killer, of course, but his attitude to women was clear. He had said that Ellie could be flirty at times. Did he misread the signs? Time will tell.

FIFTEEN

It was the Friday before the week of the Brussels show. Mid-January seemed an odd time to hold a car show, except that it gave dealers time to boost sales for the spring and summer trade.

Daniel, under the guidance of both Caroline and Stuart, had supervised the work, as well as undertaking the task of collaborating with a designer for both the stand and for the various banners and placards which would be needed. A magnificent twenty-page catalogue, showing the cars the company supplied, had been produced for issue to the serious buyers, along with leaflets and brochures for general distribution. No expense had been spared.

It had been decided that Caroline would accompany Daniel to Brussels. She was knowledgeable about the company. He knew about cars and how to sell them. They would make a good team.

Daniel checked the transport situation with John. 'How do we get our exhibit there?' he asked.

'We've hired a car transporter from Raybrook's to take our best car...'

'Which is?'

'The Mercedes AMG GTR. At just under a hundred thousand pounds, it should make a statement on our stand.'

'I was selling Mercs in my last job at Burke's, so I'll be at home with this one, just a bit of swotting at the weekend,' he said. 'Carry on.'

'It will cross the Channel, Dover to Dunkirk then travel on to Brussels. It's about five hours to Dover and a couple of hours travelling on the other side. You and Caroline will travel by car – there will be no need to travel with the lorry. We'll have an eighteen tonner with a box body, a hydraulic lift and side opening doors.'

'Why not an ordinary transporter?'

'Because (a) we're only taking one car, it's a real eye-catcher, and (b) we like to keep it secret.'

'Why secret?'

'There's a lot of car thefts happening at the moment. And this car would be worth double its money in Saudi, so we'd like to keep it under wraps, otherwise it would be followed by every car thief in the country, waiting for an opportunity to hi-jack it. Also, there's the element of surprise when it's unveiled at Brussels'

'Sounds good,' Daniel said. 'You seem to have all bases covered. Well done, John. What if we need to contact the driver on the way?'

'Raybrook's gave me his phone number. It will be in the paperwork that Susan has for you. Any questions?'

'Not at the moment. As I said, you seem to have covered everything.'

'Finally, it's a three-day-show. Susan will tell you about accommodation for the four nights.

Daniel walked across the office to talk to Susan Taylor, a plump, pleasant young lady approaching her thirties.

'I hope you've booked us in at the Ritz,' he joked.

'No such luck. The Ritz was fully booked when I rang.' He was not the only one with a sense of humour. 'Instead, you'll be in the Hotel Marie. It's close to the exhibition hall and a short distance from the city centre, not that you'll have much time for sight-seeing. Two single rooms. Dinner, bed and breakfast. All the usual amenities – Wi-Fi, tea/coffee making facilities, *en suite*, Sky TV. Is there anything else you would want?' She handed him a folder containing all the details of the trip; times, ferry tickets, hotel reservations, passes for the exhibition hall.

'Don't think so. Thanks very much for this. I'm looking forward to the trip. It's the first time I've done this kind of thing. Going abroad for work, that is.'

'You'll be OK driving on the continent, won't you?' John asked'

'Yes. Done it many times. Holidays, mainly.'

He turned and walked towards Stuart's office where Caroline and Stuart were discussing the forthcoming trip.

'I thought I'd finished doing these trips when you and Ellie took over,' Caroline was saying. 'Would you believe it's over three years since I did one? Still, it will be a nice trip to go out on. A happy memory for my retirement,' she said.

'It should be straight forward. Daniel seems to know his stuff. He'll be pleased that I've chosen the Mercedes to go there. He'll be on familiar ground,' Stuart said, as Daniel entered. 'John and Susan have done their usual excellent job of planning routes and booking transport and accommodation. Do you agree, Daniel?'

'Yes. Impressive. It's all in here.' He patted the folder that Susan had given him.

'So it's all set up for Monday. You're driving, I believe, Daniel?'

'Yes.'

'Well, drive safely. Good luck. Come back with a full order book!'

'We'll do our best,' Caroline said.

Daniel said nothing.

He and Caroline made their arrangements for meeting on Monday morning and left the office.

When he was outside the building and well away from the office, Daniel made two phone calls. The second was to Kieran Donovan.

'Hi, Kieran. We're off on Monday morning. The number of the transporter is MX71RAY, it's a Raybrook's vehicle, an Iveco.'

'Good. Thanks for that. Nice to have it confirmed.

Remember, you know nothing.'

Daniel had a warm feeling as he drove home that evening. He had done something for his boss. The wheels were in motion.

SIXTEEN

David Pollard had ridden horses in flat races since he was sixteen. Prior to that, he had lived and breathed horses. His mother had placed him on a pony almost before he could walk and he had progressed through the various grades from leading rein classes to the top pony classes. Every weekend he was at a gymkhana or cross-country event. His favourite discipline, though, was show jumping and he moved easily into adult classes, quickly becoming an international rider. The feeling of the power of the horse at take-off; the control of an obedient horse through intricate courses; the camaraderie (and rivalry) between riders; the travel around the world; the enthusiasm of the spectators. All of this thrilled him from day to day. He could recall the many winning rides at the top level, none better than the win at the Olympic Games.

Away from horses, there had been no shortage of girls in his life. He was tall, just under six feet. He was good-looking, handsome, even, with an unruly lock of hair which flopped across his eyes, giving him a boyish appearance. Many of his admirers were disappointed in their ambitions when he was taken off the market by Jenny Hill, daughter of a neighbouring farmer. They had known each other all their lives and were comfortable in each other's company.

David and Jenny lived in a bungalow that David's father, Robert, had built in readiness for his retirement, the arrangement being that he and David would exchange residences when the time came that he would retire and David would take over the running of the dairy farm. In everybody's eyes, that day was a long way in the future, and while David was not a keen dairy farmer, he never thought to voice his opinion of the difficulty of running a farm while pursuing a show jumping career.

The problem was solved prematurely when a drunk driver drove the wrong way down the M6 and collided head-on with David's parents returning from a theatre visit in London, killing both of them outright.

Over the next six months, David and Jenny sorted their lives out. Fortunately, Jenny was capable of running the farm in David's absences. The owners of his competition horses, while sympathetic to his situation, still held him to their contract when a lucrative competition took place. A substitute rider was not enough; they were paying for the best.

Disaster followed disaster as David, competing in Holland, was injured during his round. As he approached an obstacle at the edge of the arena, a protestor against animal cruelty let off a firecracker next to the fence, spooking the horse which crashed into the fence. Both horse and rider went down among the poles which flew in all directions. David's left leg was broken in two places, crushed awkwardly beneath the fallen horse. The animal, panicking in its struggles to get up, stamped a foot on David's outstretched left hand, crushing his fingers. He knew, as he lay on the ground, that his show jumping career was over.

Weeks became months as his treatment went on. Jenny's father helped her to run the farm, but in his now idle moments of recuperation, David could see it was a hopeless task.

He decided to sell the cattle from his dairy farm. He had not lost his interest in horses. He still had the farm. A new ambition was born. He would build an equestrian establishment to stand alongside Hickstead and Badminton and Burghley. We need something like this up here in Cheshire, he thought. He said nothing to anyone about these plans. First of all, he had to be sure that such crazy ideas were not the result of the drugs which he was still taking to alleviate the pain. As time went on, he became sure that his plans were sound. He built an indoor arena to ensure his income through the winter. He built a cross-country course with well-thought-out obstacles. There were tracks through the woods for other activities too, from dog walking to cross-country running. The huge cattle yard now sported a BMX cycle track and the old farm buildings became admin offices and restaurant and shops. David ensured there was something of interest to see or do for a wide variety of users.

It was to this arena that Helen made her way most Sundays, accompanied by Nick when he could. They spent time browsing in the shop which catered for all of a horseman's needs, from bits and bridles to saddles and stirrups, rugs and feed for the horse and warm jackets for the rider. Riders could get their sustenance at the Stables Restaurant next door, which had an attractive menu of lunchtime meals.

Helen's class was later in the afternoon, so they had enjoyed a leisurely lunch and wandered around the shop until it was time to saddle up and warm up her horse in readiness for the competition.

Nick was now a proficient helper rather than the awkward amateur he had been a few months previously. He watched her in the ring and met her with an encouraging smile as she came out, having jumped a clear round. He waited nervously as the jumps were raised and the shortened course decided upon. The order of jumping was drawn and Helen would go first. It would be against the clock. It was not her favourite position as it always posed a problem.

'If I go fast I might knock one down. If I go for a clear round it might not be fast enough. Either way, I'm set up to lose. I'll go for a steady clear, I think. Nero is a young horse and I'd rather bring him on slowly,' she said.

She went into the ring and Nick was pleased with her time, which was too short for the following riders, who rode too quickly in trying to beat Helen's time and had fences down. Helen's decision was proving to be correct. However, the final two riders were experienced, as were their horses, and they rode fast clear rounds, placing Helen into third place.

'As we expected,' she said, as they loaded up to return home. A rosette and a small amount of prize money was all she had to show for the day's work, but her horse was fit and well and was improving day by day.

Nick was pleased with their day out. Interest, excitement and, most important, they had been together. He had not thought about work all day. That would be on the menu for tomorrow.

SEVENTEEN

'I hope you have all had a good weekend and are ready for work,' Nick began.

'Eager as ever,' Eamonn muttered to Rob. Nick was not sure whether this was sarcasm, so he ignored it and pressed on.

'We need to work on the Bertrand's deaths. We are still not sure whether the two are connected.

'It's a big coincidence if they aren't, don't you think?' Eamonn said. He was always the one to speak up.

'Coincidences do happen,' Nick said, 'so we have to examine two possibilities. If they are connected, then Stuart Reid is our prime suspect.'

'On what grounds?' Liz asked.

'He killed Ryan out of jealousy, or revenge, because Ryan had taken Ellie away from him and he wanted her back. Then he killed Ellie because she refused to go back to him after he had killed Ryan.'

'That means Daniel Thompson and George Smith are off the hook,' Dave put in.

'Correct. On the other hand, If they are not connected, then Daniel is prime suspect for Ryan's death, to get him out of the way at the interview and George is in line for Ellie's because she refused his advances. Stuart could also be of interest, for the same reasons as before. We need to interview all three again with this in mind. On the plus side, we don't have to go to Liverpool again to see Daniel as he's now at Bertrand's. There's one other thing. I have an email from Anu and guess what? The DNA showed that Stuart was the father of Ellie's unborn child. I wonder where this fits in. Does it mean he would or would not have killed her? It could point either way. I can't be sure. Let's see how our interviews pan out.'

'So who does what?' Dave asked.

'Eamonn and Rob can go round to George's house this afternoon. He'll be asleep this morning, so I don't want it to look like harassment. You and I, Dave, will see Stuart this morning and while we're at the office we can interview Daniel as well.

Nick and Dave walked into the Bertrand building. A brunette receptionist sitting at the table where they had seen George previously, looked up.

'Can I help you, gentlemen?' she asked. They showed their warrant cards.

'No thanks. We know where we're going. Bertrand's.'

'If you need the lift, it's free at the moment.'

'Thank you,' Nick said as they walked across the floor and entered the lift.

They walked into the office and Stuart looked up and saw them through the glass. He waved them in.

'Have you got any news?' he asked.

'No news. But we'd like another word with you and Daniel.'

'I'm available, though I am very busy. There's no Daniel, I'm afraid. He and Caroline are on their way to the Brussels Motor Show. They'll be back next week. So I'm here on my own, which is why I'm busy. What can I do for you? Take a seat.'

'First, I'd like to run through the morning of Ellie's

death. We've been informed that you were seen waiting in the car park instead of coming into the office. Can you explain this?'

'I've no idea who would have said this. I arrived just before Caroline did. I looked over the other cars to see if she had arrived. She's usually not far behind me. Then I saw her by the door, so I walked across to her and we came into the building together.'

'She came up in the lift, I believe.'

'Yes. I walked up. Keeping fit, as I told you before.'

'What was your relationship with Ellie?'

'I've already told you this.'

'Just remind me.'

'We were a couple, until Ryan arrived.'

'That must have been difficult for you, working in the same office.'

'It was. But I tried to be adult about it, not letting my personal feelings affect business decisions.'

'Very commendable, I'm sure. Didn't you try to win her back?'

'Privately, yes. But with no luck, I'm afraid.'

'What do you mean, privately?'

'I sent her a couple of texts and I met her one evening, by accident, She was fixed on Ryan. Plenty of money. Flash car. I'd got no chance.'

'You met her? What happened.'

'We had a drink and went our separate ways.'

'Just a drink?'

'OK. We had more than one drink.' His tone showed that he was getting defensive, holding something back.

'Anything else?'

'You know something, don't you?'

'Just wondering when you're going to tell me the truth.'

'We went round to my flat for a night-cap and went to bed. She realised that she shouldn't have left me. Or perhaps it was the effect of a couple of drinks, I don't know.'

'This would have been about three months ago?'

'Yes, how did you know?'

'The DNA swab you gave matched the DNA of Ellie's unborn child.' Stuart's mouth dropped open as he gasped for air.

'She was pregnant? With my child?' Stuart broke down into tears which flooded down his face as he recalled that wonderful night of exciting sex. Thoughts tumbled round in his head. They were meant to be together. The knowledge that Ellie was pregnant would have fulfilled his wildest dreams. She would surely have dumped Ryan and come back to him.

'You've got to find out who killed her – and my child. We could have had such a good life together, as a family.' He gripped Nick's arm for emphasis and held on as his head bowed and he fumbled for his handkerchief with his other hand.

Nick waited until the grip was released and looked across to Dave. He spread his hands, shrugged his shoulders and tilted his head as if to say 'That tells us everything.'

When Stuart had regained his composure, Nick said 'Let's talk about Ryan's fall.'

'OK. But I know nothing about that.'

'You said that you saw him go out to the roof while you were in the meeting.'

'Yes.'

'Shortly afterwards, you left the meeting and were seen running down the corridor.'

'Yes.'

'Why?'

'I needed some figures from the accounts department.'

'Who did you see there?'

'Nobody. They were in a presentation in the boardroom.'

'What did you do then?'

'I went back to the meeting without the figures.'

'Did you see anyone else in the corridor?'

'There was a young man coming away from the roof. I didn't recognise him at the time, but at the job interview I realised it was Daniel. You're not suggesting that he had anything to do with Ryan falling off the roof, are you?'

'We don't know what happened out there. We're still trying to find out. I think we can call it a day now, but we may want to see you again. Daniel is away until next week, you say. We'll wait until then.'

Dave put away his notebook and they left a very sad Stuart pondering over what might have been.

EIGHTEEN

Ken Harvey's day had started very well. His girlfriend, Shona, who worked in the offices at Raybrook's, had allocated him a trip to Brussels. He would spend a couple of days in Belgium before bringing the car back to Chester, two days in which he could do a couple of pick-ups and deliveries over there, which Shona had arranged with one of the many contacts she had in the business. As long as he paid for the fuel, that is. John Raybrook had no objection to his drivers taking on private work as long as they looked after the vehicles while doing it. And as the longest serving driver in the company, Ken was trusted implicitly not to overstep the mark.

He had spent the morning at Bertrand's, loading up the Mercedes, then had a quick, farewell lunch with his girlfriend. His pet name for his lorry was Bella. He had wanted to call it Shona, after his girlfriend, but John Raybrook had vetoed the idea. Two Shonas about the place would be confusing.

He and Bella drove down the M6 until he reached Junction 1 at Rugby. It had been voted the Number 1 Motorway Services for the second year running and he knew why. Everything was new, spacious and spotless; he always found it restful to stop there. The food was good, too. After a leisurely meal he wandered out to his vehicle once more. There was no hurry. He was booked on a late ferry from

Dover. The journey from Dunkirk tomorrow would take only a couple of hours. He would deliver the car to the exhibition hall then the day would be his.

Back at Raybrook's base near Chester, Shona checked the tracker on Ken's lorry.

'Ken's at Rugby Services, John,' she reported to her boss. 'He likes it there. He'll probably have a kip after tea.'

Ken walked back to Bella and found that an identical vehicle had parked next to his, a little too closely for his liking. Raybrook's had no lettering on their vehicles. Neither had its neighbour. A white cab and a blue body was the only identification they had.

As he stood there between the lorries, a bearded man wearing a woolly hat appeared at the front. Ken turned to go back, and found another man blocking his way. There was no escape. He realised that the lorries were close together for a reason.

The men pulled down the front of their hats, revealing that they were wearing balaclavas. Ken recognised the situation immediately. Trapped between the two lorries with both exits blocked, anything that happened here would be unnoticed by anyone outside. It was a hi-jack. John Raybrook had always said, 'If it comes to a fight, let them take the lorry.'

The taller of the men said, 'If you do as we say, nobody gets hurt. Understand?'

Ken nodded. 'OK. What do you want'

'Your keys and your papers. We'll take it from here.'

'You don't know where I was going.'

'But I know where I'll be going.'

'You won't get very…'

A heavy thump on the back of his head rendered Ken unconscious and the men lifted him into the back of his lorry. They used duct tape to bind his hands and feet, with a strip across his mouth for good measure. They set about transferring the Mercedes from his lorry to theirs, using the hydraulic lifts available on both. They opened the cab and found his documentation. They flung his keys in before setting off in their lorry, taking the Mercedes with it.

Shona had stayed late at work. Ken's tracker still showed that he was at Rugby. She tried ringing him but he failed to pick up. Now worried for Ken's welfare, she rang John to advise him of the situation.

'Thanks, Shona. I'd better go down there to see what's happened.'

'I'll come with you. I hope he's all right,' she said.

'No, you stay here in case he rings. Keep me informed.' It would take almost two and a half hours to drive to Rugby. John set off determined to investigate.

It was dark when Ken recovered consciousness and he slowly realised what had happened. His head ached, he had difficulty breathing and his bones ached from lying on the lorry floor. He also realised that there was very little he could do to improve his situation. Many of the lorries around him were parked up for the night, their drivers listening to the radio or watching TV. He rolled about, and after half an hour, he achieved a comfortable position, lying on his side. He then used his feet to thump the sides of the lorry, hoping that someone would hear him above the sounds of their entertainment.

Voices outside gave him some hope.

'Hey up. Has he got a horse in there?'

'Shouldn't think so. It hasn't got a ramp.'

'Are you OK in there?' Louder, this time.

Ken thumped the side.

'That's no good. One for yes, two for no. Are you OK?'

Thump. Thump.

'Can we help you?'

Thump.

The back door opened slowly. One of the car park's floodlights revealed the solitary figure of Ken inside the empty cavern of the trailer body, bound and gagged, breathing with difficulty through his nose.

Two young men vaulted in beside him and immediately set about removing the tape around his arms and legs. They cast doubtful looks at the tape across his mouth.

'I think we'll let you take that off. It could be painful.'

It was, but Ken was so relieved to be able to breathe normally again that it didn't matter.

'I'd better report this to the boss as soon as I can,' he said and walked round to the cab to pick up his phone. It wasn't there.

'They took my phone as well,' he said.

'Hang on. Is this it?' One of the men had noticed it, glinting in the floodlight. 'It's been smashed.' The screen had been stamped on, rendering it useless.

'Borrow mine to ring your boss,' the other man said and handed his phone over.

Ken dialled the office; the phone was normally diverted to John's home at night, but Shona answered.

'What are you doing in the office at this time of day?' Ken asked.

'More to the point, what are you doing? You should be on your way to Dover by now,' she retorted.

''I've been hi-jacked. They've taken the car. I've still got Bella. And I've got a headache and a lump on my head to prove it. Not bad for a day's work. Can you tell John?'

'You'll be able to tell him yourself soon. He's on his way down. We noticed your tracker hadn't moved and you weren't answering your phone, so he thought you had a problem. He left over an hour ago, so he'll be with you in about an hour. I'll ring him and let him know what's happened. Are you sure you're all right?'

'Yes, I'll be fine. A bit sore, but it'll pass.'

'I do worry about you, you know,'

'I do know. But there's nothing to worry about now. My phone has been smashed so don't try ringing me. Otherwise, I'm OK.'

'Except for a lump on your head. You could have been killed, Ken.'

Having dealt with the business side of the situation, she was becoming aware of the personal effect. The lump in her throat grew and grew. She was on the verge of tears It was better to finish the call. Ken would get a loving welcome when he returned home.

Ken decided to go back into the service area and buy some painkillers.

'We'll come with you.' The two young men, Chris and Mike, were not letting him out of their sight. Ken took a couple of pills and the trio sat in the cafeteria, sipping tea, swapping tales of experiences on the road. They were good company and the time passed quickly until John Raybrook came in, concerned for his driver. They brought him up to date with what had happened. John looked out across the car park.

'I see you've still got Bella,' he said.

'Who's Bella?' Chris asked, fearing that they had somehow overlooked a passenger.

'Ken's beloved truck,' John replied. 'If they'd taken that he would have put up more of a fight,' he added with a smile. 'Which brings me to what they did take,'

'Just the car. They came prepared with a truck like Bella with a hydraulic lift,' Ken said.

'They obviously knew what they were after,' John said.

'What kind of car?' Mike asked.

'Mercedes AMG GTR,'

Whistles of amazement came from the two men and Mike said 'I'd kill for one of those...Sorry Ken, I didn't mean… I meant…'

'It's OK. We know what you meant,' Ken replied.

John tried to change the subject.

'It's a good job you boys came along when you did or we might not have known until the morning.' he said.

'We only opened the doors to let him out. Then we stayed with him to keep him awake after a bump on the head. Concussion and all that, you know.'

'You did the right thing, so well done and thank you, both of you.'

'I'll second that. I must say I'm feeling better already,' Ken put in. 'Let us have your details in case we need to get in touch.'

'Good idea,' John said, 'and I'll ring the police to get the ball rolling.'

Chris and Mike scribbled their phone numbers on a paper napkin and said their farewells then left John and Ken to make phone calls, John to report the theft to the police and Ken to reassure Shona that he was well and would be home by morning.

Two constables arrived swiftly, having been patrolling the motorways nearby.

Ken described the thieves as best he could, though 'Two tall men with black beards, dressed in black with black balaclavas' was not the most helpful description they had heard. He had no idea which direction they had taken when they left, as he had been lying in the back of Bella at the time. Escape routes included M6 Northbound, A426/A14 East bound, M1 both north- and southbound. The sucking of teeth from the constables at the impossibility of the task made Ken feel like apologising for not being hi-jacked somewhere more -or less- accessible.

When it came to a description of the vehicle, more head-shaking and tooth-sucking took place. 'White cab and blue body' covered thousands of vehicles on the road. Stop and search would create chaos. The constables were not optimistic. They saw this as just another car theft. They left with the comment that car thieves were getting more adventurous, as though it was not worth taking the matter any further. The case would probably be shelved amongst the domestic violence and shoplifting cases that warranted less attention.

John was not looking forward to ringing Stuart Reid in the morning to report the loss of their most-prized car. Nevertheless, he had rung Stuart's mobile number several times but got no reply. 'He's either asleep or his phone's switched off,' he concluded, and gave up at midnight. He sent a text instead,

'Stuart, Ring me. Important. John.'

NINETEEN

Daniel and Caroline travelled together. He was keen to show off his Mercedes and spent most of the journey in the outside lane of the motorway at eighty miles an hour, sometimes more. They therefore made good time for the journey to Dover, even allowing for a coffee stop on the way down.

'The lorry won't be here for a while. He's booked on to a later boat, anyway,' Daniel explained. 'We'll meet him at the exhibition hall in the morning.'

Caroline was glad to arrive at Hotel Marie and the privacy of her room. Daniel was all right in small doses, she decided. But an afternoon filled with him boasting about his car, about how successful he was as a salesman, about how lucky Bertrand's were to get him, had bored her to distraction. No doubt he would bore her with his knowledge of wines and continental cuisine at dinner later. She was dreading the rest of the week. Her knowledge, acquired over many years as a stand rep, would count for nothing when they were in the exhibition hall, she was sure. He would know it all.

The evening went as expected, and Caroline took refuge in her room after dinner, feigning a headache and wanting an early night to be fresh for the next day.

Next morning, they turned up at the nearby exhibition

hall at 7am to find that their stand had been erected in accordance with their specifications. They set about unfurling banners and flags to decorate it, in anticipation of the arrival of their exhibit, the Mercedes AMG GTR.

Paul Dubois, the exhibition overseer, visited them as they worked.

'Caroline!' he said and greeted her with kisses on both cheeks and a hug. 'I am so pleased to see you again. I thought you had stopped coming here.'

'No. We had some big changes and I have been pressed into service once again. This is Daniel Thompson, who will be doing this job from now on.'

Paul turned to Daniel and welcomed him to Belgium, to Brussels and to the Show with a flourishing handshake and a question about the main eye-catching banner which now stretched across the stand.

'Is this your work? I like it. *We supply nothing but the best!* he read. But where is it?' he waved an arm across the empty space in the centre of the stand.

'It will arrive this morning. It shouldn't be far away by now. You will be surprised and impressed!' Daniel promised.

'I will look forward to it. We open at 12 noon.' Paul said and hurried off to continue his welcoming inspections.

Caroline set about connecting her laptop to the wi-fi and laying out the brochures and leaflets that they had brought. Daniel was more than a little twitchy, she thought. He constantly looked towards the door, expecting the car to arrive. He was probably nervous at his first trade show. He had organised it under supervision, of course, so nothing should have gone wrong. She hadn't liked his boastful slogan, but he over-rode her opinion. Hadn't he devised the successful Burke's slogan? He knew what he was doing. As time went on, Caroline herself became nervous as their exhibit was still not there.

Daniel had been telling other exhibitors how they

would be amazed by the Bertrand's exhibit, creating an air of anticipation throughout the morning.

At eleven o'clock, Caroline's phone rang.

'Hi Caroline. It's Stuart. We have a problem. Raybrook's rang me to say that their driver was attacked and the lorry has been hi-jacked. I don't have any other details at the moment. But you will not have an exhibit. Just turn around and come home. Apologise and explain to the management, of course. This is a disaster.' His voice was full of emotion. This had never happened before.

'I'll tell Paul Dubois right away.'

'Is he still doing that job? Yes. Tell Paul. He'll understand. But there's no point in you staying there any longer. Get Daniel to book you on the first available ferry and come home.'

Caroline cut the call and walked across to Daniel who was talking to the reps on a BMW stand. She took hm to one side.

'That was Stuart on the phone. The lorry has been hi-jacked and the car stolen. We're to go home right away.'

'What? Hi-jacked. So we've no exhibit.'

'Keep your voice down. We don't need to broadcast it.'

Too late. The BMW reps had heard every word and took great delight in ridiculing Daniel and his non-existent car.

As Caroline was busy repacking the leaflets and brochures, one of the neighbouring reps had lowered the banner, deleted the last three words and hauled it back up.

'Take that down,' Daniel shouted, which alerted others that something was amiss. Peals of laughter rang out as people could see a banner reading '*We supply nothing*' over an empty stand.

Caroline, holding back her tears, took command. She hauled the banner down and told Daniel 'Wrap it up quickly. I'm going to find Paul.' She was ever conscious of Bertrand's reputation. She had guarded it all her working life. This scene would do no good. Daniel's shouting merely attracted attention. Press reporters arrived like vultures around a carcass, to find out what was happening. The BMW reps were only too glad to provide a well-embellished story. It would be all over the trade press. As Stuart had said, it was a disaster.

TWENTY

The humming was subdued as The Pastor climbed up to his pulpit. He faced his congregation, slowly raising his open arms from waist level to above his shoulders, at the same time raising the volume of the humming to its highest, then, with a quick side-to-side hand movement, stopped it as if it had been cut with an axe.

With hand movements now moving in the reverse direction, he indicated that the congregation should sit. His voice boomed out in the small chapel'

'Cassie Morgan! Step forward.'

The girl approached the dais more confidently than on the previous occasion. She climbed up on to the dais, into the spotlight which beamed down from above. She had stood here at each gathering since she trod the sinner's path a month ago. Not one member of the congregation had spoken to her in that time. Today would be the end of her punishment, her penance. The Pastor's voice boomed out once more

'Here you see a sinner, but now a sinner who repented. She has borne her punishment and has promised to mend her ways. We will welcome her back into our family as a new member.'

Cassie's parents were first to run forward to hug their daughter, followed by the remainder of the congregation. Cassie wept tears, this time of joy, as smiling face after smiling face approached, hugged her and passed on. She sat happily with her family, vowing never to steal or stand in that dreaded spotlight again. The Pastor's voice brought her back to reality once more.

'You have all heard of the death of our beloved sister, who has passed away in suspicious circumstances. A month has passed and her family are with us today. We will join together to share their sorrow.

Organ music filled the room to be joined by the voices in a sad rendition of *Nearer, my God, to Thee.*

TWENTY ONE

Nick and Dave sat at the boardroom table at Bertrand's. They had been invited by Stuart Reid to a meeting of people who had recent dealings with the company. Across from Nick sat John Raybrook. Next to him was an empty seat, apparently for Neville Formstone, who had suggested the meeting to Stuart and, as CEO, would be chairing the meeting. Caroline Paterson, who had arrived back from Brussels that morning, sat next to Nick. Daniel Thompson, who had driven back in one hop from Brussels, had cried off on the grounds that he needed to sleep and, anyway, Caroline could report everything that had happened as they had been together the whole time.

At 10am prompt, Neville Formstone entered the room and made sure that everyone had been introduced. However, Nick had a word to say.

'Before we start, Mr Formstone, I'm not entirely sure why we're here. Has something happened that we should know about?'

'Yes, something has happened which affects the company and you may as well be in at the start as we decide what to do. Our attendance at the Brussels Motor Show was a disaster, due to the fact that our intended exhibit, a top-of-the-range Mercedes, was stolen at Rugby Services, on the way down.'

'It may be asking the obvious, but did anyone get in touch with the police down there?' Nick asked.

John Raybrook replied.

'Yes, I got there about two hours after it happened. A

couple of constables came in response to our call. I must say I wasn't impressed. The assailants were in black and wearing balaclavas, and if you look round the high street, everybody wears black these days, My driver did see that they had black beards before they pulled their balaclavas down prior to attacking him and tying him up. They put him, unconscious, in the back of the lorry. Their vehicle was identical to mine, same make, white cab, blue body. Again, that's a common combination on the roads these days, so the constables took what details they could and would set the wheels in motion, but they were not optimistic about tracing the lorry or the men. In addition, Rugby services is near the junction of the M1 and M6 and not far from the A14. Nobody saw which way they left the Service area and we didn't know the registration number of the lorry, so again, a search would be difficult and time-consuming.'

'Thanks for that, John,' Neville Formstone said. 'It seems that the only thing stolen was our car and the only injuries were to your driver. We'll have to be in touch with our insurance companies this morning.'

'I'd like a word with your driver. Where is he now?' Nick asked.

'On the way back, I should think. He'd had a knock on the head and I suggested that he get checked out at a hospital down there before returning. His girlfriend works in my office and she spoke to him before I left. She said he sounded OK.'

'Could I have your card, John, please? I'd like to have a word with your driver. I can come round this afternoon.'

'That's an encouraging move. I'm glad we asked you to come here this morning.' Neville felt happier that a positive move was on the cards.

'I'll do what I can,' Nick said. 'There's a lot of trade in the export of stolen high-end cars these days. We might need to get in touch with the NCA…'

'NCA?'

'Sorry, the National Crime Agency. Organised crime might be involved and NCA are the experts. I'll do what I can and let you know how I get on.'

'Thank you,' Neville said. 'Now then, Caroline, can you tell us what happened at Brussels.'

'I can see how Daniel reckons he's a good salesman. He's loud, over the top, really, and he makes people listen. It's not my style, but there we are. When we arrived at the exhibition, he let everyone know we were there. We put the banners up and prepared the stand for the arrival of the car. The main banner read *'We supply nothing but the best!'*

'Good slogan,' Neville muttered.

'He prides himself on his catchy slogans. But I'm afraid that this one backfired on him.'

'How come?' Stuart had approved the banner and was interested in what had gone wrong.

'When we received your phone call that the car had been stolen, he made a loud fuss. The people on the neighbouring stands – BMW of all people - all knew what had happened. One of them altered our banner by crossing out the last three words.'

Neville was trying to work out what was left. He asked 'What effect did that have?'

'We had a banner above an empty stand, reading *'We supply nothing.'* We were the laughing stock. Reporters were on to it like a shot and we'll be all over the trade press, As we returned on the ferry, I even saw it on the television news.'

'There have been phone calls this morning. I've instructed my secretary to field all calls and to say we have no comment at the present time,' Neville said.

'I'm afraid that Daniel's brash approach did us no favours. I'm sorry, Neville, but I could do nothing about it.'

There were sympathetic murmurs all around the table as Caroline dabbed her eyes with her handkerchief. A lifetime supporting Bertrand's had gone down the drain in a stroke. She felt that she would be retiring from a broken company.

Her pride in a lifetime of loyalty would be forever tainted by this disaster.

Whatever optimism had been generated by Nick's involvement had been overshadowed by Caroline's input. The meeting was closed by Neville Formstone, giving Stuart the task of contacting their insurers and hoping that Nick would have some success, though he felt that he would never see the car again.

TWENTY TWO

Bella rolled into Raybrook's yard with Ken Harvey at the wheel. Ken was looking forward to an afternoon in which he could relax and recuperate. After the thump on the head and a sleepless night in the cab of his lorry, the anticipation had filled his mind all the way back from Rugby. He was sure that John Raybroook wouldn't grudge him some time off as the hospital had recommended two days. Shona ran out to greet him as he climbed down from the cab, flinging her arms around him and planting a welcoming kiss on his lips. Ken, not one for being overly romantic, glanced around to see if any of the mechanics and other drivers on the yard were observing this show of affection. No-one had, so he returned the kiss without the ironic cheers that would have come from his colleagues, had they been watching. He patted her bottom as they turned and walked towards the office.

'How's your head today?' Shona wanted to know.

'It's just a bit sore. And I'm tired. Looking forward to going home, having a shower and having a kip in comfort.'

'No such luck,' she replied. 'John says there's a copper coming to see you today. He didn't say what time. You'd better come into the office and have a cup of tea. I've brought some sandwiches for lunch.'

John Raybrook came into the office as they were eating their lunch.

'We had a meeting this morning. Bertrand's, me and the police.'

'Why the police?'

'Bertrand's CEO decided to ask them to attend as

they are having a lot to do with the cops lately, a couple of sudden deaths and so on. He thought they would be useful for a bit of advice. And they were, which is why…' – he consulted a business card for a name – …'DI Nick Price is coming to see you this afternoon. He thinks there may be connections to organised crime.'

'I hope he's not thinking I was part of the theft!'

'Course not. But he needs to talk to you. Tell him what happened.'

'Right. Let's hope he gets here soon. The hospital recommended a couple of days off with a head injury. I'd like to get home.'

There was not long to wait as Nick's car appeared on the yard and parked outside the office. John introduced Nick to Ken and Shona, then left to set about his other work; he was already behind because of that morning's meeting. At least he didn't have an insurance claim to deal with. That was Bertrand's problem. Shona returned to her desk; the phone was ringing incessantly as news of the hi-jack filtered through the drivers' grapevine and other owners wanted to know the details.

Ken and Nick moved to a quieter room for their conversation.

'You've had a rough time, Ken. Are you feeling OK?'

'Yes. I'll be fine. I might just drop off to sleep, though. I spent the night in the cab after a long wait at the hospital. Not much sleep, with lorries arriving and leaving.'

'Well, let's see if we can get you home before you drop off,' Nick smiled. 'Do you mind if I record our conversation? It's not official, you understand. Not taking evidence or anything. Just saves me scribbling as we talk.'

'That's fine by me,' Ken replied. He liked this copper. He was not a bully. He explained things.

'So, you were parked up at Rugby Services. Had you ever noticed whether you were being followed on the way down the motorway?'

'No.'

'What was the first sign of trouble?'

'The first thing, that I didn't notice until later, was that the next lorry was very close to mine. I was standing between them when a man came round at the front. He was tall, dressed in black, black beard, wearing what turned out to be a balaclava, which he pulled down over his face. I turned to run, but another man, dressed identical to the first, came up from the back. I was trapped. That's why the lorries were close together, there was no escape. They said if I did as they said, nobody would get hurt. They got that wrong.' he said, rubbing the back of his head and went on. 'I asked what they wanted and the first man said 'Your keys and your documentation.' I gave them the keys…'

Nick raised his eyebrows as if to say 'Why?' but Ken had his explanation ready.

'John has always said, 'If it comes to a fight, let them take the lorry,' so I did.'

'OK. So you gave them the keys and..?'

'I got hit from behind and that's the last thing I remember. They must have used the keys to get into the cab, I suppose. I was unconscious by then. My paperwork was missing when I finally got in. They'd left the keys in the cab.'

'So why didn't they steal the lorry? Surely it would have been easier to dump you in the trees and take the lorry with the car in it?'

'I don't know. It would definitely have been easier than transferring the car over, even though both lorries must have had hydraulic lifts. I know mine did. I assume theirs did, otherwise they would never have got the car on board.'

'Have you any idea where they might be headed?'

'None at all.'

'There are so many car thefts these days, is there anywhere that you know of that is a regular destination?'

'No.'

'Nowhere mentioned when drivers get together?'

'No. It's not something that many people know about. If you know about it, the chances are you're involved with it. A dead give-away, so it doesn't get talked about.'

'That makes sense, I suppose,' Nick said. 'I'm puzzled about why they would want your paperwork. Any ideas?'

'Not really.'

'When would it be checked – officially, I mean?'

'At Dover, by the port authority and as we went on to the ferry. Then on the other side as we entered France at Dunkirk.'

'So that means they were intending to cross the Channel. That's why they needed identification.' Nick felt a buzz of excitement as this ray of sunshine cast some light on the case. Ken was not so sure.

'But the number plate would give them away. The vehicle number was on all the documentation these days. Including on the pass for the exhibition lorry park. It wouldn't tally with the number on the vehicle.'

'At least we can be sure they were crossing the Channel. I need to make a phone call. That car was stolen to order and it's on its way to its new owner. I think you can go home for that well-earned rest, Ken. I might want to see you again when I know some more.'

'You'd better ring Shona first thing if you're thinking of coming soon, just to make sure I'm in. Couple of days off, the hospital said.' Ken left it at that as he departed.

He turned and went through the door as Nick took out his phone to ring Liz.

'Hi Liz. Can you make a couple of calls for me, please? The Port Authority at Dover and the DFDS Ferry Office at Dover as well. Tell them we have a case of a stolen car and we'd like them to check their CCTV and boarding records for yesterday's sailings to Dunkirk. Find out who I'll need to speak to and I'll ring them tomorrow morning. Also, make an appointment with the NCA. Tell them about the case and again, find out who I should speak to tomorrow.'

Nick then went through to Shona's office, told her what Ken had said and made a note of the number to ring in the morning.

He looked at his watch. An early finish was in order and perhaps a quiet night in with Helen. He would pick up a bottle of wine on the way home.

TWENTY THREE

Years of bachelorhood had turned Nick into a proficient cook, so when Helen arrived home that evening after a busy, strenuous day schooling young horses, she was relieved to find that Nick had prepared their evening meal. Having changed out of her heavy jumper and jodhpurs, she showered then dressed in a blue blouse and grey slacks.

She walked down the stairs, savouring the interesting aromas coming from the kitchen and went through to investigate, only to be playfully banished by Nick and directed to the dining table. She sat, full of anticipation. A few moments later, Nick appeared with the food and they sat down to chicken in a white wine sauce with garden peas and fluffy mashed potatoes. The flickering candle on the table sparkled through the glasses of Pinot Grigio, matching the sparkle in her eyes as she looked across at Nick. They blew kisses, happy in each other's company.

The food was excellent, the wine was satisfying and the conversation as lively as two people in love could make it. They related their day's happenings as briefly as they could. Nothing out of the ordinary had happened. Nick's case broadening out to include the NCA was about the high spot. Whether it would continue to be interesting after it had been handed over remained to be seen. Helen had taken on a new young horse and its training would be a slow job, but would be fruitful in the long run.

The dessert of a fresh fruit salad with thick cream was light but filling and they took their coffees out on to the small balcony to enjoy the setting sun as it dipped down over the Welsh mountains.

'I love being here with you, Nick,' Helen said as she stretched out in the reclining chair.

'Not hankering after the rolling acres at your parents' home then?' Nick asked. 'I thought you would feel hemmed in here in my little flat.'

'I'm very content here. There's no sudden emergencies at night like there are at home.'

'Emergencies?'

'A mare foaling, perhaps. They always seem to do it at night. Or sometimes a horse opens its stable door and goes walkabout and needs to be brought back. That's if you can find it in the dark. There's nothing like that here. It's so relaxing.'

Nick felt that he ought to mention his call-outs, often at night. 'In the last few weeks since you've moved in,' he said, 'I haven't been called out at night, though that's when a lot of crime takes place, fights, burglaries, RTA's, murders and so on. As I said, we've had a clear run lately. But it does happen.'

'I can live with that,' she said. 'I'm happy with you, that's the important thing. And I don't have to worry about family things.'

'Such as?' he said, hurriedly adding 'If you don't mind me asking, of course.' He had thought that her family, outwardly so well-off, didn't have domestic problems. Obviously, they did.

'No, I don't mind. You would have to know at some point. I have a brother,'

Nick looked surprised.

'He's twelve months older than I am. Malcolm. You could say he's something of a black sheep.'

'In what way?'

'To start with, you might expect him to be involved with horses, wouldn't you? The whole family, aunts, uncles, grandparents have been horsey. My dad's father rode in the Grand National many years ago. You've seen us all at Chester Races. But not Malcolm. He seemed to hate horses from the word go. He was a tear-away at school. Suspended a couple of times but never expelled, fortunately. Mummy would have had forty fits if he had been. Skipped university and vanished into Liverpool as soon as he was able. We rarely see him' but when we do, he's very evasive. We don't know what he does for a living, but he always seems to have plenty of money. The general feeling is that he is up to no good. If you ask what he's doing these days, the best you get is 'This and that.' Infuriating.'

'He must be good at it, though, if he's managed to stay out of jail.'

'That's true. We just hope he's not involved in crime. Whenever we see a report of crimes in Liverpool on television we wonder 'Is it Malcolm?' But so far, 'No,' is the only answer.'

'That must be worrying for your parents.' Nick said. 'You don't want the family name dragged through the mud when everything is going so well.'

Helen said 'Hmm,' hoping that it would be taken as agreement. It might also have been an expression of doubt.

She thought of how her father had kept up the family tradition of a small racing stable which produced runners in the big races year after year. Ross Fletcher's horses were always runners to be reckoned with. Then there were always a few young horses to be brought on, to be trained for racing or, if not found suitable, would be handed over to Helen. Having recovered from her back injury, she had left her secretarial job at Thornhill Hospital and worked full-time with her father, bringing horses on as show-jumpers. She was a calm, sympathetic rider who managed to bring the best out of her horses in competitions.

Her horses were always well-mannered and used to crowds. She took them to local shows and gymkhanas, anywhere there was a crowd of people, dogs, children, loud music, flapping banners and discarded paper blowing in the wind. Consequently, her animals were classed as bomb-proof, always an advantage when it came to selling them on.

'There's another indoor show next Saturday at Pollard's. Would you like to come with me?' she asked.

'Of course I would. I'm looking forward to doing something together,' Nick said.

It was the end of a perfect evening.

TWENTY FOUR

'I've spoken to the port authority at Dover, the DFDS office and the NCA,' Liz said as Nick settled behind his desk next morning. She handed him a piece of paper with the names and numbers of the persons to ring, as he had requested. 'Also,' she went on, 'I took the liberty of telling them the nature of your enquiries. They'll be ready for you when you ring today.'

'Thanks, Liz. You're a gem. I'll get to it right away.'

His call to the Port Authority at Dover was unproductive. Without a registration number, there was no way in which they could help, and searching the CCTV for a blue and white vehicle was a needle in the haystack job which they were reluctant to undertake. Nick supposed he would get the same response from DFDS, so he decided on another angle of attack. He rang Shona.

'Good morning. Raybrook's. How can I help?' she sounded cheerful.

'Morning Shona. It's Nick Price from Cheshire Constabulary. Could I have some details about Ken's trip yesterday, please?'

'Yes...' There was a short delay during which Nick heard her tapping her keyboard to call up the correct page. 'Here we are,' she said. 'Booked on the 21.30 sailing from Dover to Dunkirk. Paid for on 21st of last month. Returning this Friday on the 07.30 sailing, Dunkirk to Dover.'

'Thanks, Shona. Incidentally, what is the registration of Ken's vehicle?'

'That will do you no good. It's back here on the yard.

It won't appear on CCTV down there.'

'Nevertheless, what is it, please?'

'MX71RAY. I hope it helps.'

'I hope so too. Thanks again. Bye.'

Nick's next call was to DFDS, where June of Customer Services took his call. He explained what he thought had happened so far, including the Port Authority's inability to trace the vehicle. He told her that she would probably have the same problem, but asked if they had a late arrival, perhaps replacing a lorry that didn't arrive, despite having booked in advance.

'What was the registration of the one that didn't turn up?' June asked.

Nick told her. Key tapping followed, then June said, 'Ah. Here it is. That vehicle arrived and was loaded on time. Have you got the right number?'

'Positive. Was it an Iveco, white cab, blue body?'

'I'd have to look at the CCTV.'

'I'll be grateful if you would.'

He arranged for her to email him a copy of the CCTV when she found it and went on to ring the National Crime Agency, where he spoke to DS Matt Crewdson. He explained what he knew of the case so far and said he felt that NCA might be interested in the case as it fitted in with so much car theft involving organised crime.

'So what have you done so far, Inspector?'

Nick told him.

'And you didn't think that someone in Raybrook's might be the guilty party?'

'No. They all seem to be above board.'

'You've forgotten your A B C, haven't you? Assume nothing. Believe nobody. Challenge everything. In addition, you've now alerted them to police interest, making our task even more difficult.'

'I'm sure that's not the case. I followed things as far as I could, saving you time if it became necessary. Nobody has been accused or arrested. Will you be taking it on from here?'

'We'll be in touch.' Was the curt reply, leaving Nick up in the air. Should he carry on or not? Crewdson's attitude set him thinking. Perhaps it was an inside job. He ticked them off in his mind.

John Raybrook had gone down to Rugby after the theft. Was he checking that it had gone well? Was his interest just a whitewash?

Ken Harvey is unlikely to volunteer to be hit over the head. But was he hit? Or was it just a sham? No ambulance had been called. There was only Ken's word for it. And his descriptions of the men were next thing to useless.

Shona had done all the booking. She knew all the details of the journey. Was she a useful cog in someone else's machine? Was her relationship with Ken just a cover for something more sinister?

Nick made his way out to Raybrook's once more. An email had arrived on his phone from DFDS. June had been busy and had found the CCTV image of a vehicle boarding the ferry. He needed to show it to them all at Raybrook's.

Sitting in the office with John, Ken and Shona facing him across the desk, he opened his phone and selected June's email.

'What do you make of this?' he asked and pressed 'play'.

The on-board camera showed a head-on view of a lorry entering the ferry. It had a white cab, a blue body and the number plate showed that it was MX71RAY.

'That's our lorry!' John said.

'No it isn't,' Ken joined in.

'Of course it is, Ken. Look at the number plate.' Shona was adamant.

'How do you explain this?' Nick asked.

'Look through the window,' Ken said, with the beginnings of a smirk on his face. 'I'm the only one who spotted it.'

'Yes, that's Bella on the yard,' they all agreed.

'And what's written above the windscreen?'

'Her name. Bella.' John said, then looked again at Nick's phone. 'And that one doesn't have it. False number plates.'

Nick thought hard. Who knew the number of the lorry taking the Mercedes? Shona for sure. Ken, of course. And John, naturally. He would need more evidence before going further. Perhaps Crewdson at NCA had been right. Perhaps it was an inside job. He would hand it over to NCA as soon as he could. He left Raybrook's saying he would be in touch.

TWENTY FIVE

Nick Price knocked on the door of DCI Tom Cameron's office and entered when he heard 'Come' in his boss's loud voice.

'Have you a few minutes for me to bring you up to date with the Bertrand's case, sir?'

'What's going wrong with it? It's not like you to come to tell me unless there's a problem. I usually have to call you in to keep me up to date.'

'Nothing wrong, sir. But there have been ...developments that I should inform you of.'

'Go ahead, then.'

'First of all, there has been no progress on the murders. The remaining suspect will be interviewed again this afternoon. I have interviewed Stuart Reid. Davidson and Carr have spoken to George Smith. I have their report on my desk. However, the company was exhibiting a car, top of the range Mercedes, at the Brussels Motor Show, but the driver of the transporter was attacked and the car was stolen *en route*. I was invited to a meeting with the management of Bertrand's and Raybrook's...'

'Raybrook's? Who are they?'

'John Raybrook owns the transporter, sir. I was invited in what I thought was an advisory capacity but I have become involved in investigating what had happened. I knew that the theft-to-order of high-end cars would be of interest to the NCA, so I have rung them. I spoke to a DS Crewdson, who seemed to think I should have told them earlier and so on, you can imagine. He said they would be in touch, which is why you need to know what went on. If they are taking it on, their Chief will no doubt ring you officially.' He then continued to tell his boss a potted version of the case so far, leaving out his doubts about it being an inside job.

'Right. A full, written report on my desk before lunchtime, please. Then you can get back to chasing the murder case. It's time we had some results on that one. Off you go.'

Nick left, feeling that he had done the right thing. Crewdson would be sure to get his boss to ring and he would only speak to Cameron. At least, he had got in first. He returned to his office and typed out the report.

Rob Davidson and Eamonn Carr had eventually seen George Smith. Nick had their report, but as they were in the office, he called them over.

'I know I've got your report here, but tell me about your visit to George Smith,' he said. 'What was the house like?'

'Clean. Tidy. Probably wanted a woman's touch. Everything was where you would expect, but somehow it was different,' Rob said.

'Well, I suppose that's to be expected. He's been a widower for three years.' Nick thought back to the days of his bachelorhood and the change in his flat since Helen had moved in.

Eamonn joined in. 'It needed my missus to go round there. She can spot a speck of dust at ten yards.'

'So what about pictures on the walls? Anything that would confirm his need to be close to women?'

'Nothing. There was a black and white wedding photo on the sideboard, presumably George's wedding but no other pictures. We talked to him about his current job. Eamonn got in a few quips about working with all these young women coming in to book holidays from the travel firm, but there was no reaction, even when Eamonn said he would swap jobs with him, all he said was 'I'd go back to policing any day.' We tried talking about his previous job at Ellesmere Port. Eamonn mentioned that Bridget had been transferred here but he showed no interest other than to say she had been a good cop and hoped the move worked out for her.'

Eamonn took up the report.

'We mentioned Ellie's death. He was sad about that, he said. She'd been a pleasant girl. He only saw her as she came in and out at night and morning. She could be a bit flirty if Ryan wasn't with her. He was on duty the night she died but had heard no disturbance or screaming. Definitely, nobody had gone out through the back door – closing it would have been too noisy.'

'It seems he's sticking to the story he told me,' Nick said. 'Whether that's a suspicious, well-rehearsed script or not, I'm not sure. With his experience, he'd know we're on his tail and he thinks he can put us off the scent. He's not in the clear by any means.'

With that report out of the way, Nick turned his attention to his remaining suspect, Daniel Thompson. He rang Stuart Reid.

'Hello, Stuart. Nick Price. I wonder if you have a room available for me to have a chat with Daniel this afternoon. It will save bringing him into the station.'

Stuart sounded relieved as he replied. 'Yes. The little room you used before is available. Shall I tell him you're coming?'

'No thanks. As long as it's OK to take him away from work for a short time.'

'That will be fine. See you soon.' Stuart was happy to think that Daniel was still under suspicion. Perhaps that meant that he himself was off the hook.

'Sorry to take you away from work,' Nick said, as Daniel came into the room. 'Have a seat.'

'Do I need a solicitor?' he asked.

'Not unless you think you need one.'

Daniel recalled Kieran's advice. 'Tell them a good story and stick to it.'

'No, I've nothing to hide. Nor anything to add to what

I said before. Am I still under suspicion?'

'You were the last person to see Ryan alive, so yes, you are a suspect. Now, who did you say passed you in the corridor as you came back off the roof?'

'I didn't know at the time, but I recognised him as Stuart, the Office Manager, when I was introduced at the interview.'

'Whose idea was it to go up on the roof?'

'Ryan's. I didn't know the roof existed. He was showing me round.'

'And what did you do up there?'

'We talked about the job. He pointed out what we could see off the roof. Liverpool one way. The Welsh mountains the other. Apparently they used it to get some fresh air, to get away from the air conditioning.'

'It would have been cold at that time of year, wouldn't it?'

'Yes. That's why I came down before him. And he'd texted someone. I thought he was waiting for them to turn up.'

'How do you think Ryan came to fall off the roof?'

'I don't know. I didn't see him, did I? Walking too close to the edge, I suppose. Showing off, close to the edge. It was windy. Perhaps a sudden gust overbalanced him and he'd have gone over the side. I'd told him it was dangerous but he said he'd be OK. Famous last words, eh?'

Nick noted this new knowledge. Was this true or was Daniel embellishing his story? Time for a change of tack.

'You were in Belgium last week, weren't you? Good trip?'

'Yes. Disappointing, though. The car we were supposed to be exhibiting got stolen, so we came home.'

'We?'

'Me and Caroline.'

'Who booked the transport?'

'John in the office. He used Raybrook's for the transporter and I took Caroline in my car. I'd been telling everybody there about our exhibit, got them all excited, then we heard the car wasn't coming. Embarrassing or what?'

Nick got the impression that Daniel didn't share in the embarrassment, but said nothing about it.

'Not a good start for you here at Bertrand's, then?'

'That was nothing to do with me. John booked it.'

Defensive? Why? Nick thought.

Nick folded up his papers.

'That will be enough for now.'

'Does that mean I'm in the clear?'

'Afraid not. Not until I can prove for sure that you could not have been involved in Ryan's fall. Difficult, I agree. I'll see you again, perhaps at the station.'

Daniel felt he had done enough to deflect suspicion. He had even warned Ryan about the danger.

Nick felt even more sure of Daniel's guilt. Where did the new information about the warning come from? Did Daniel need to emphasise his innocence?'

Progress.

TWENTY SIX

'Hello. DI Price? It's DS Crewdson of NCA.'

Nick's heart sank. His previous contact with Crewdson had been frosty. Would this be another lecture on procedure?

'Hello. You're back sooner than I expected.'

'Yes. We've looked into this and we think that it will be better for you to carry on with the investigation.'

'Any reason why?'

'It looks like a one-off theft. Perhaps someone trying to muscle in on the trade in high-end cars, so most of the evidence will be at your end. You are the man on the ground, as it were, so you will be the best one to investigate. You won't be on your own, though. We'll help all we can, but, like everyone else, we're shorthanded and overloaded.'

'I'll certainly need help dealing with the European side of the case. Interpol, etcetera.'

'That's your first problem, you won't be dealing with Interpol. This will have to go through Europol, a different organisation. They are a support organisation covering the whole of Europe.'

'Support?'

'Yes. They have nearly a thousand agents in Europe, but their function is to collect and analyse information on serious and organised crime. They do not arrest people. They give the information to national police forces for them to deal with. They will help you and we will act as a go-between if needed.'

'Sounds like I'm going to need them, and you.'

'Yes. After we last spoke, my boss rang yours, Detective Chief Inspector Cameron, and went through this with him. Your boss said that you were 'eminently capable' - his words, not mine - of dealing with this, so here we are.'

Nick realised that this explained Crewdson's change of attitude, a change for the better if they were to work together.

'My first question, then, is what happened on the other side of the channel? The fact that the transporter had the same registration as the original one suggests to me that they had false number plates to match up with the paperwork. Can CCTV on continental roads, the autobahn etcetera, identify the vehicle? What if they dumped the plates when they crossed over?'

'Their agents are pretty good. Let's see how good they are. That will be my first call for you. Once I've set the ball rolling, you can take it over. Just let me know the registration of the lorry and the VIN number of the car. Presumably, it wouldn't have been registered until it was sold.'

'True enough. I'll make a couple of calls and ring you back.' Vehicle Identification Number for the Mercedes should be easy to find and he already knew the registration of the lorry.

'I'll await your call. By the way, I'm Matt.'

'And I'm Nick.' He hung up.

A new partnership had been formed.

He then rang Stuart Reid to obtain the VIN of the stolen car, and passed it on to Matt Crewdson with a description of the lorry, sparse though it was – white cab, blue body. The ball was rolling.

TWENTY SEVEN

Saturday at Pollard's was going to be interesting. Helen was taking two horses, Nero and a youngster, Gordonstoun Rambler, predictably known, in the stables, as Flash, for his first competition. She also needed some professional help, so Linda, her father's groom, went along with Helen and Nick in the horsebox.

It was an opportunity to introduce Flash to the world of shows, with crowds of people, dogs, children, loudspeakers, banners and other horses. Linda would walk him round occasionally, ride him sometimes, acclimatising him to the new environment. An experienced horse-woman herself, she had a calming influence on horses, a benefit felt by both Helen on her show-jumpers and the jockeys who rode Ross Fletcher's horses on the racecourse.

Nick was also becoming acclimatised to the environment. He enjoyed the freedom from the responsibility of his work. He was a learner here, learning fast about procedure at the show, how the classes were arranged, how courses were built; it was all new to him.

'We've got plenty of time before the first class,' Helen said. 'Nick and I can go round the shop and perhaps a bit of lunch.'

'I'll be fine here,' Linda said. 'I've got my usual packed lunch. I'll stay with the horses.'

Helen and Nick walked off, her hand nestled in his, happy to be together.

'Feeling lucky today?' he asked.

'I feel lucky every day,' she said. 'I've got you

and...'

She paused, as a frown crossed her face.

'What's that all about?' Nick asked.

'I thought I saw... I couldn't have. Just saw someone I didn't expect. I've got you and my horses, what more can a girl want?' she finished her sentence gaily, without explanation.

Nick wondered but didn't ask. An ex-boyfriend? An old competitor? A ruthless horse dealer? It was no business of his so he gave up, though the detective in him stored the frown in his memory-banks for future reference.

They strolled on, into the tack shop, though they browsed rather than purchased anything, then found their way into the restaurant, where they chose a light lunch and enjoyed each other's company before returning to the horse-box and Linda, to prepare for Helen's class.

'Next we have Helen Fletcher riding Gordonstoun Rambler,' came over the loudspeakers.

Helen circled the ring and wanted to give Flash a good view of the first fence, but, inexplicably, she missed the start gate, thus failing to start the timing mechanism.

'Unfortunately, that is elimination for Helen and Gordonstoun Rambler for failing to go through the start,' the announcer explained for the uninitiated.

With her face red with embarrassment and holding back tears, Helen returned to the horse-box and leapt from the saddle.

'I'm so stupid,' she exclaimed. 'I took my eye off the line I was taking and went too wide. All because....'

'All because what?' Nick asked, as she had stopped speaking.

'All because I saw *him* in the crowd.'

She pointed at a young man who approached, rather shame-faced. He was almost as tall as Nick, with blond hair and blue eyes.

'Sorry, Sis. You weren't supposed to see me. I tried

to keep out of the way.'

Helen turned to Nick.

'My brother, Malcolm. Who has the knack of turning up at the wrong time. Malcolm, this is Nick.' The two men shook hands following the brief introduction, though Nick was not sure whether or not to be too gushing with his welcome for the black sheep of the family, so he restricted himself to 'Hello' as did Malcolm.

'I'm not sure that there is a right time for me to turn up in our family,' he said, with a smile, then turned to Nick and said 'I'm the black sheep, in case she hasn't told you.'

Nick thought he seemed to be a pleasant enough young man with enough of a sense of humour to smile about his title.

'What brings you here?' Helen asked. 'It's not like you to come to a horse show.'

'It's not like you to miss going through the start, either, but you did. However, I felt like a change from the city streets and I saw an advert for Pollard's so I thought I would venture into Cheshire once more. I admit that I half expected to see you, though I didn't expect such disastrous results.'

Linda stood nearby with Nero. She pulled down the stirrups in readiness for Helen to get mounted, rather noisily, Nick thought, as if to attract attention to the job in hand.

'I've got to go. We'll talk when I come back.' With that, Helen mounted up and rode off to the collecting ring. Malcolm and Nick both shrugged and said, 'Shall we?' and walked to the ringside.

'At least she won't miss the start this time,' Malcolm said.

'Helen told me you hated horses. So you can see why she was surprised to see you here.'

'Yeah, well, it wasn't the horses I hated when I was growing up. Both of us could ride almost from the cradle, it was that kind of family. I just wanted more out of life. I couldn't stand routine, whether at home or in school.

Consequently, I didn't fit in anywhere.'

'So how did that affect your career?'

'Career?' Malcolm laughed. 'I've never had one.'

Nick looked at Malcolm's smart suit. He had already noticed the expensive watch on Malcolm's wrist and the gold ring on his finger.

'You seem to be doing all right for yourself,' he said.

'Oh, yes. Just odd jobs, this and that, here and there. Helping people mainly. It pays the bills.'

'Which city were you escaping from this morning?' Nick asked, making conversation, though he was aware that it might sound like police questioning.

'Liverpool. I've lived there for years, since I left school. Living on my wits. All legal, of course,' he laughed.

Nick heard Helen's entry to the ring over the loudspeakers and watched her circle the ring before starting her round. There was no silly mistake this time. She was determined to do well, especially with her brother watching. Nero jumped well and produced a satisfyingly clear round. Linda met her as she came out of the ring to take Nero back to the box, while Helen rejoined the two men.

'You haven't lost it, have you, Sis?' Malcolm said as she walked up to them.

'You could have done the same if you'd stuck with it,' she replied.

'Well, you know me. I need to be on to something new all the time.'

'So what are you doing now? And don't say 'this and that'. You've put Mummy off with that answer for years, but it doesn't wash with me.'

'You mean, what am I doing today?'

'Yes. You're always up to something, so come on. Tell.'

'Just keeping an eye on things for somebody.'

'What things? What somebody?'

'Can't tell you that. The cat has to stay in the bag, I'm

afraid.'

'Legal?'

'Might be.'

'You are infuriating! I give up. At least it's nice to see you again. I can tell Mummy I've seen you and that you look well. She always asks.'

Just then, Nick's phone rang.

'I need to take this,' he said. He turned and walked away.

'Perhaps, I should visit more,' Malcolm continued. ' but we always end up having a row which is usually about what I do for a living.'

'OK. But it's only because we care about you.'

'It's also because I haven't become a solicitor or something "respectable" - he drew the inverted commas in the air - like you did. So let's change the subject, shall we? Tell me all about Nick. Boyfriend? How long have you known him?'

'We've been together for a year or so and we live together in Chester.'

Nick returned, tucking his phone into his pocket. Malcolm turned to him.

'And what do you do, Nick? Something respectable, I bet. Salesman? Estate agent?'

'Wrong and wrong. I'm a policeman,' Nick replied. 'It depends on your point of view whether you think it's a respectable job or not.'

'To be on the safe side, I'll say it's respectable. Will you excuse me for a moment?'

He turned and ran off towards the toilet block'

'That was sudden,' Helen said.

'Taken short, I suppose. Happens to all of us. He seems to be someone I could get on with,' Nick said. 'He has restless eyes, as though he's searching for something. I don't know what.'

'He's always been like that. On the lookout for

something new,' Helen said.

'Yes. I noticed he took great interest in the junior jumping ring. He's over there now.'

'I wonder why,' Helen said. 'He said he came out to Cheshire for a change of scenery, but I think there's another reason.'

'Really?' Nick asked.

'I know my brother,' she replied and left it at that.

They walked across to the horsebox where Linda was walking Nero round in readiness for the jump-off.

Malcolm returned a short time later.

'Sorry about that. Needs must...' he said. 'Anyway, you'll be going into the jump-off soon, so I'll leave you to it. Love to Mum and Dad. Nice to meet you, Nick. Hope to see you again. Bye, Sis. Good luck.'

He hugged Helen, shook Nick by the hand and moved away, melting into the crowd.

Later, heading for home, Helen hung a red rosette on the rack in the horsebox.

'Nero did well. He's very good against the clock. He's responsive. He seems to enjoy the speedy competition.'

'Something to do with the rider, as well,' Nick said, as Linda drove the box towards the gate out of Pollard's yard, heading for home and though she was driving slowly, the box lurched as she slammed her foot on the brakes to avoid the ambulance which was turning into the yard, blue lights flashing.

Helen heard Nero trying to maintain his footing in the box and got out to make sure that he was all right. Nick appeared at her side.

'Is he OK?' he asked as she closed the side door after her inspection.

'Yes, he's fine. It was as well to check.'

'I wonder what the ambulance is for?' Nick said

'I don't think it would be for any of the riders. We'd have heard of any fallers over the loudspeakers,' Helen replied.

'There's quite a crowd here today. It could be for anyone in the shop or the restaurant or around the rings, I suppose,' Nick concluded.

Helen turned to a passer-by who was leaving on foot.

'Any idea what's happened?' she asked.

'Horse ran into an old woman and knocked her over.'

'Loose horses are always a danger,' Helen said.

'This one wasn't loose. There was a kid on it. Just rode it into the crowd. Laughing his head off.'

Helen and Nick got back into the cab.

'Nothing we can do,' they concluded, though it had put a dismal end to a good day out.

TWENTY EIGHT

DCI Tom Cameron called Nick into his office.

'Good weekend?' he asked.

'Yes, thank you, sir. Helen was competing at Pollard's.'

'Then you'll be just the man for this job. Leave DS Martin to run the murder case for now and take our new recruit to Pollard's. There was an accident there yesterday and David Pollard has reported that the person involved may have been on drugs. He thought we ought to know.'

'It must have happened as we were on the way out, sir. We met the ambulance as it came in. We heard just the bare bones of what happened. A boy on a pony ran into the crowd.'

'Then get over there and put some flesh on the bones. Have a word with PC Williamson. He was called out and did a drug test which turned out positive. The boy was allowed home afterwards. We need to know where these drugs are coming from, whether it's County Lines or some other supplier. And keep me informed.'

With Dave in charge, the murder case would be in safe hands, though the shortage of evidence in Ellie's case was a problem. All three suspects could be in the clear. Where would they go then? Ryan's case could be written off as suicide. Or could it? Again, lack of evidence would mean a killer went free.

Having given Dave his orders, Nick collected Bridget Carson and drove over to Pollard's. On the way, he told her as much of David's history as he could remember from Helen's description of the man. On arrival, Nick found that David Pollard had taken useful notes of the previous day's events.

David reported that Mrs Hilda Benfield had been run into by a pony, ridden by a competitor, Jamie Turner. As Helen had been told the day before, he was riding uncontrolled, laughing and shouting, through the crowd moving between the junior ring and the car park. The pony had been stopped, whether by the rider or by the crowd was not clear, and the boy, just 14 years old, had been dragged off its back by a bystander, a Paul Renton, and taken to David's office.

David had meticulously taken contact details for everyone involved, from Mrs Benfield, the first-aiders who had called the ambulance, PC Williamson, Paul Renton and a couple of ring stewards who had tried to head off the galloping pony.

'What about Mrs Benfield? Was she badly hurt?' Bridget wanted to know.

'She was shaken up. Luckily, there were no cuts and no broken bones, but there may be bruises this morning, as she fell against a fence post. She was taken to hospital but went home after examination.'

Nick was grateful for the details that David had recorded, then asked 'What do you know about this boy, Jamie Turner? Is he a regular competitor here?'

'Yes. If you'd asked me this yesterday morning, I would have said he was lively, full of beans, a good rider and a pleasant lad to have about the place. Now, I think he's taken his liveliness to another extreme. The paramedics told me there were signs of drug taking, which is why I contacted the police.'

'What was he like when he was brought to you?'

'To say he was behaving strangely would be an understatement. He was saying things like 'I can rule the world' and 'I can fly'. He felt no remorse about running into an old lady, in fact, he thought it was funny. 'Ninepins' he said, meaning Mrs Benfield. He was an embarrassment. I was glad when they took him away. We were lucky that this was the only injury he caused.'

Nick thanked David for his information and he and Bridget left.

'First stop, Mrs Benfield,' he said, and Bridget set the satnav to the postcode that was on David's sheet of notes.

A round, rosy-cheeked lady answered the door at Nick's knock.

'Mrs Benfield?' Nick asked.

'Yes, luv. Who are you?'

'I'm Detective Inspector Nick Price from Cheshire Constabulary and this is Detective Constable Bridget Carson.'

'Oh, what a lovely name. Bridget. I suppose you've come about yesterday's accident, have you?'

'Yes. Can we come in for a short chat?'

'Course you can. Shall I put the kettle on?'

'Thanks, but not for us. We have a lot to get through this morning.'

Mrs Benfield led them along a hallway into a small, neat kitchen. Neat but at the same time, lived in. Fridge magnets covered the fridge door from places as far apart as Cornwall and Scotland and many places in between.

Bridget commented, 'You seem to have been everywhere, but not abroad?'

'No, I haven't seen everywhere in this country yet. Albert and I used to go on coach tours. Always to interesting places. Now take a seat. I always think that round the kitchen table is the best place to talk, don't you?'

Nick agreed, and they all sat on the kitchen chairs as Bridget took out her notebook.

'First of all, how are you feeling this morning after

the accident?' Nick asked, thinking that she was showing no signs of injury.

'I'm fine. Luckily, I saw him coming and I was turning away when the pony bumped me into the fence. I'm well-padded, as you can see, but they took me to the hospital to get checked out. Luckily, my daughter had taken her little girl to get an ice cream or I would have had the little one in the pushchair and that would have been dangerous.'

Nick agreed.

'What did you think of the boy on the pony?'

'He seemed mad. Big stary eyes. Shouting 'I can fly' Stripped to the waist and waving his shirt over his head. And he laughed when he bumped me into the fence. That hurt more than falling into the fence. I'm all for kids enjoying themselves, but that was too much. No respect for age.'

'Well, I'm glad you are ok this morning. Thank you for talking to us. Now we must get on.'

'If the police are involved, will he go to jail?'

'No, he's under age. But he will have had a good telling-off. He'd be wishing he could fly after that.'

Nick and Bridget left and made their way to the home of Jamie Turner. On the way, Nick used David Pollard's list to ring PC Williamson on hands-free, who responded after a couple of rings. Nick explained who he was and asked about the drugs test.

'I used a drugalyzer,' Williamson said, 'which showed the presence of drugs in his saliva. On looking at the boy, I could see his pupils were dilated and he was sweating and grinding his teeth. He also seemed unconcerned about what he had done. When searched, he had two Ecstasy pills in his pocket. I arrested him for possession. He was allowed home in the care of his mother.'

'Ah, Ecstasy. That will explain his attitude to the accident. That feeling of euphoria is one of the known effects of Ecstasy,' Bridget said.

Nick thanked the constable as they drew up to a house

in the country. A neat stable yard was nearest to the road with white-railed paddocks visible beyond, in one of which a pony grazed quietly, only lifting its head when the car drew up, resuming grazing when it found no interest in the new arrivals. A young girl, about fourteen years old, Nick guessed, appeared at one of the stable doors, broom in hand.

'Can I help?' she asked, explaining that there was nobody in at the moment.

'Any idea when they'll be back?' Bridget asked.

'No idea at all. Jamie was ill in the night. Mrs Turner called the ambulance and they've taken her and Jamie to Thornhill Hospital.'

'What about Mr Turner? Is he about?'

'No. He works in Liverpool. He's an architect. I usually see him at weekends but he's away this week, abroad somewhere.'

'What's your name, by the way?' Bridget said.

'Penny. Penny Carter.'

'Oh, you're not Jamie's sister, then. Girl friend?'

'No. Just his groom. I work here at weekends. I'm here today because it's half-term week, otherwise I'd be at school.'

'What kind of a lad is Jamie?' Nick asked.

'Wild, I would say. Daredevil. Always up to something.'

'Same school as you?'

'No. I'm at St James's Secondary. He's at Thornhill College as a day student.'

Nick explained to Bridget that Thornhill College was a private school.

'Were you at Pollard's with him at the weekend?'

'Yes. I looked after the pony. We won the prize for Best Turned Out. That was down to me.' She was obviously proud to be associated with a successful family.

'Did Jamie win any classes?'

'Yes. Two. And a cup.'

'Did you see what happened towards the end?'

'No, I was too far away, the other side of the ring. I said he was wild, didn't I? Well after he won the cup he said he'd got a headache and his friend Macca had given him a headache pill when he went to the toilets. He took it with a drink. It cured his headache, I think, but he started acting silly, saying he could fly and laughing and galloping around. Mrs Turner tried to stop him, but he took off his shirt and waved it like a flag. Then he ran into an old lady and someone stopped the pony. The pony wasn't hurt. I took it back to the box and made ready for home, but by then the police had taken Jamie away. Mrs Turner and I came home alone and she went to collect him later.'

'Thanks for talking to us,' Nick said. 'but we must get on. Good luck in the future, Penny,' He and Bridget got into the car and left.

'That was very useful, getting an opinion from someone about Jamie's own age. 'Wild' would seem to be a good description of him. And did you notice, she said 'The pony wasn't hurt.' That's horsey people for you. As long as the pony's ok, it doesn't matter about Jamie or Mrs Benfield getting hurt. Let's go over to the hospital and see what's happening there.'

TWENTY NINE

It was Jim Lewis's turn to drive along the autobahn. He and Allan Brewer had made good time so far and a comfort stop near Nuremberg was called for. Jim pulled into the lorry park and drove to the far side near the trees well away from the restaurant.

'It's nearly dark now. A good chance to get rid of the number plates,' Jim said as they stretched their legs and eased their backs.

'I've more to get rid of than a pair of number plates,' Allan said as he unzipped his jeans, while making for the trees.

This isolated spot was ideal cover for them to remove the number plates to reveal their original ones beneath. Allan returned at length, now relieved, and helped Jim to conceal them in the waste ground beyond the trees.

'Job done,' said Allan as they made their way towards the restaurant. 'A good meal now and a night's sleep will set us up for another ten-hour drive tomorrow. What do you say?'

Jim agreed. Over a good meal, they discussed the operation. Neither had done this kind of a run before though both were experienced in driving on the continent. Sat-nav was a great help in finding detours around road works. But carrying stolen goods was new to them. Hence, the touch of nervousness they both felt. The papers they had taken from Ken showed the destination as Brussels, which was a day's driving behind them. Their papers were never checked, and careful driving would ensure that they did nothing to interest the Polizei. They did their best to keep it that way.

'Do they speak English in Turkey?' Allan asked.

'I should think so. There's always someone who speaks English. And there's no money to change hands, so it should be straightforward. Take photos of everybody at the hand over, that's what we were told and that's what we'll do. Mind you, I'm wishing you hadn't tapped the other driver so hard. He seemed quite prepared to let us take his load. Almost as if he expected it.'

'Well, he might have got a look at our faces. I just didn't want him remembering too much about us.'

'I suppose that's reasonable.'

After a full day together, conversation drifted off until both agreed that it was time to settle down for the night. Tomorrow would be another long day.

At noon the next day, Nick Price's phone buzzed.

'Hello Nick. It's Matt Crewdson, NCA.'

'Hi Matt. Don't tell me you have news already!'

'I have, and it's all good. Your lorry has been identified on the autobahn. It spent the night in a car park near Nuremberg.'

'That's good news.'

'It gets better. The drivers removed the false number plates there and dumped them in a field.'

'I'd like those back as useful evidence. I hope the Polizei haven't messed up any fingerprints.

'They've been very careful. We're talking about Germans here, so 'meticulous' would be a better word than 'careful'. The Polizei are very keen to interrupt the flow of smuggling through their borders, in both directions. Their ANPR picked up the lorry twenty kilometres outside Nuremberg and they suggest that they follow it to its destination, just in case it turns off routes that are covered by ANPR. It may also bring more illegal goods, or even immigrants, back on the return journey. If so, they want to know about how and where they are picked up and find out what they can about the main dealers in this game.'

'That sounds excellent. Will they let us know the original number of the lorry, so that we can watch for it when it returns?'

'Yes, of course. We'll be on to it straight away and let you know. In view of the seriousness of this case, you'll be able to track progress on HOLMES.'

'That'll please Liz Marston. She's our computer queen. She'll love getting on to the Home Office database.'

'Sounds like I've made everybody's day,' Matt said.

'You certainly have. Thanks, Matt. We'll keep in touch.'

Nick had been right. Liz was thrilled to be following the case on the computer. And this time, there was no rush. All they had to do was wait for the lorry to return.

THIRTY

Nick enjoyed visiting Thornhill Hospital. It was where he first met Helen, when she had been the CEO's secretary and he had had a case to solve. He looked back fondly to those days.

He enquired at A&E about Jamie Turner and was directed to a side ward, where a nurse at the door asked whether he was related to Jamie. When he explained his reason for visiting, she told him that the boy may have overdosed on drugs – Ecstasy, she thought - and was very ill. They agreed that it would be better for Bridget to remain at the hospital and to ring Nick later, when it might be possible to speak to Jamie.

Meanwhile, Nick returned to his office. On the way, his thoughts went back to Pollard's. He had thought it odd that Malcolm had rushed off to the toilet, yet moments later, he was down near the Junior ring. And when he'd returned to them, he gave the impression that he had just come from the toilet. Why the subterfuge? And Penny Carter had said that Jamie had a headache pill from his friend Macca. Couldn't 'Macca' be a shortened form of 'Malcolm' - a kind of nickname? He thought over how Malcolm had described his work. '…odd jobs, this and that, here and there.' The vague description he had been using to fob his mother off for years. To cover up what he was really doing perhaps? 'Helping people mainly' was another of his phrases. Helping them to do what? Helping them to forget the world? Helping them to feel good? To stop feeling anxious? Ecstasy could do all of those things.

But Malcolm was Helen's brother. Nick would have to bear all this in mind before taking any positive steps. He would certainly need more concrete evidence before making an arrest or even an accusation. He would keep his suspicions to himself for now.

THIRTY ONE

Daniel walked into Kieran's office with a selection of motoring magazines under his arm and a big grin on his face.

'I thought you'd like to see these reports of the Brussels Show. The motoring press is full of the theft,' he said.

Kieran picked up the top one and read 'THE MOTOR'
'The Brussels Motor Show was overshadowed by the theft of a Mercedes which was to be shown by Bertrand's of Chester but was hijacked on its way to Brussels. Bertrand's representative, Daniel Thompson, formerly of Burke's, told us that it was a very sad event indeed for his new company, to lose a car in this way.'

He turned to the second, which was MERCEDES TODAY.
'The theft of a Mercedes on its way to the Brussels Motor Show is nothing but tragic for Bertrand's of Chester. Not only did they lose a car, they also lost the faith of their customers, though Daniel Thompson, their representative, said they had done their best to take all security precautions to protect the vehicle.'

BMW ROUND-UP was less sympathetic, with a photograph of their representatives smiling joyfully on their stand at Brussels, next to a photograph of Daniel's defaced banner prominently displayed over the empty Bertrand's stand, announcing *We supply nothing.'*

Even more damaging was the report in the MOTOR DEALER'S DIGEST, highlighting Bertrand's current problems, as if anyone needed reminding.
Bertrand's of Chester, for so long a leading dealership, have hit a

new low. In the last few months, two of their staff, well-known to most dealers, have died, with their deaths still unexplained. Then, to cap it all, their prize exhibit for the Brussels Motor Show, a Mercedes AMG GTR, was the subject of a hi-jack. The car has not been seen since.

The company has suffered both financially and in its reputation. We can only hope that a recovery is on the way.

However, morale in the company was at an all-time low. The question in everybody's mind was 'If Ryan and Ellie could be killed without obvious reason, it could happen to anybody.'

There was no pattern to their deaths. Ryan had died on a day when all the staff were in. Ellie had died when she was alone in the building. What was there to prevent a member of the accounts team or HR being a target? Resignations followed, weakening the company further.

Daniel reported this state of affairs to Kieran, who took it all in with a satisfied smile on his face.

'It's all going my way,' he said, 'but what's the situation with the police? Are you still a suspect for the first one?'

'They haven't said I'm not. They seem to be digging around and finding nothing, but I'm sticking to my story, like you said.'

'Good. I don't want to make my move too soon, but see what you can find out about that detective. We might need to put some pressure on him to get him off your back.'

The telephone rang. Kieran answered it.

'Yes? Who's that? ...Oh, Macca. Problems?'

Daniel could only make out a garbled version of the caller's message and judged from Kieran's changing attitude that something was amiss.

'What d'you mean, in hospital?'

More explanation from Macca followed.

'Well it must be a bad batch. How many did you give him?...Three? Well don't give 'em so many to start off. Gently gently. And be careful. You've started off ok, so don't spoil it. It's a new area for us. Cheshire's a big county. We could have good pickings there.'

He slammed the phone down.

'Bloody Macca. Overdoing it again,' he said.

'Sorry, I'm not with it.' Daniel said.

'It's best you don't know too much about it, so forget you ever heard that conversation.'

Daniel knew enough not to press the point, so he remained silent. It was obviously to do with another of Kieran's interests. If Macca was working in Cheshire and he was preparing the ground for Kieran to take over Bertrand's, it was clear that his boss was expanding his business interests in a new area in a big way. If Daniel played his cards right he could become important in Kieran's organisation and make himself a lot of money in the process. Keeping his ears open and his mouth shut would be the way forward.

THIRTY TWO

'Hello, Bridget.'

Nick had been expecting a call, but not so soon. He might now be able to speak to Jamie this afternoon rather than wait until tomorrow.

'Hi, boss.' Her voice was subdued, beneath the hubbub of the hospital corridor with the rattle of passing trolleys and the hum of voices in conversation.

'Speak up, Bridget. I can hardly hear you,' Nick said.

'I'm outside the ward. Sorry, boss, but Jamie has just died.'

'That's bad news. I was hoping to get some information from him. So what happened?'

'They've just wheeled his body out of the ward, going to the mortuary but the pathologist hasn't seen him yet. Should I stay here or would you like to come to see his mother? She's still here, of course.'

'It's too soon after his death to talk to his mother. We don't want a complaint on the grounds of intrusion, but if it's possible, have a brief word with her. Ask if we can visit her at home. Impress on her that we're on her side and we're keen to find out where he was getting drugs from and who was supplying him. We also need to know who his friends were, though Penny Carter might be more helpful on that, she's more his age. Then come back here and we'll decide on further action.'

He put the phone down. He now had a problem. Those thoughts about Malcolm became important. Where did he fit in?

Bridget arrived at Nick's office an hour later.

'I had to hang about for a bit, but I eventually had a word with Mrs Turner. She was, naturally, overcome with events, but said we could speak to her tomorrow morning. And Penny Carter would be there as well. It's half-term.'

'Good work, Bridget. That's what we'll do.

Next morning saw Nick and Bridget driving out to the Turner house, arriving as Penny was grooming a pony tied to a ring on the stable wall. A grief-stricken Joyce Turner greeted them on the garden path and invited them into the house.

'Can we talk in the kitchen?' she asked, assuming agreement as she led them into a spacious kitchen, luxuriously fitted out with oak cupboard doors and an array of machines, food mixers and coffee makers, electric can openers and shining kettles, arranged on the granite worktops.

'Tea or coffee?' she asked.

Nick turned to Bridget. The coffee machine was clearly up to making a variety of coffees to equal high-street coffee houses, but they kept it simple by ordering tea.

Joyce Turner seemed bright enough, though to Nick's practised eye, her brightness seemed a little forced. Her eye make-up failed to disguise the sleepless, tearful night she had spent, without the comfort of her absent husband or the chatter and noise of the now-deceased Jamie. She was glad to have company, even if it was a couple of coppers making enquiries. Nick decided to keep it conversational, enquiring about how she felt and sympathising over the loss of her son. He encouraged her to talk about Jamie, though she found difficulty in referring to him in the past tense.

'He's a wonderful boy. Full of fun. The house is so quiet without him.' She dabbed her eyes with her handkerchief as the need for a past tense hit home. She went on. 'Adventurous as well. A wonderful rider. Always wanted to try something new. He was never satisfied with just riding a pony, like other children. He wanted to do something different. He thrived on competition. He found polo exciting, and after we had a holiday in Canada, Western barrel racing and the bucking bronco caught his interest.'

These Canadian events went clear over Nick's head, but he kept his silence rather than show his ignorance by commenting.

'Was he a popular boy?' Bridget asked?'

'Oh, yes. Both at school and in our riding club. Rugby team captain at school and team leader in the show jumping team at the club.'

'Responsible positions, so yesterday's performance was not his usual behaviour?'

'Quite out of character. And to run into that poor woman. How is she, by the way?'

'A bit sore, but otherwise ok. We saw her yesterday,' Nick replied, pleased that Joyce Turner had enquired.

'I'm glad she wasn't hurt. He was so boisterous; I couldn't control him.'

'Had he been like this before?'

'No. They said at the hospital that he'd taken drugs or something. That's the first I've heard of them. Where he got them from, I don't know.'

'Did he ever mention anyone named Macca?'

'No. Not at all. Does he have something to do with this?'

'We don't know. It's something we're looking into at the moment.'

Bridget decided to ask a question.

'Can you give us the names of some of his friends? We'll need to speak to them.'

'I could mention a few, but the club are having a rally at Pollard's tomorrow, as it's half-term. You might be better turning up there tomorrow. His closest friend was Tom Hassall. He's sure to be there. His mother phoned me this morning. He and Tom were inseparable. Tom even came to see him that evening after the show. I heard them laughing in the games room. When I asked what they were laughing about, they said it was about Jamie getting arrested. I told them I didn't find it funny and sent Tom off home as Jamie needed to rest.'

'Any girlfriends?' Bridget asked.

'Jamie and Annabelle Hart have been close recently. How serious this was I'm not sure, but he may have confided in her as well. In fact, Penny, our groom, is nearer Jamie's age. She might be able to give you more information.'

Nick thanked Mrs Turner for her hospitality and for telling him about Jamie. They left, saying that they would keep her informed as the case developed.

Penny had just put the pony back in the stable as Nick and Bridget approached.

'It's so sad,' she said.

'Yes,' Nick agreed. 'A young life wasted.'

'I meant about the pony, Jasper. There's no-one to compete on him now and he's so fit. He's ready to go on winning.'

Nick looked at Bridget and raised his eyebrows, reminding her of his previous comment about horsey people. Bridget smiled and nodded in acknowledgement.

'Penny, can you tell me about Jamie's friends at the riding club,' Nick asked.

'He was friendly with everybody.'

'What about particular friends. Tom, for instance.'

'Tom Hassall is a creep. He only pretends to be friends with Jamie.'

'Why do you say that?'

'They were great friends at one time. I think Tom was in Jamie's shadow, like a lap dog. Then, after last year's Christmas party at the club, things changed.'

'In what way?'

'Tom's girlfriend, Annabelle, left the party with Jamie. She's been with him ever since.'

'So Tom is jealous?'

'Yes. He wanted Annabelle back but she wanted to stay with Jamie.'

'Would Tom do anything to harm Jamie, do you think?'

'I wouldn't be surprised. He's so slimy, he's capable of anything. Two faced, that's what he is. He'd love to get Annabelle back, but she's seen through him now. He's got no chance.'

'And what about Annabelle?'

'She's lovely. Everybody likes her, She always helps the little ones in the club to tack up their ponies and she's often helping the mums when there are refreshments to pass round or washing up after parties.'

'Except last year's Christmas party,'

'Yes. She was stuck on Jamie then.'

'No other friends close to Jamie?'

'Not really. Not close. Except me, of course, but I'm a different kind of friend. I just look after Jasper for him.'

Nick thanked Penny for talking to them and they made their way back to the car.

As Bridget drove back to Chester, Nick's phone buzzed. It was Anuradha Rintoul, the pathologist.

'Hi Anu,' he said. 'I didn't expect you to ring so soon.'

'I was working in the mortuary when this boy was brought in. My preliminary diagnosis is that he died from a drug overdose. Ecstasy would be my guess. I thought you'd like to know as soon as possible. You usually do. I'll be doing a full *post mortem* tomorrow.'

'Thanks, Anu,' Nick said and closed the call.

As they passed through the leafy countryside, Nick made his plans. He would get the team together for a briefing tonight and deliver a plan for tomorrow.

THIRTY THREE

While his team were gathering for the briefing, Nick rang David Pollard.

'I understand your riding club have a rally with you tomorrow.'

'Yes,' David said. 'It's just a private thing, just for the juniors as they are all off school this week. It's not open to the public.'

'That will help. I have a favour to ask, David. As you know, young Jamie Turner has died, and your rally will be a good chance to have a word with some of his friends. However, I don't want to appear heavy-handed in this by turning up with a team of officers, but it will be quicker to interview some of them if I do. Hopefully, their parents will be with them.'

'Yes, driving their horse-boxes and trailers.'

'Good. Is there any way we can have separate areas to talk to them?'

David thought hard and suggested that, as the restaurant was closed, four interviews could be done in the corners of the empty room. He asked if a couple of empty stables would be suitable.

'Ideal,' Nick said. 'Nice and informal. I don't want to frighten anyone, especially kids. We want their help, after all.'

They discussed a few other details then Nick went through to speak to his team, who had arrived in the incident room.

'You've all heard about the boy at the riding club who died of drug overdose. We need to interview some of his friends which we will do tomorrow, before they get started on a rally at Pollard's. Ten to fifteen minutes should be enough for each one, longer if you need it. We must be there early. You will all be in separate places, some in the restaurant and some in the stables, so that there will be an air of confidentiality. They will each have a parent with them.'

'What are we trying to find out?' Eamonn asked.

'Make a note of how well they knew Jamie Turner - that's the boy who died. Did they see him on Saturday last, if so, what was he doing? Did any strangers speak to him, particularly adults? If so, get a description. Basically, we need to know more about the drugs scene, where they come from, who brings them in, and so forth, so anything you can find out, will help towards that end.

Next morning, they were all in place well before the riding club junior members arrived. Nick wanted to avoid facing them with his team behind him. That would be a daunting sight for these young people. As it was, he asked the youngsters to gather in front of the restaurant before unboxing their ponies. When all were present, he spoke to them and their perplexed parents.

'Good morning. I am Detective Inspector Nick Price of Cheshire Constabulary, and this is Detective Sergeant Dave Martin, and we've gathered you all here because we need you to help us. I was here last Saturday, I think I recognise one or two faces. I was with my friend Helen Fletcher in the senior ring.'

He needed them on his side, so a bit of name-dropping would do no harm at all. There were smiles and murmurs of approval at the mention of Helen's name.

'We would like to ask you a few questions,' he went on, 'just five or ten minutes of your time before you start your activities.'

A tall man at the back interrupted. 'It's going to take more than that to talk to this crowd.'

'Not really,' Nick replied. 'First of all, we would like

to talk to the ones who are twelve years old and upwards, so the younger ones can now go back to their ponies.'

He waited until they had moved off before continuing.

'Now, there are officers waiting to talk to you around the complex. It's nothing to worry about. We're not here to arrest anybody. We're just looking for information. And we would like the parents to come in with them.'

'You could have done this down at the station without all this palaver.' The tall man was determined to make his presence felt.

'Well, let's get the interviews on the way and I'll tell you why when they've started,' he said, handing over to Eamonn to direct youngsters and parents to the waiting officers. Nick approached the tall man with a smile and led him away from the waiting youngsters.

'Now, Mr er…'

'Hassall. Joe Hassall.'

'Well, Mr Hassall, we are investigating a death here. You may have heard about Jamie Turner. It's a lot for youngsters to take in. I think, if we had tried to speak to all these people by visiting them at home it would take a vast amount of time and effort. As it is we have narrowed down the possible helpers and we will have spoken to all of them within an hour without frightening any of them. A much better plan, don't you think?'

Joe Hassall shuffled from foot to foot and grudgingly agreed. 'If you say so.' He turned and returned to his horse-box, a large vehicle with 'J. HASSALL HORSES' emblazoned along the body in a script-like font and an artistic impression of a horse's head and a couple of rosettes and a silver cup filling up the corners. As he did, Dave Martin appeared from the other side of the box, leading a young boy.

'Here! What's going on?' Joe Hassall shouted.

'I saw this young man walking off with the little ones. I'm sure he should be here with the older ones,' Dave said.

'What have you been up to?' Joe asked the boy.

'Nothing, Dad. Honestly.'

'You'd better be right,' his father growled.

'So you must be Tom Hassall?' Nick asked. 'You were Jamie's friend, weren't you?'

'How do you know that?' Joe said, before Tom could open his mouth

'It was mentioned in a conversation earlier,' Nick said, 'Come with me, please. It will be quieter in here.' He led the way into a loose box which had a wet floor and smelled of disinfectant, having been cleaned out that morning.

'It's very hard to lose a friend, Tom,' he said. You must be very upset.'

'Yes,' Tom said.

'When did you last see Jamie?'

'Saturday.'

'Here, at the show?'

'Yes. Afternoon.'

'This is an informal interview, so you're not under caution, but I do expect you to tell me the truth. So I'll ask you again. When did you last see Jamie?'

'Saturday. Evening. We were in the games room at his house.'

'What were you doing there?'

'He wanted to celebrate winning a cup at the show. His mum gave us some cans of cider.'

'So you were having a good time?'

'Yes. And we played pool.'

'Who won?'

'I did. For once.'

'You're good at pool, are you?'

'Better than Jamie. He didn't cheat this time.'

'Who is Macca, Tom?'

'He comes …' Tom stopped, realising he had fallen into a trap.

'Go on. You were saying.'

'Just that Macca is someone who comes here from Liverpool now and again.'

'What does he look like?'

'Tall. Fair hair. That's all I know. I've only seen him once. Jamie knew him better.'

'Sadly, he's not here to ask. Why do you think Jamie charged around at the end of the show?'

'No idea. Excited at winning the cup, I suppose.'

'Showing off to the girls, perhaps?'

'He didn't have to do that. He could have any girl he chooses. '

'Like Annabelle?'

Tom's face fell.

'Like Annabelle,' he agreed.

Joe Hassall interrupted.

'I thought Annabelle was your girlfriend?'

'She was. Until Christmas.'

'You didn't tell me about it.'

'It wouldn't change anything, Dad. What Jamie wants, Jamie gets.'

Nick wanted to proceed. He changed the subject.

'Do any of the kids round here take drugs?' he asked.

'No idea. I don't.'

'Good job too or you'd feel the weight of my belt,' his father thundered, and Tom flinched at the memory of the last time he'd felt the belt, following an evening when he and Jamie had opened, and sampled, one of his father's favourite whiskies, a Penderyn Legend. Jamie had got off scot free, of course. His mother's only comment was 'Boys will be boys' and laughed it off. Tom's punishment left marks on his back for weeks.

'Did Jamie take any drugs?' Nick asked.

'Not that I know of.'

'Well, I said ten minutes. Thank you for talking to me, Tom. You've been very helpful.' Nick shook hands with Joe Hassall. 'And thank you, too. Enjoy the rest of your day.'

Tom and his father returned to the yard, with Tom being quite pleased that his lies had not been detected.

Tom having lied about Saturday evening, Nick wondered how many of Tom's other answers had been truthful. Dave met Nick as he emerged from the box.

'That's everybody finished.'

'OK Dave. Let's get back and see what we've got.'

THIRTY FOUR

The incident room filled up quickly as the team returned from Pollard's. With notebooks at the ready, they waited as Nick began proceedings.

'Well done, this morning. It all went according to plan.'

'That's the first time I've been in a restaurant and not even had a cup of coffee,' muttered Eamonn.

'I'm sure you'll survive,' Liz replied.

'OK. Let's get on,' Nick said.

'Excuse me boss,' a constable said, 'but there's a couple of us with nothing to report.'

'How come?'

'The children we saw only knew Jamie briefly. New members and so forth. They hadn't seen him on Saturday except when he was in the ring competing.'

'Right. So let's go to those with something to report. Bridget. Who did you see?'

'I saw Annabelle Hart. She was Jamie's girlfriend. She spent a lot of time with Jamie on Saturday. He said he had a headache and went to the toilets and came back saying he'd met his mate - Macca he called him – and he'd given him a pill. It must have worked because he appeared to be a lot brighter after that. She said she didn't know why he wanted to race around at the end. She was rather shy to start, but she eventually said that earlier in the afternoon he had cornered her in a horsebox, one kiss led to another, but he wanted to go further, but she had refused. That was why he complained of a headache and went off to the toilets.'

Eamonn was quick to say 'That's a change, It's usually…'

'OK. Leave it, Eamonn.' Nick shut him down quickly.

Bridget continued. 'When he returned, Annabelle had decided that their relationship wasn't working and told Jamie so. He flung a few insults at her, said he could find a better girlfriend anytime and then jumped on his pony and galloped off around the arena. She was concerned about the lady who was injured. She felt partly to blame.'

'Thank you, Bridget. Eamonn, you're next.'

'I saw Ian Simms. He didn't like Jamie at all. Said he was big-headed. Moody, like when his mood changed on Saturday. They didn't go to the same school, so he didn't know him apart from seeing him at the riding club.'

'Rob. Who did you see?'

'Jeremy Tate. He goes to the same school as Jamie. He said that Jamie was captain of the school rugby team. Something of a bully. Mocked those of them who didn't play rugby. Called them wimps. He was the same in the riding club, but he didn't throw his weight about when the adults were nearby. Crafty like that. Jeremy didn't trust him. He saw Jamie talking to a man in the toilets, but he didn't hear what was said and he didn't get a good look at the man's face, so apart from tall and wearing dark clothes, there's no description.

Liz was next to report.

'I saw Belinda Johnson. She had been Jamie's girlfriend before Annabelle 'got her hooks into him' as she put it, so there's no love lost between the two girls. Since then, she had realised he had been controlling everything she did, everything she wore. On one occasion he had tried to get her to take drugs. She had refused. She was glad to be away from him. She tended to ignore him at riding club, so was no help with descriptions.'

'What have you got, Dave?' Nick asked.

'I saw Emma Sage. A shy little girl, more interested in ponies than in boys. She saw Tom Hassall and Jamie deep in conversation earlier in the afternoon. About an hour later, she saw Jamie with Annabelle near the horseboxes. They were arguing. Annabelle shouted 'Forget it!' and walked off. Jamie shouted some insults after her and went to his pony and rode round like a maniac. That's Emma's words, not mine.'

'That's everybody,' Nick said and reviewed the note he had made. 'There's no description of Macca, who seems to be a vital character in this. I'd like to know more about him. Jamie wasn't as popular as his mother would have us believe. In fact, he was a controlling boyfriend to Belinda and seemed to be going that way with Annabelle. There again, I don't think any of them wanted him dead, not enough to give him an overdose. Tom was non-committal when I asked him if Jamie took drugs. Another word with him when his father wasn't around might get us nearer the truth.

THIRTY FIVE

Jim Lewis sat in a corner booth in a roadside café just off the autobahn.

'The A3 isn't what it's cracked up to be,' he commented. Their sat-nav had shown three sets of road works ahead of them and had suggested a detour on to minor roads. The café at Legenhof had seemed inviting, its Bavarian style with a steeply sloping roof and timbered façade reminding Jim of his childhood story books with tales of Hansel and Gretel.

Inside, it was warm and welcoming, though the coffee was stronger than they would have had at home. They ordered Wienerschnitzel with two eggs and chips. A noisy game of cards was in progress. The players slammed down their cards and shouted as the game got under way, and Jim was pleased to find a relatively quiet corner for their break from driving.

They reviewed their trip so far.

'Successful trip, I would say,' Jim said.

'Yes' Allan replied. 'We found the destination easily enough, though I was a bit worried when they put that guy in the cab with us to guide us down to the docks.'

'You worry too much. What are they going to do? Slit our throats and dump us in the sea?' Jim laughed at the idea.

'You never know.'

Their food arrived and they ate in silence for a while.

The meal over, Jim wiped his mouth and continued their review of the trip.

'Well, we got photos of everybody and they were

happy for us to take them as proof of delivery.'

'True. The Arab guy was a bit twitchy when they suggested craning the car up to put it on the yacht. He wasn't the only one. I felt the same.'

'They thought they knew what they were doing. Until he got the captain to reverse the yacht up to the slipway. They pressed a button and the back opened up and he drove the car into the yacht.'

'I've never seen a garage on a yacht before,' Allan said.

'Neither have I . That's what you call luxury. It was a ten-million-pound yacht, so the car has gone to a good home.'

'The tips weren't bad, either. A thousand between us.'

'That's Arabs for you. They don't mind paying for good service.'

'We ought to do this more often.'

'You've changed your tune. On the way here you were looking for a police car behind every lamp-post.'

'Well, you never know. I'm more relaxed now the car's gone. But I agree, we haven't had any trouble so far. Let's hope our luck continues.'

They paid for their meal and returned to their lorry for the last leg of their continental tour.

THIRTY SIX

Janet Bagley was neat and methodical in all she did, the result of having lived with her mother for most of her life. Elizabeth Bagley had been a stickler for perfection. Whether baking, crafting or something as mundane as ironing, she produced an immaculate finish to her work. As a result, Janet was also obsessed with getting things right. At the office, the area around her desk was always tidy. Her work was meticulous and always up to date. Having worked at Bertrand's since leaving school seventeen years previously, she was a patient trainer for new recruits, instilling in them the need for accuracy. Following Elizabeth's death five years since, she had moved to a smaller house near the canal, where her mother's influence still took precedence.

It was later that morning that Roberta Nicholls, Head of Accounts at Bertrand's, tapped the door and, when invited, entered the CEO's office.

'Good morning, Mr Formstone,' she said. 'I think we have a problem.'

'It's not like you to have problems, Bobbie,' he replied. 'You're very good at solving them usually.'

'We have a young lady in tears.'

'Oh?'

'Janet.'

'What's up with her?'

'I've had three phone calls already this morning and it is still only half past ten. All three were suppliers requesting payment of their invoices.'

'And?'

'Janet says she hasn't seen their invoices. She thinks I'm accusing her of something.'

'And are you?'

'Not at the moment. But it's highly suspicious for a batch of invoices to vanish like that, don't you think?'

'What kind of amounts? Do we know?'

'Website hosting is a hundred pounds for last month. Seventy five pounds for cleaning supplies and two hundred and fifty pounds for stationery supplies.'

'That's not good, then.'

'No, it isn't. They are all in a position to harm the company if it gets out. Wayne Sanderson will shut the website down straight away if he doesn't get paid. Remember what he did to that double-glazing company last year? They've never recovered. Rumours get round. Bad news travels fast.'

Neville thought for a moment. 'You get back to work, then. I'll have a word with Janet later on. She's one of our best. She'll be able to explain it, I'm sure. I'll get to the root of this, don't you worry.'

As the door closed behind Roberta, Neville's telephone rang.

'It's Mr Hannemann from Mercedes for you,' Naomi, his secretary, said. 'Shall I put him through?'

A frown crossed Neville's face. He wondered whether this would be on the same errand as Roberta's previous calls. He picked up the phone, gingerly, as though it was hot.

'*Guten morgen, Waldemar. Wie geht's*,' he said, trying to sound jolly with his limited knowledge of the German language.

'It goes very well with me,' the German replied in impeccable, unaccented English. 'But I wonder if all is well with you.'

'Yes, all is well.'

'I read that you had a problem with one of our cars at Brussels.'

'Yes. Our police are trying to trace it.'

'It's just that I wondered whether the theft had affected your ability to pay for the car. You owe us the balance of fifty thousand euros. You have our invoice already, I think.'

Neville thought hard. His conversation with Roberta suppressed his ability to sound confident about invoices.

'Don't worry, Waldemar. Must be a glitch in the office. I'll transfer the money this afternoon.'

'You realise, of course, that we expect prompt payment for our cars. The fact that you lost the car is between you and your insurers. It is an unfortunate incident, but it should not affect your ability to pay.'

'Of course. Of course. As I said, the payment will be with you this afternoon.'

'I look forward to receiving it, Neville. It would be a pity for this to be known in the trade. You have your reputation to protect. Goodbye, Neville.'

'Goodbye...' Neville's voice trailed off as the thinly-veiled threat echoed in his ears.

It took some time for the importance of his situation to filter through the panic in Neville's mind. His fingers pressed into his temples as he tried to concentrate. What was happening to the company? Waldemar's attitude had changed from friendly to threatening. Why? Where did the Brussels fiasco fit in? Things were starting to go wrong. It was up to him to stop it. He thought of going into the accounts office to question Janet, but then decided that it would assert his authority for her to come to him.

He picked up the phone and asked Naomi to get Roberta to send Janet in to see him.

There was a gentle tap on the door, to which he said a loud 'Come!' Janet timidly entered and closed the door behind her. She moved towards a chair facing Neville across the desk.

'Stand there!' he commanded.

Red-eyed from crying after Roberta's questioning, Janet stood before him. Late thirties, slightly round-shouldered from years in clerical work and with spectacles that gave her an owlish appearance, she cut a pitiful figure.

'Stop the sniffing and tell me about these invoices.'

'I…I…I've never seen them,. Honestly.'

'According to Roberta they must have arrived, so somebody…' he jabbed a forefinger in her direction… 'is lying!'

His phone rang.

'What?' he almost shouted into the receiver.

'Sorry to interrupt, but Roberta thought you would like to know that John Raybrook rang. It's another invoice problem.' Naomi said, which added to his discomfiture. He slammed the phone down, unable to speak. Janet took in a deep breath.

'It's nothing to do with me. You know how conscientious I am. I would never do anything to harm the company. I'm as mystified as anyone. All I know is that I haven't seen them.' The courage it had taken for her to put the outburst together ran out and she dissolved into tears again.

'We'll have to search the office, then,' he said.

'We've already done that. Everybody searched but we found nothing,' Janet said.

'Right. Go back to your desk. Ask Roberta to come in.'

Janet scuttled out, relieved that the dreaded interview was over.

Minutes later, Roberta tapped the door and entered and sat opposite her boss.

'Well, Bobbie. We do have a problem. Janet tells me you've had a search and found nothing.'

'Yes. I put the whole staff on it, but we found nothing except a pair of scissors and a hole punch that went missing weeks ago. But no invoices. Perhaps they've been taken out of the office, or destroyed, though I can't think why. They have no value.' Roberta's report enabled Neville to put his mind in order.

'I'll organise another search,. Your staff searching their own office is all very well, but there is always a tendency to make assumptions about familiar places. I'll arrange someone else to do it. I'll have a word with Caroline. And while you're out there, pay Mercedes fifty thousand euros. It's the balance due on the car that we lost. You've got their details from when we paid the deposit.'

Neville walked up to the Show Team office. Caroline had been with the company for ever. She was level-headed. She would help him decide what to do.

He told her of the disastrous situation developing in the accounts office and of his thoughts of an independent search. She approved of his idea, though as everyone in the Show Team was familiar with the accounts office, they could be counted out.

She thought hard.

'Except…'

'Except what?'

'Except Daniel. He's not been here long enough to know much about the accounts office.'

'Of course. I knew you would come up with something.'

He looked across to Daniel, who was sitting at a neighbouring desk.

'What do you think, Daniel?

'I couldn't help overhearing you. I'd be glad to help. I'm not familiar with the accounts office or anyone in it.'

Neville felt a weight lifting from his shoulders.

'Of course,' he said. 'The ideal man. New blood. Come with me. There's no time like the present. Well done, Caroline!'

Neville strode into the accounts office, followed by Daniel.

'Listen up, everybody.'

There were surprised looks on the staff faces as they looked up. This had never happened before. The CEO had never raised his voice to them. This was serious. Neville continued.

'These missing invoices must be here somewhere. I appreciate that you have searched and found nothing, but a fresh pair of eyes may spot something that your familiarity may have overlooked, so I have asked Daniel to conduct a search. He must look everywhere, including personal bags and cases, so you will give him any assistance he needs.' He turned and left, slamming the door as effective punctuation to his words.

Daniel looked around the room.

'I'm looking for invoices which also may be in envelopes. That is all I'm after, I will not be reading anything I find and if there is anything personal in your desk, don't worry, it won't be mentioned,'

He started his search at the nearest position. He opened drawers, looked into cupboards. Brief cases revealed nothing more than packed lunches and magazines, raising his eyes at one or two titles which he promised not to reveal. He flicked through piles of papers. He worked his way to the small kitchen area at the end of the room. The cupboards revealed no surprises and it was clear that Roberta insisted on complete cleanliness and tidiness in that area.

He moved on to the coat racks next to the kitchen. An array of overcoats, anoraks and puffa jackets faced him and he ran his hands over them all, hoping to hear the rustle of paper within.

'What's this?' he said. Behind the coats was a Tesco bag-for-life.

'That's Janet's old shopping bag. It's been there for weeks. They won't be in there,' a young man replied.

Daniel brought the bag on to the nearest desk and looked inside.

'And what have we here?' he asked, trying not to be

too melodramatic as he lifted out a bundle of envelopes.

Roberta hurried across the office and took them from him. She opened a couple, revealing some of the missing invoices. She turned to Janet.

'What have you got to say to this?'

Janet was open-mouthed.

'I...I...I don't know. I didn't ...Someone must have put them there. It wasn't me.'

Her denials tumbled out of her lips. She trembled and tears were not very long in coursing down her cheeks.

'Why would I hide them?' She tried to be defensive.

'You tell me,' Roberta said. 'Better still, you can tell Mr Formstone. Come with me.'

She led the way to Neville's office and entered without knocking.

'We've found the invoices, Mr Formstone. In Janet's shopping bag!' She could hardly contain herself.

'But I didn't put them there!'

The normally timid Janet dug her toes in. How long her strength would last was uncertain.

'They would be no good to me,' she continued, 'They have no value. Why would I hide them?'.

Neville asked, 'Did you think that you were doing the company a favour? If the invoices vanished it would save us money?'

'No. It would be stupid to think that. I swear, I have never seen these invoices. Why don't you believe me?'

'Was it an attempt to cut down your work-load?'

'No!' She was almost screaming. 'I'm always up-to-date. Ask Roberta.'

'That is what bothers me,' Roberta replied. 'Is the work too much for you? Would you like some time off? Go back to your desk and let me discuss it with Mr Formstone.'

'Thank you,' Janet sniffed and closed the door behind her.

'What was that all about? Don't tell me you're going

soft, Bobbie.'

'She was right. She is always up-to-date and there is no value in the invoices, so there would be no point in stealing them.'

'Well, I'm a firm believer in punishment. If someone does wrong, they should be punished accordingly.'

'But there's no proof that she hid the invoices. Anybody could have put them there.'

'Who do you suggest?'

'Someone with a grudge against us.'

'Any suggestions who that might be?'

Roberta had no response. It had to be internal, but no obvious culprit came to mind. Neville broke the silence.

'We'll sack her on the spot. They were in her bag. She did wrong. She must pay.'

'It doesn't work that way these days. You'd end up on the wrong end of a tribunal. There is no evidence of wrongdoing. We could suspend her while we investigate further.'

'I suppose you're right, but it still feels wrong to me. Two weeks suspension it is.' He was glad to get the matter out of his hair, if only temporarily.

THIRTY SEVEN

Liz Marston called Nick over to her desk.

'Look at this, Nick.'

She had been following the route of the lorry across Europe from the reports on HOLMES, the Home Office website.

The German Europol officers had been as meticulous as Matt Crewdson had predicted. Frequent updates told of stops, both overnight and meal breaks, some of which had provided opportunities for inspection of the lorry while the drivers were absent. No contraband nor illegal immigrants had been detected in those inspections in either direction. The false number plates had been recovered and were on their way back to UK by courier and the lorry's original number had been recorded making identification possible. The destination of the stolen car was in Turkey and there were photographs of it being put aboard a luxury yacht in Silivri Marina on the Sea of Marmara.

'Why didn't they make an arrest at that point?' she wondered.

'Because Europol only collect information for the rest of us to use. NCA will be on to this, I'm sure.'

'I see the lorry is entering Belgium, Nick.'

'Thanks,' he said and picked up his phone.

He rang June at DFDS and asked her to be on the look-out for the lorry and to let him know when it disembarked at Dover. Matt Crewdson agreed to have the lorry followed from Dover and would report its destination when it finally reached it. Nick would take over from there.

The false number plates arrived from the Polizei by motor-cycle courier and Nick had them fingerprinted in readiness for the arrival of the lorry. All he had to do was wait.

He reviewed his case-load so far.

It was still not clear whether Ryan's death was the result of accident, suicide or murder and there were no positive indications of guilt in the suspects. Ellie's death was definitely murder, but George Smith was only a tenuous suspect. The theft of the Mercedes had landed on his plate and he had also acquired the investigation of the death of Jamie Turner and the importing of drugs into Cheshire. His suspicions about Helen's brother were an added complication.

Another visit to Bertrand's was called for.

THIRTY EIGHT

Nick wondered what he would find as the lift ascended to the top floor of the Bertrand building. Whatever guesses he might have made were nowhere near the mark. As he exited into the long corridor, he met two women approaching the lift.

One was tall, slim, elegant, with white hair, wearing clothes that Nick guessed must have cost a pretty penny. Her make-up was immaculate and her fingers bore expensive rings. Her commanding voice completed the picture of a wealthy lady who was clearly used to having her own way.

The other lady followed her meekly. Equally well-dressed, but failing by a mile to match the elegance of the former, she presented a dumpy figure. Nick guessed there would be at least thirty years between them in age, mother and daughter perhaps, his thoughts confirmed when the younger one said, 'Oh mother, don't make a fuss.'

They were followed by Neville Formstone, flustered, trying to speak to them but hindered by the adamant statements of, 'I've made my mind up, Neville. It's no good arguing.'

They paused as they came face to face with Nick and Neville took the opportunity to speak.

'Mrs B. This is the detective I was telling you about. Come back into the office, please. I'm sure he has news for us,'

This had the desired effect, and they all turned back into the CEO's office, where Neville made the introductions.

'This is Detective Inspector Price, Mrs Bertrand and

her daughter Louise, directors of the company. We were just discussing the situation here when you arrived.'

'Situation?' Nick asked.

'Yes. We've been getting a bad press lately. We lost two young members of staff, as you know. Then our display car was stolen. I'm hoping you have news of that. And some payments were not made. Doubts were expressed in the trade press and in the Chester Chronicle about our financial stability. As a result, two of our accounts staff have resigned this morning. The value of the company is dropping through the floor. I hope you have some uplifting news about the Mercedes.'

'Yes and no.' Nick said. 'Yes, we know where it went. No, we haven't got it back. It was put aboard a super-yacht in Turkey and is probably on its way to Dubai or somewhere similar by now. International police are trying to keep tabs on it, so there may yet be a chance for it to be returned.'

'That's something, at least.' Neville clutched at straws to ease the tension in the room.

'Perhaps I should explain what has happened here this morning, as Neville has omitted to tell you.' Mrs Bertrand began, in a manner which commanded attention. 'My daughter and I are the surviving directors of the company. My husband, who founded the company, passed away thirty years ago and we have been happy to leave the running of the company in Neville's capable hands. Well, they were capable until recently.'

The barb struck home and Neville made to remonstrate, but Mrs Bertrand silenced him with a raised finger, then continued.

'What was a successful company, well-respected in the trade, is suddenly a laughing stock. It's worth very little in comparison to its heyday, so Louise and I have decided to sell. Neville wants to improve things before we sell, but I have no confidence in his plans. Our decision is to sell the company and that is final. Come along Louise.' She gathered her handbag and walked out through the door. Neville followed her.

'But Millicent, please…' he protested.

'I will sell it. The company. The building. The whole bloody lot.' She made for the lift.

Daniel, smiling, closed the toilet door softly. He had overheard the previous outburst and had come out to investigate. Hidden in the toilet, what he had just heard was music to his ears. He would text Kieran immediately.

THIRTY NINE

Robbie Sylvester and Laura Bishop were students, studying Business Studies at Chester University. Housed in student accommodation in a block which overlooked Chester's canal area, they had spent many an afternoon becoming familiar with each other's naked bodies – the soft, curvy parts, the hard, rigid parts and everything in between. Not that they were studying anatomy, of course. They were clearly in love, and without the possibility of parents walking in on them, they had consummated that love – regularly.

Laura lay in bed, watching Robbie walk across to the table, where a bottle of wine and two glasses awaited his attention. She thrilled at his muscular legs, his lithe body and his broad shoulders, the result of many years of swimming training.

He turned back to the bed, glasses in hand and stopped.

'Jesus!' he exclaimed and returned the glasses to the table quickly.

'What's up?' Laura said, alarmed at the sudden change of direction. Robbie was reaching for his jeans, which lay over the back of a chair.

'Someone has just fallen in the canal.'

'They'll get out. They always do,' She was impatient to get back to their love-making.

'Not this one. It looked deliberate.' he said, making for the door, calling over his shoulder, 'Ring 999 We might need an ambulance.'

He ran across the garden area in his bare feet. As a

swimmer, he had a great respect for the dangers of deep water. A fully dressed woman would not last very long in the cold waters of the canal, hence his urgency. He reached the canalside to find a woman face down in the water, her head under the surface. He jumped in beside her and tried to lift her face out of the water, but her upper body seemed unnaturally heavy. He found that her shoulder bag was holding her down and further investigation showed that it contained bricks. She had no intention of surviving the event. Robbie lifted the bag off her shoulders and let it fall to the muddy bottom, then turned her over on to her back. She spluttered and fought him.

'No. Let me go. Please.'

'Don't worry. I've got you,' he said as he held her chin out of the water and pulled her towards the side.

'Please. I want to die.'

'We can get help.' He was in uncharted territory. He had received training in life-saving and brought her, efficiently, to the side, but dealing with an attempted suicide and a determined one at that, was something else.

The sight of a semi-naked man running across the garden and jumping into the canal had been enough to bring inquisitive sight-seers from a nearby pub. Some, with glass in hand, cheered as the rescue was completed, thinking it was a student stunt. Others, realising the seriousness of the situation, rushed to help Robbie to lift the woman out of the water and on to the path. She was still protesting and coughing. She had not been in the water long enough to take in much water. What little she had swallowed came back as she vomited violently. Robbie did not need to perform CPR on her. He sat with her as they waited for the ambulance, both shivering without any extra garments to counteract the cold and the wet. The woman wanted to leave, full of embarrassment, but Robbie dissuaded her as Laura ran across with a couple of coats, all she could find in Robbie's room.

'Let's wait for the paramedics,' he said, helping her into one of his anoraks, not knowing what to do next.

'I'm so embarrassed. You should have let me drown,' she said through her tears.

'What made you do it?' Robbie asked.

'Work. I don't want to talk about it.'

The crowd slowly dispersed, the pub television holding more attraction, now that the rescue had been completed. The paramedics arrived and took over and insisted that she went to hospital to be checked out.

'You'll need your bag,' Robbie said.

'No, no. Leave it.'

'It's no trouble.'

Robbie ran across to a moored-up narrowboat and borrowed a boat hook. He knew better than to dive into the canal. Instead, he probed the bottom until the hook caught into the straps of her bag and he lifted it out. He handed it to a paramedic, who suggested that Robbie should accompany them to the hospital.

'I'll be fine,' he said.

'Yes, but you've been in the canal. So have rats, and there is a possibility of Weil's disease. You'll need a blood test and possibly antibiotics.'

Robbie shrugged. 'OK, I suppose.'

He ran across to Laura to explain.

Their afternoon of lovemaking was over.

FORTY

'Still no progress on the Bertrand's murders, then?'

'No, sir. They seem to be going cold. Lack of evidence. Lack of suspects. But I am keeping them under review.'

'Good.' Tom Cameron was not known for being satisfied with his men's work. Nick was surprised. He continued.

'However, I'm not sure about the staff situation at Bertrand's, so I'll be there later to chat to Caroline Paterson. She's been with the firm from its inception, years ago. She's like the mother hen. Perhaps she will be able to point out things that newcomers would miss.'

'Sounds like a good idea. Anything else?'

'Yes. The transporter that took the stolen car is due back up here. It arrived at Dover overnight and we've been tracking its progress on HOLMES. It's being shadowed by the NCA, and DS Crewdson will let me know where it finally ends up and I'll be there, ready to arrest the driver and his mate. I'll also be able to find out who hired it and give that information to the NCA for them to follow it up.'

'That's excellent news. It's just as well to keep in with NCA.'

'Will that be all, sir? I'd like to be on my way.'

'Of course. Good work so far.'

Nick pushed his chair back and left.

Five minutes later he and DS Dave Martin drove out to Bertrand's offices.

Ten minutes later, they were seated in their now

familiar interview room with Caroline Paterson.

'I don't need to tell you that we have made little progress investigating the two deaths. It's very frustrating. I get the feeling that nothing happens here without your knowledge, so I'd just like to have your help in bringing me up-to-date with what goes on here.'

'I'm flattered. A lot has been happening since you were here last. The Brussels fiasco did us no good whatsoever. It generated a lot of bad publicity, particularly in the trade press, with some filtering out into the local press. Chester Chronicle and the Liverpool Daily Post have already carried articles expressing doubts about our viability.'

'I've seen some of these reports. It's not good, I agree.' Nick said.

'Then two days ago, some invoices went missing and as a result, some important payments were missed. People talk and bad news travels fast, especially in the motor trade, Mr Price, so our company's reputation, which I have cherished for years and struggled to defend, has suffered once more.' She dabbed away a tear. She could never have admitted this to anyone in the office, but to these two strangers…

'I can see this is difficult for you, but can you tell me any more about office life?'

'We eventually found the invoices, unfortunately in an employee's bag. The employee concerned, Janet Bagley, has been suspended for two weeks until we could investigate further. In the meantime, two of our accounts staff have resigned, leaving us short-handed and reducing our efficiency.'

'Do you think Janet is the guilty person, then?'

'Everybody thought so, but I was doubtful. She was such a reliable worker. I'm not overstating her case when I say she was conscientious; meticulous. She had worked here for years with not a blot on her record.'

'Did you have any suspicions about what happened?'
'Yes.'

'Tell me.'

Caroline went on to tell him about the finding of the invoices; how Neville Formstone had demanded a search of the office and how Daniel had been selected to conduct an independent search. It seemed like a good idea, to have a fresh pair of eyes searching, but it had seemed too pat for her. But she could not see what he had to gain. In many ways, Daniel had been a great addition to the team. He had supported her at Brussels and seemed to be enjoying his new job. He had become the hero of the hour in finding the invoices. On the other hand, Caroline was sure that Janet was not the guilty party. It was not in her nature. Another tear was dabbed away as she mentioned Janet and Nick wondered why.

'How has Janet taken suspension?' he asked, remembering his 'mother hen' description from earlier.

'Not very well. We heard this morning that she tried to drown herself in the canal yesterday afternoon. Luckily, a student from the university rescued her in time. I shall call in to see her after work this evening.'

'If you find out anything useful, perhaps you could let me know,' Nick said. There was no useful purpose to be served by a visit from the police. They could hardly get involved in a few missing invoices, but if it was serious enough for someone to attempt suicide, then there may be more to discover. Caroline's visit to Janet later may be fruitful.

At six o'clock that evening, a grinning Daniel walked into Kieran's office, proud of what he had done.

Did you like my text?' he asked.

'Yes, I did. Sit down. Tell me all about it.'

'From the beginning?'

'From the beginning.'

Daniel reminded Kieran about his mission to discredit Bertrand's and told of how, a few days ago, he had gone into work early and took the day's post from George on the front desk, up to the office. He recognised some of the letters from logos on the envelopes, particularly the Mercedes one. He hoped that it might be the invoice for the car which went missing and decided to hide them in the accounts office to delay payment. Even if it was just correspondence, it wouldn't look good for no reply to have been sent. The invoices were well hidden, so when they couldn't find them, it had been suggested that he could be a fresh pair of eyes. His plan worked. They were so used to seeing an old shopping bag hanging on a coat rack, nobody searched it. The girl whose bag it was, was suspended and the phones were red hot, with people wanting their money – including a big payment to Mercedes The papers got hold of it…'

'How?'

'Need you ask?'

'Ok. Go on.'

'Then the next day the directors came in and had a bust-up with the CEO and said they were going to sell the company before things got worse. I just happened to overhear what they said, and I texted you. So, it's all going our way.'

While Kieran was pleased with progress, he was concerned that Daniel would overstep the mark. He would have to keep him in check before he brought the whole deck of cards tumbling down.

'It's worked this time,' he said, 'but don't do any of your schemes without consulting me. We don't want the police anywhere near us.'

'They're stuck on the murder cases. I don't think they're getting anywhere with the hi-jack and the missing invoices are a purely internal matter. I saw a couple of cops in the office this morning, but they only spoke to Caroline, not me, for once. It looks like I'm in the clear.'

'Don't you believe it. They're like a dog with a bone. They'll nibble away until they get what they want. So don't get too cocky. Take your time. Give it a rest now and leave it to me. You've done well so far, but you've a lot to learn.'

'Ok. You're the boss.'

Although Daniel agreed, he was confident that he could contribute more to the downfall of Bertrand's. He needed to impress Kieran further.

FORTY ONE

DS Matthew Crewdson rang Nick.

'We're just following your transporter up the M6,' he reported. 'It's on its way to Frodsham.'

'You've tracked it down then?' Nick said.

'Yes. We've followed it from Dover. DVLA check says it is owned by RP Hire of Frodsham, so we knew where it was headed. If you meet it there, you could arrest the two crew as they arrive. Keep us informed of anything you find out. We've taken opportunities to check the vehicle over and found no sign of drugs or illegal passengers, though we'll be very interested in any smuggling activity you discover. Probably only a few cigarettes or booze, but they can be disregarded in the general scheme of things. The car export will be much more important.'

'Will do,' Nick said, and mobilised Dave Martin and a couple of his DC's with a couple of unmarked cars to be the welcoming party. They made their way to Frodsham, the constables parking out of sight, away from the yard. They would pull into the yard only after the lorry arrived.

Kieran's phone buzzed. It was Jim Lewis, his driver.

'Job done, then, Jim?' he asked.

'Yes. We're coming up the M6. Allan's driving. We'll be back soon.'

'Any trouble with police?'
'Nope.'
'Border Force?'
'No. Sailed through.'
'Car delivered OK?'
'Yes. No problems.'
'Good. See you soon.'
'We'll take the lorry back to Reg first.'
'Of course.'
'See ya, boss.'

Jim and Allan were congratulating themselves on a successful trip, with the hefty tips they had received in Turkey being the icing on the cake.

Kieran then rang Reg Potts.

'Hi. Just reporting that your transporter is on its way back. My drivers will be with you within an hour. Everything's gone well, they tell me. We might be able to do it again. Watch this space.'

'Right. Thanks for letting me know. By the way, I don't have your name. Just for the records.'

'You don't need it. You don't need to keep any records. That's why I paid you in cash. No records. Get it?'

'Yes. I suppose so.'

The line went dead.

Nick arrived at Potts's yard and introduced himself and Dave to the owner.

'You'd better come into the office,' Reg Potts said. 'It's not often we have a visit from the police,' was his jolly remark.

He was a portly little man with rosy, round cheeks and a button nose. His flat cap was pushed back to his receding hairline and a fair-isle sweater was stretched across his ample stomach.

It struck Nick that this man was quite relaxed about a police visit. He looked at Dave with raised eyebrows, who nodded, indicating that he felt the same.

Reg offered them a seat in his office, then sat behind his desk to face them.

'Well, what can I do for you two gentlemen? Nothing serious, I hope?'

Nick pushed a piece of paper across the desk, On it, was written the registration number of the lorry.

'Is this one of your vehicles?' he asked.

Reg looked at the number, recognising it immediately, and a frown crossed his face. The coincidence of Kieran's call and the arrival of the police rang alarm bells. He decided to brazen it out

'Yes. Out on a week hire. Should be back today or tomorrow.'

'Tell me how this works. Do you ask what a hirer is going to do with a vehicle they've hired?'

'None of my business. They are expected to treat it as their own. As long as it comes back clean, there's no problem. If it doesn't, then they lose their deposit. If it's damaged, either the insurance covers it or we charge to repair it ourselves.'

'Who hired it this time?'

'I don't know.'

'How come? You must have some record.'

'No, sorry. It was an odd one. A guy phoned in an order for a transporter with a hydraulic lift. He paid in full, in advance, in cash. He sent the money with his drivers on the day they took it.'

That's not normal, is it?'

'Not at all. But money's money. What have they been doing with it, then? Something illegal?' Nick ignored the question.

'It's due here soon and I want you to stay in here while we go and greet the drivers.'

Dave hid a smile at the thought of 'greeting' the drivers. What a welcome they would receive!

Reg Potts had no choice but to remain in the office

while the policemen met the lorry. He fell back on his original comment that what the drivers were involved in was none of his business, though he would like to give the vehicle the once-over before the drivers were taken away.

Five minutes later, the lorry came into view, turning into the yard, followed by the two unmarked police cars which parked so that the lorry could not be reversed.

Allan Brewer looked into both wing mirrors and saw a car in each. He knew they were trapped and immediately guessed why, when two constables came out of the cars and stood alongside his lorry. He turned to Jim,

'Remember,' he said. 'The deal. We plead guilty, take our punishment and he'll pay us well when we get out.'

'I hope he keeps his promise,' Jim said. 'At least we'll get a rest in jail.'

Nick and Dave left the office and approached one driver each, issued their formal arresting speech and bundled Jim and Allan into separate cars for onward transmission to Chester.

Reg found no fault with the condition of the vehicle and was content for them to be taken away. Who they worked for and why they hired the lorry was, as he maintained, none of his business.

On arriving at Chester, they were put into separate interview rooms and spoke to confirm their names, the fact that they were free-lance drivers, and that there was nobody else involved in the actual hi-jack. They were only carrying out instructions, they said. Any other questions about whose instructions they were working to were met with 'No comment.'

Nick decided to leave them to stew for a while. The threat of serving a long sentence for the theft and sale of the Mercedes would weigh heavily on their minds. By their next interview, their solicitor may have talked some sense into them.

FORTY TWO

Mrs Millicent Bertrand sat at her desk in her Cheshire home. She enjoyed all the sumptuous furnishings, the luxurious sun-room looking out on to manicured lawns with a distant view of the Welsh hills in the background.

She was not looking forward to this interview. It felt disloyal. The company had been her late husband's pride and joy for years. Indeed, it had provided her with an envious way of life. Whatever she wanted, she could have. Clothes from the best shops. A new car every year. A hot tub on the patio. And this house. Formerly a manor house, now modernised into a home worthy of entry in any lifestyle magazine.

All of this would remain after the sale, and she would hope that Roger Bertrand would understand, wherever his spirit dwelt in the after-world.

She heard the crunch of gravel as a car arrived. The car door slammed and she heard the footsteps on the gravel, approaching the door. The bell rang.

'Very well, Louise. Let him in,' she said to her daughter, 'And there will be no need for you to stay for the meeting.'

'But ...' Louise got no further.

'I will deal with it. Now go to the door.'

Dutifully, reluctantly, Louise walked to the door to admit a tall man, wearing jeans and a check shirt, sleeves rolled to half-way up his forearms, revealing a gold watch on his wrist. His fair hair was of medium length, tousled but not untidy, quite attractive, really.

He entered the office and strode across to her with his hand outstretched for a handshake.

'Good afternoon, Mrs Bertrand. I'm Kieran Donovan. It's good of you to see me at short notice.'

She waved him to a seat.

'Yes, though I'm intrigued to know how you knew that I was considering selling the company.'

'News travels fast in the motor trade, Mrs Bertrand.'

'You are in the motor trade?'

'Yes. Burke's. I have a Mercedes dealership at Anfield, looking to expand into Cheshire. This seemed a good opportunity to do so.'

'Well, as you know, we are a well-respected company in the motor trade. We own the building that houses our head office in Chester, plus a showroom on the outskirts of the city. We also have showrooms in Liverpool and Crewe. We have the top floor of the building in Chester, and there are tenants on the other floors. Just to be clear, I am not selling the building, just the Bertrand dealership.'

'So, if I were to buy your company, I would continue to be your tenant.'

'Exactly. But you could move the business to wherever you wish, though I think it would be unwise to sever our connections with Chester.'

'I agree, though you said 'well-respected'. That may have been true at one time, but not now. So many things seem to be going wrong in the company. Reputation will need to be reflected in the price I'm prepared to offer.'

Millicent winced inwardly. She knew that this would come up, however much she wanted to avoid it.

'I will need to think about it, of course. There will be a lot of negotiation before we establish a price. Our solicitors on both sides will need to discuss terms. I must say, however, that a connection with a Mercedes dealership in Liverpool would be advantageous. Thank you for your interest.'

'Have you a price in mind?' he asked.

'That's something I will need to discuss with my legal team. It's early days.'

They exchanged names and addresses of their solicitors and he gave her his card and left, saying that he looked forward to a successful transaction. He had started the ball rolling. Perhaps he had better do more towards devaluing the company to help Millicent to decide in his favour.

Having shown Kieran out, Louise returned from the kitchen.

'That went well,' she commented.

'Were you listening in?' Millicent asked.

'Of course. I am still a director of the company. I need to know what's going on. And I think he's too good to be true. How did he know you wanted to sell? Who told him? Neville? Roberta? Caroline? Who will benefit from a sale?'

'You have more sense than I gave you credit for,' her mother said. Louise nodded her agreement. The nod said 'I told you so,' but it was a rare compliment which did not warrant a clever reply. 'So tell me, my clever daughter, what you think.'

'All three could retain their jobs, so no clue there.'

'True.'

'Neville might feel threatened after you tore into him. You weren't very complimentary about him when you spoke to the policemen, either.'

'Also true. He's let it go to pieces. Perhaps it's his way of getting rid of me.'

'Roberta is a highly qualified accountant. She could get a job anywhere. She would not fear losing out in a take-over.'

'And what about Caroline?' Millicent asked.

'She's been with the company for ever. New owners would find her knowledge invaluable.'

'Yes. Ever since your father died she has been an absolute rock. She guided me over the rough times when you were growing up. I knew nothing about cars. She knew everything. It was more her company than mine. No, Caroline would not have spread the news. We will have to keep an eye on Neville.'

FORTY THREE

Nick's telephone buzzed. It was Caroline Paterson.

'Good morning, Nick. I said I would ring you when I had seen Janet. I saw her last evening. She is feeling very aggrieved about this whole business. All her loyalty over the years and all her hard work have counted for nothing. For nobody to have believed her and to be sent home was very degrading. She had denied ever seeing the invoices, but Mr Formstone just shouted at her. She was treated as guilty from the beginning, hence her frustration, which led to trying to end it all in the canal. She thought that Roberta, the leader of the accounts team, seemed to believe her, but Mr Formstone was so agitated about it, there was no arguing with him.'

'And it was Daniel who found the invoices in Janet's old shopping bag?'

'Yes. He volunteered when Mr Formstone was looking for an independent searcher.'

Although Nick could hear his grandmother's voice in her Cheshire accent saying 'Them as hides can find,' he could not see that Daniel joining the search was more than coincidental. Nor could he see what Daniel had to gain from hiding the invoices to then find them later. A silly prank gone wrong? Horribly wrong as far as Janet was concerned. That was highly unlikely.

'Have you spoken to Roberta about this?' he asked.

'Yes, I have. She said that she could not believe that Janet would do this. She spoke highly of Janet's dedication to her work and to the company. She could well understand that Janet felt betrayed and unsupported by the company as a whole.'

'Will Janet go back to Bertrand's at the end of the two weeks?'

Caroline thought for a moment.

'I would think so. It's all she knows. She came to us from school. After me, she's the longest serving employee.'

'She'll be worth keeping on, then. Thanks for the call, Caroline.'

They agreed to keep in touch and closed the call.

Nick couldn't keep Daniel out of his head. He was still a suspect in Ryan's death, less so for Ellie's death but not entirely off the hook. His trip to Brussels had ended in disaster for the company and now he turns up in the case of the missing invoices. The company had operated successfully until he appeared on the scene. Perhaps he was more involved than Nick had thought. But why? Daniel seemed not to benefit from anything that had happened – except perhaps Ryan's death had opened the door for him to gain entry to the company. That could hardly have been planned, though. He dismissed the thought.

Instead, he gave some thought to his other case, the death of Jamie Turner.

Tom Hassall was a worry. Penny Carter described him as a creep. Other descriptions described him, more precisely, as two-faced, slimy and capable of anything. Nick knew he had seen through the first one, concerning the last time Tom had seen Jamie. From that point on, he could assume that everything he heard had been a lie. It would only be a matter of time before the rest of Tom's lies were uncovered. Further questioning would be necessary.

If he assumed that all Tom's replies had been lies, Macca would not have fair hair, Tom would know that local kids were on drugs, and he would have known that Jamie was on drugs. How many would be proved correct?

In defending Jamie, Tom was defending himself. But as Jamie's behaviour changed after a meeting with Macca and he had taken an overdose after an evening with Tom, indications were that Tom was lying.

Macca's identity remained a mystery. Nick resisted his conclusions about Helen's brother but was finding it difficult. Malcolm's evasiveness over his occupation was definitely suspicious, as was his behaviour at Pollard's, his interest in the junior rings and sudden visits to the toilets – notorious places for drug dealing.

FORTY FOUR

The humming reached its crescendo, then died down as The Pastor got to his feet. The faithful bowed their heads until he instructed them to sit, followed by a further instruction to kneel.

They all knelt.

'We will now give thanks for Saint Oda, our patron, who keeps us on the straight and narrow path to salvation.'

The humming resumed, together with chanting, as, with hands clasped, the kneeling congregation thanked the Lord for the life of Saint Oda, who had been the Archbishop of Canterbury over a thousand years previously. He had been responsible for writing royal and ecclesiastical laws and was known as Oda the Good, also Oda the Severe. It was this latter name that was followed by the Odonian Church, which insisted on strict adherence to the laws as set down in the Bible.

The Pastor completed their obeisance by instructing them to resume their seats.

When the shuffling and grunting had ceased, he continued.

'You are all aware of the need to support our church financially and you have done so willingly over the years. However, it has come to a point when the church requires even more support. The decision has not been taken lightly, but from next month, the church expects your contribution to rise to twelve per cent of your income, and the treasurer will take the new contribution next month. Are there any questions?'

A silence followed until one man raised his hand.

'Some of us are finding the current ten per cent difficult. Twelve per cent will make life very difficult with a family to support.'

'What value do you put on your spiritual life? Your heavenly home will be at stake without these contributions, or would you prefer Purgatory and Burning Hell for your family?'

The man backed down, unwilling to enter into a philosophical argument with The Pastor. No-one else ventured a question for the same reason, so The Pastor carried on with his service, satisfied that the funds would be forthcoming. His theme today was 'Jesus, the Good Shepherd' but it was the congregation who were being fleeced.

FORTY FIVE

'Another day at Pollard's. Let's hope for better luck this time,' Nick said.

Helen was keen to give Gordonstoun Rambler some ring experience, following her previous mistake, and had left Nero at home.

Pollard's was crowded when they arrived, a testament to the popularity of the venue and David Pollard's foresight in building it.

Nick recognised one or two faces among the juniors from his previous interviews and his name-dropping at the time bore fruit as two little girls shyly came up and asked Helen for an autograph, which she gladly signed.

'How did they know I was here?' she asked.

'Maybe something I said last time I was here,' Nick replied, busying himself with running a brush over the horse. He realised that in the only photographs of Helen that these girls would have seen in *Horse and Hound* she would have been wearing a riding helmet, jacket and jodhpurs. Seeing her now in her jeans and boots, with blonde curls blowing in the wind, there would have been no recognition. Could they have recognised Nick from that morning and remembered what he said at the time? Very possibly, but he thought it better not to mention it.

Fortunately, Helen was too busy preparing for the competition to continue the conversation.

Now fully attired in her riding kit, Helen went off to walk the course, striding the distance between jumps to enable her to match Flash's stride, and familiarise herself with what lay ahead. Nick watched her go, when he heard a familiar voice.

'Morning, Nick. I hope she remembers which way to

go this week,' he said.

Nick turned to find Malcolm also watching his sister walking the course..

'She won't make that mistake again,' Nick said. 'But what brings you here again?'

'Just need to keep an eye on things,' Malcolm replied.

Another off-hand remark designed to tell Nick nothing, which Nick found as infuriating as Helen and her mother did when hearing a similar reply.

'Oh, excuse me a sec. Needs must. Tell her I'm here. It'll avoid surprises.' Malcolm smiled and rushed off towards the toilets. Nick noted that Tom Hassall had gone in before him.

Helen returned and reported that the course was as straightforward as it should be for novice horses. She felt Flash would do well.

'We've just had a brief visit from Malcolm,' Nick said.

'What? Here again? He's up to no good, I'm sure. Where is he now?'

'He went off to the toilets.'

Nick was reluctant to let her know about his suspicions, so let the matter drop with a comment about weak bladders.

Helen mounted up and rode off to the practice jump in the collecting ring. Nick watched as her turn came and she rode an impeccable, uneventful clear round, then he congratulated her as he met her outside the ring.

* * *

Tom and Annabelle sat on the tailboard of Joe Hassall's horse-box.

'You'd think his mother would have asked me to ride Jasper for her,' Tom said. 'I was his best mate, after all.'

'She probably had her reasons, or perhaps she wanted to give Penny a chance to go in the ring. She does all the work at home, doesn't she?'

'She's only a bloody groom, though.'

'You're miffed because you only came third,' Annabele said.

'And you're feeling smug because you came second.'

Annabelle was concerned that the conversation was going the wrong way.

'Anyway, what are we arguing about? We were beaten fair and square on the day. Penny deserves a bit of success. And when Mrs Turner decides to sell Jasper, your Dad will be first in the queue and you'll have Jasper all to yourself.'

Tom brightened a little at the thought.

'Very true. You and I were Jamie's only friends, so let's talk about us.'

'How do you mean - us?'

'Well, now that he's out of the way, I was hoping we could go back to how we were.'

'Before Christmas, you mean?'

'Yes. Why not?'

'I was thinking that way myself, but let's take it easy, not be in a rush. There's no need to tell anybody yet.'

'They'll guess anyway, when they see us together.'

'True.'

They enjoyed a brief silence, considering their decision, then Annabelle asked 'What did Jamie die of? Have you heard?'

'We don't have to talk about him now, do we?'

'Not if you don't want to. I just wondered if it involved drugs. Something the policeman said that night.'

'Why? Are you interested in drugs?'

'Not really. Jamie tried to get me to take one of his pills but I refused. He didn't like it. Me refusing. He always wanted his own way. I was going off him. In fact, I had told him so that afternoon. We had a row.'

'So that was the bad news he'd had. He told me, but

didn't say what it was. He had a pill to get over it.'

'Yes, From his friend Macca. That's what he told me. Who is this Macca? I've never heard of him.'

'Just a guy who comes down from Liverpool now and again.'

'Why? Does he have a horse?'

'No. He brings things.'

'Don't be evasive, Tom. Does Macca bring drugs?'

'Why assume that?'

'We're a long way from Liverpool and putting two and two together, he's not going to come all this way to deliver aspirins on the off chance that someone will have a headache, is he?'

'Well keep your ideas to yourself. It could get both of us into trouble.'

'Both of us? Why? Are you into drugs as well?'

'I've said enough.'

They fell into a miserable silence, Tom wondering whether to tell Annabelle the full story, Annabelle wondering about a future with Tom

* * *

Nick left Helen with the horse and wandered down the line of parked horse-boxes. Some of the owners and competitors, having completed their jumping, were enjoying the afternoon sun, sharing a picnic as they sat in their folding chairs. Others were busy preparing for the next class, oiling hooves, donning hair nets and neatly tying a cravat, or stock as they are known. He heard one of them say that this judge had already sent one competitor out of the ring for being improperly dressed – her green school blazer was unsuitable!

Nick kept on walking, until he reached the palatial vehicle owned by Joe Hassall. There was no sign of Joe himself - he was probably in the bar – but Tom was sitting on the tailboard with Annabelle Hart, both looking unhappy.

Nick wondered whether Tom was trying to reignite his relationship with Annabelle, now that Jamie was gone. Not wishing to interrupt, despite his hope of speaking to Tom, he smiled and said 'hello' and made to walk on.

'Are you checking on me?'

Tom's question took Nick by surprise.

'Not at all,' Nick said. 'Though I was hoping for a word if I saw you.'

Tom still felt under pressure.

'You didn't believe me last time, did you?'

'I just have to decide if people are lying to me or not.'

'You thought I was lying.'

'You lied when you said you last saw Jamie in the afternoon. So how many other lies did you tell?'

Tom went on the attack.

'Do you want to search me?'

'No.'

'I'll show you then!'

He began emptying his pockets, slamming down a handkerchief, a fistful of coins, a hoof-pick, a bunch of keys...

'What's going on here?' Joe's voice thundered as he rounded the horse-box. 'Are you searching my lad?'

'No. This was his own doing.'

'Is that right?' Joe glared around the group.

'Yes,' Annabelle broke the silence.

'Stupid tart,' Tom spat out, proving to his father that Annabelle had been correct.

'If that's what you think of me, goodbye!' She turned away, in tears, any hope of a reconciliation vanishing out of the window.

'I'll speak to the Chief Constable about this,' Joe threatened

'Do so. But speak to your son first.' Nick responded, turned on his heel and left.

Further along, he caught up with Annabelle.

'Are you OK?' he asked. 'You looked very unhappy when I saw you with Tom.'

'Yes. I'm fine. At least, I know where I stand with him.'

'What were you unhappy about?'

'It started because Tom was hoping that Mrs Turner would have asked him to ride Jasper, Jamie's pony.'

'Didn't she?'

'No. She asked Penny Carter to ride him instead and she won the class. Tom was third.'

'Who came second?'

'I did, but I didn't expect to beat Jasper anyway.'

Nick was pleased for Penny. She did all the work at home, grooming, mucking out, exercising in all weathers, she deserved the ride.

'I thought at first that you and Tom were getting together again,' Nick said.

'So did I. But he's got no chance now, after calling me a stupid tart.'

Nick was quiet on the way home, silently debating the possible connections between Malcolm, drugs and Tom Hassall. He had not expected Tom to empty his pockets as voluntarily as he had. Perhaps the boy was innocent of drug dealing after all. But why had he turned on Annabelle. Had she ruined an opportunity to put Nick in the wrong? And why would he want to do that? The only thing he could think of was guilt.

Tom and Jamie had been close and Tom had been the last person, apart from Jamie's mother, presumably, to see him on the night before he died. Tom had to be a person of interest.

FORTY SIX

Daniel drove slowly, parked at an isolated spot beneath some trees and walked around the corner into a cul-de-sac, at the end of which was his target bungalow.

He tapped on the door.

A thin female voice called out 'Who is it?'

'I have a message from Stuart, Mrs Reid. May I come in?'

'It's not locked. Come in.'

Using a handkerchief, he pressed the handle and opened the door, to find himself in a hallway, to the right of which was a pleasant lounge, neatly furnished, with expensive ornaments, a large television screen on the far wall and an old lady in a wheelchair turning away from morning TV to see him as he entered.

'Who are you?' she asked.

'I work with Stuart. He asked me to look in on you as he's busy this morning.'

She gripped the handle of her walking stick more tightly.

'He doesn't usually 'look in on me' as you put it. What's going on?'

'He wasn't sure that Cathy would be on time and he wanted to make sure you were all right. I would be passing, so he asked me to pop in.' He hoped that using Cathy's name would be reassurance that he was genuine.

A long chat with Stuart the day before had told Daniel that the carer, Cathy, visited his mother three times a day, her second visit being at 11.00 for coffee. Then, having prepared a cold lunch for Mrs Reid, Cathy would be on her way to her next client.

'It's a lovely home you have here. Quiet, in the cul-de-sac, too. Did Stuart tell me you have a terrific view across the hills from the kitchen window?'

'I do. I used to walk across those hills when I was a girl. Can't do it now.' She brought her hand down on to her lap as though to punish her old legs for denying her of the chance to repeat the walks. She relaxed a little. This young man wasn't going to be a problem after all, she thought, as he showed an interest in her home and the views.

'Mind if I have a look?' he asked.

'Not at all. It's through there.' She pointed with her stick.

Daniel walked through to the kitchen. As he expected, Stuart's tidiness in the office was repeated here at home. There was no problem in finding the coffee jar. Wearing nitrile gloves, he removed the lid and tipped in a small amount of a brown powder, then replaced the lid and removed his gloves. He returned to the lounge.

'You're right. It's a terrific view. Must put thousands on the value of your bungalow.'

'Perhaps it does, but it will be to Stuart's benefit when I've gone.'

'Well, let's hope that won't be for a long time yet. Perhaps I could call round when the weather improves and take you for a trip up into the hills again.'

'I'd love that,' she said. 'The neighbours will think I've got a boy-friend.' Her eyes twinkled, mischievously. 'By the way, what is your name? You didn't say.'

'Dave,' he said. 'I'd better be off, now that I've seen you're all right.'

They said their farewells and he left, using his handkerchief again to ensure that no fingerprints remained as evidence of his visit. He walked to his car and drove off, satisfied with a job well done.

* * *

As Cathy Turton finished her circuit for the day, her final call would be to Mrs Reid. It was always a pleasant call. Mrs Reid often shared a few pleasantries with her. She never complained, except to express her exasperation with the physical limitations of old age. It was a visit to which Cathy looked forward. Added to the fact that it was the last call of the day and she could get home to Andy and the kids.

As she turned into the cul-de-sac, she found police cars everywhere, She undid her seat belt and picked up her bag off the passenger seat and hastily got out of the car.

'What's happening?' she asked the nearest constable as she rushed towards the bungalow.

'Can't go up there, miss. It's a crime scene.'

'Why. What's happened? Is she all right?'

'The inspector will tell you. Who are you?'

'I'm Mrs Reid's carer.'

'The inspector would like a word with you.' He waved across to Nick, who was already striding across.

'Cathy Turton?' he asked.

'Yes,' she mumbled, looking around, scared at what she could see. People in white suits entering Mrs Reid's bungalow. People taking photographs – police, press or public, she was unsure.

'I'd like a word,' Nick said. 'We can sit in here.' He opened the rear door of the nearest police car.

She hesitantly got in and Nick followed her. He introduced himself.

'Well, Cathy. Mrs Reid has been found dead this afternoon…'

Cathy's hand went to her mouth.

'Oh, no!' she said. 'How did it happen? Did she fall?'

The questions came tumbling out.

Nick continued. 'Your agency tells me that you were to call at Mrs Reid's at eleven o'clock. Is that right?'

'Yes. I was there at ten fifty five. It's on my time sheet, in my bag, here.'

She took it out and handed it to him.

'Tell me about your visit.'

'It was just as usual. She's a very tidy person, so there was nothing to do. I made her a coffee. We chatted as I made it and I left.'

'Do you have coffee with her?'

'Sometimes.'

'But not today?'

'No.'

'Why not today?'

'I knew my next call would be a long one. An old man, bedridden, doubly incontinent. I knew I'd have to change his sheets and put them in the wash. Which is why I was early at Mrs Reid's, to get ahead of schedule.'

'Was there anything odd about your visit today?'

'No, not really. Though our conversation was a bit odd. I wouldn't have said she had dementia or anything like it, but she told me she had a young boy-friend who was taking her up in the hills in the summer. Old people do ramble, sometimes, back into their childhood, so I just smiled and took no notice.'

'And was Mrs Reid OK when you left?'

'Yes. Perfectly. Enjoying her coffee and watching TV.'

'Was she a difficult customer in any way?'

'Not at all. She's a lovely lady. Generous at Christmas. She always gives me a little something for my boys' birthdays, perhaps a fiver each. She never complains. But can you tell me what this is all about?'

'Mrs Reid was found dead this afternoon and you were the last person to see her alive, so you can see...'

'But I didn't...she can't be...how did it happen?' Cathy burst into tears, tears of sadness for Mrs Reid. Surely these policemen wouldn't suspect me? I'm a nurse. I wouldn't harm Mrs Reid.

'Well, Cathy, that will do for now, but we may need to speak to you again,

Cathy went to her car and left.

Maggie Talbot was being a good neighbour, providing Stuart with tea and sympathy at her bungalow next door, which is where Nick found him.

'I'd like to have a few words with Mr Reid,' he explained. 'Could we do it here, Mrs Talbot?'

'Of course. I need to do a bit of gardening out back, anyway.' She left and Nick and Stuart sat down in the kitchen.

'Tell me about your day, Mr Reid.'

'It's been a normal day at the office. I had been in a meeting just after lunch-time with the CEO when a call had arrived on my phone. I hadn't noticed it until later, about three o'clock. It had been from my mother. She had left a garbled, unintelligible message, it's still on there, you can listen to it if you like. She sounded frightened between bouts of vomiting, so I rushed home to find her dead on the floor. You saw the scene. I rang 999. The paramedics hadn't moved her because they thought it could be a crime scene and called you.'

'I had a word with the Forensic Pathologist and her initial feeling is that your mother might have been poisoned. The question is, Mr Reid, who would want to poison your mother? Do you have any ideas?'

'None at all. She left her friends down south when she moved up here to live near me, but there's no-one who would want her dead.'

'Neighbours?'

'There's only Mr and Mrs Roper next door on the other side. They're in Australia for six weeks. He's retired..

And you've met Mrs Talbot. She's a great neighbour.'

'Have you any brothers or sisters, Mr Reid?' Nick asked.

'No. I'm an only child. So were Mum and Dad. Mum and I are the only members of our family left. My father died when I was three. I have no aunts, uncles, cousins. Grandparents are long gone. Longevity is not a strong suit in our family. Now there's only me,' he finished ruefully.

'That'll be all for now, Stuart. I'm sorry for your loss.'

Nick left and back in his office, settled down to consider what evidence he had.

'I could do without this case,' he said to Dave, 'but the chief thought that as I'm working on the Bertrands case, there might be a connection with Stuart being on the staff there.'

'Sounds feasible. It's got to be more than coincidence that all these things are happening there.'

'Mrs Reid had nothing to do with the firm.'

'No,' Dave agreed, 'But does Stuart need money? Perhaps he wants to buy into the company or start another company and needs his mother's money to get going. That's an expensive bungalow that she lived in.'

'Yes. We had two suspects. I feel that Cathy would be innocent. She could have introduced the poison, but why? She had no motive. She had nothing to gain from Mrs Reid's death. The old lady was not a problem, unlike the doubly incontinent old man. Ask Rob and Eamonn to dig around to see if she could have been tempted to poison Mrs Reid. On the other hand, Stuart could have a motive and, of course, he's still a suspect for Ryan's death. And not entirely in the clear in Ellie's. We have work to do, Dave.

FORTY SEVEN

Nick and Dave walked into Anuradha's office when bidden by her receptionist.

'Morning, Anu. You have news for me, I believe.'

'Yes. It's very interesting. This is not your usual case. No blunt instruments. No firearms. A puzzle solved by research.'

'Sounds complicated. Tell me more,' Nick said as they settled into chairs and Dave took out his notebook, pen poised as Anu began.

'As I told you at the bungalow, it looked like a case of poisoning. Questions arising - which poison? And by whom was it administered?'

'How do you identify all the possible poisons? There must be hundreds,' Nick asked.

'With modern toxicology, no substance, poison or otherwise, is ultimately undetectable. To cut a long story short, this lady shows all the signs of aconite poisoning. She will have had a horrible death, not knowing what was happening to her body. Starting with severe stomach pains, she would have sensed a feeling of pins and needles around her mouth. She would have been sweating and the abdominal pain would have prompted vomiting. In trying to get out of her chair to get to the toilet, her weakened muscles would have let her down and, with her eyesight suddenly failing, she would have fallen to the floor, with profuse vomiting. At length, her heart would be racing, her blood pressure would plummet, she would convulse and death would follow.'

Both Nick and Dave shuddered at the thought.

'How do you know it was aconite poisoning?'

'We found it in her vomit, in her half-empty coffee cup on the table and then a brown powder mixed in the coffee jar.'

'Does that tell us anything about the poisoner?' Nick asked.

'Quite a bit. It suggests that the poisoner had no particular target in mind. Anyone who was served coffee out of that jar would have been a victim. It also suggests that the carer would not have been guilty. If she intended to poison Mrs Reid, she would probably have put a pinch of the powder in her victim's coffee and that would have been that.'

'If she knew anything about the amount required,' Nick added.

'But that would have pointed directly to her. She didn't join Mrs Reid for coffee that morning, which would be suspicious, so mixing the powder in the coffee jar would deflect any guilt.'

'Agreed. There were two sets of fingerprints on the coffee jar, the carer's and Stuart Reid's. It's reasonable for both to be there, which gets us no further.'

'What about the source of the powder?'

'Herbal shops sell it.'

'What? A poison on sale?'

'Aconite is used medicinally for pain relief in many Far Eastern countries. There is no quality control over its production and the tiny amount required for pain relief is dangerously close to a lethal dose. There are many instances of accidental overdosing.'

'So, of our two suspects, the carer is less likely than Stuart to be the poisoner. Without a motive, she seems in the clear, but that would have been true of Harold Shipman, and look what happened there.'

'Other matters in this case,' Anu continued.

'Yes?'

'We checked all round for fingerprints. Door handles; window catches; kettle and coffee jar. There were none other than Stuart's, his mother's and the carer's. So either nobody else has been in there or someone has been very careful to leave no trace. We also found Mrs Reid's mobile phone. She called her son at about one pm on the day she died. You'll need to check his phone.'

'We've already done that. He told us about the call and I've listened to the message she left. He described it as unintelligible and garbled, which was accurate. What I heard would have been the result of the suffering you described. It was two hours later when he raised the alarm. Poor woman, to have to suffer like that.'

Nick and Dave made their way back to Chester, mulling over what they had heard.

FORTY EIGHT

'How are things going on at Bertrand's?' Kieran Donovan asked Daniel, who had come into his Liverpool office, having travelled up the M53 at the end of his day's work in Chester.

'Very well. Your scheme to run its value down is going to plan. The team manager, Stuart Reid, is now a suspect in another case. Murder, this time.'

Kieran looked interested.

'How come?'

'His mother died in suspicious circumstances and he's one of the suspects.'

Kieran could tell from the look on Daniel's face that he was bursting with news, so he played along.

'I take it you had something to do with it.'

'You could say that.'

'OK. Out with it. Tell me what happened.'

'I've been reading up on poisons, and I decided on aconite. You can buy it over the counter in Indian herbal shops because it's used to relieve pain in foreign countries, but anything more than a tiny bit is poisonous. I went round to Stuart's mother's house and talked my way in and when she wasn't looking I mixed some powder into her coffee jar and left.'

'So how does an old lady dying help to devalue a car

dealership?'

'Because Stuart will be the prime suspect and may be sacked, even if he doesn't go to jail. The company will be less efficient without him and its name will be mud, with another dead body in the news.'

'And what if you are arrested?'

'I won't be. Nobody knows I went there. No CCTV. No fingerprints. If I'm questioned – and they have no reason to question me – all I say is 'I was never there.' They can't prove I was, and why would I go there anyway?'

Kieran was wary. His fate might be nestling in the wrong, inexperienced, hands

'As long as this never finds its way back to me. If we both end up in jail, you will regret it so be careful.'

'Of course. I've been careful so far, haven't I? They haven't arrested anyone for Ryan's death. I arranged the hijack without suspicion and now this. I take a pride in my work, you know.' He was hoping to impress Kieran

'They haven't arrested anyone, yet.' Kieran emphasised the last word. 'They're still working on it.'

'I'm still on their list, but I'm sticking to my story. I could do with getting Detective Price off my back, though.'

'Well, that could be your next project. Find a way of getting rid of the policeman. It would do me a favour as well. Moving deliveries into Cheshire is getting difficult. Macca does his best but it's small scale at the moment. He had a kid die on him last week which is of great interest to the police. If we had a pet policeman who could turn a blind eye to some of the goings-on, it would be worth a fortune to me. Think about it. See what you come up with.'

Daniel brightened at the prospect of pitting his wits against the police, and Kieran's valuation of the project tempted him. 'A fortune,' the man said. He licked his lips. Second-in-command of Kieran's empire would be a worthwhile target. Everything is possible.

'Leave it with me,' he said as he left, confident that

he had impressed Kieran at last.

As he opened his car door on the forecourt, one of Kieran's men was brushing the yard. He would pick his brains.

'Hi Josh.'

'Hi Dan.'

'You go to Cheshire quite often, don't you?'

'I do a few deliveries, yes. Horse shows mostly.'

He had no need to explain the connection between horses and a car dealership. Daniel was already aware of Kieran's other enterprises.

'Is that because you like horses?'

'No. Don't be daft. There's loads of kids. Rich kids, with daddy's money sticking out of their ears, looking for excitement. Know what I mean?'

Daniel knew exactly what he meant.

'So business is good?'

'It was until one of the kids died and to top it all, one of the lady riders is partner of a detective – Price, his name is - , so he's always there cramping my style. Just have to be extra careful. He hasn't noticed me so far, though.'

He went on to describe the difficulties of his job. He found that hanging round outside schools was a waste of time. Not having a child to collect, he stood out among the parents crowding around the gates, and parents were so suspicious these days that he would soon be reported to the police. Trawling around housing estates was better, but changing the car was necessary to avoid police suspicion. The downside was that his regular customers didn't recognise the car. 'I could do with a jingle, like the ice-cream man,' he joked as he put his brush to work once more.

Another piece had fallen into place in Daniel's jigsaw mind. DI Price had cropped up again. Another good reason to get rid of him.

FORTY NINE

'What you call a 'tap on the head' might be seen as something quite different by the owner of the head.' Nick said.

He was sitting opposite Allan Brewer and his solicitor, Gerald Bolton, in the interview room, turning his attention to the hi-jacking of the Mercedes.

'There were two of us there. P'raps it wasn't me.'

'We know it was you.'

Allan got agitated. Was their agreement disintegrating?'

'What d'you mean? Did Jim say it was me?'

'He didn't have to.'

'Could you explain why you are so sure?' Bolton asked.

'The victim had a view of his attackers before they pulled their balaclavas down. Although they were unknown to him, he knew that the first man who spoke to him had a beard. Your client is clean-shaven. So , Mr Brewer, you're facing a charge of GBH as well as theft of the car. And of course, a guilty plea could lead to a lighter sentence. So what do you think?'

Allan thought hard. It really had been just a tap on the head. Nothing 'grievous' about it. The driver was ok, wasn't he? He would brazen it out. He could always change his plea later if it suited him. He looked across to Mr Bolton, who nodded to affirm the decision they had previously discussed.

'Not guilty,' he said.

'Suit yourself,' Nick said, realising that this was now going to be a longer job than he thought. The National Crime Agency had decided to leave prosecution of the case to the local police, as none of the information they had amassed pointed to any organised crime.

'Reg Potts told me that you and Jim paid him for the hire of the truck when you took it. In cash?'

'Yes.'

'Where did you get it from/'

'It was left on Jim's door-step in a Tesco bag.'

'Sounds a bit risky.'

'Not really. The owner was sitting in his car across the road. He wouldn't have let it out of his sight until Jim picked it up. He rang Jim's mobile to say it was there.'

'Who was he?'

'Jim didn't say.'

'What car was it?'

'You'll have to ask Jim. I wasn't there.'

Nick shuffled some papers and brought out an official-looking report from the German police.

'Quite a trip across Germany, wasn't it?'

'Suppose so.'

'Where did you dump the false number plates?'

'I know nothing about false number plates.'

'Nuremberg, wasn't it?'

'No idea.'

'Wasn't all you needed to get rid of, was it?'

'Don't know what you mean.'

'Weak bladder or the effects of a long journey?'

'Is that on there?' He pointed at the report.

''Fraid so. There's also a note of what you ordered for your meal in the restaurant that night.' Nick was impressed with the German efficiency. He went on 'And, guess what, I have here some number plates with your prints on them.' He reached to the side of the table and revealed an evidence bag containing the plates and spoke into the recording machine. 'I'm showing Mr Brewer Exhibit 1, a pair of number plates. Do you recognise these, Mr Brewer?'

Allan could see everything going against him; this detective seemed to have evidence for everything. Had the cops really been following them across Europe? However, without Jim to discuss it with, he was still reluctant to go for a guilty plea.

'No comment,' was the best he could manage.

'We'll call a halt there. Interview ended at 10.34,' Nick said, to give Allan time on his own, back in the cells, deprived of Gerald Bolton's advice. He would have time to mull over his story, confusing himself before their next interview. He returned Allan to the cells.

Following a short break, Jim Lewis replaced Allan Brewer in the interview room and Nick went through the same series of questions as he had asked Allan.

Answers were similar. Obviously, they had decided on their approach and were, so far, sticking to it.

'Who do you work for, Jim?' he asked.

'I'm free-lance.'

'Both of you?'

'Yes.'

'So who hired you this time?'

'Didn't know his name. People are very secretive in this business, you know.' He smirked slightly at his humorous reply.

'Reg told me that you paid for the truck hire. Where did you get the money from?'

'The guy rang me the night after we'd been hired and said the money for the truck hire was on my doorstep for me to take to Reg. I went to the door and there it was.'

'Did you see him?'

'Not really. He stayed in his car across the street. He flashed his lights when he was sure I'd picked up the money and drove off.'

'What car was it?'

'Don't know.'

'Come on, Jim. You're a lorry driver. You spend your life looking at cars. What car was it?'

'Could've been a Merc. It was dark outside.'

'Colour?'

'Silver, I suppose.'

'Number?'

'Didn't notice. He shot off once I'd picked up the money.'

'When did you get paid for the job?'

'We haven't been, yet.'

'You're very trusting. I thought you'd be wanting cash up front.'

'There's some people you can say that to and some you can't. This one you can't.'

'Dangerous, is he?'

'You could say that.'

'So you know who he is?'

'I just know he's dangerous. That's as much as I can say.'

'Come on, Jim. Tell me his name?'

'No comment.'

Which was the response to all of Nick's further questions, resulting in Jim being returned to the cells and leaving Nick with the worrying question – who is this dangerous mystery man?

FIFTY

On returning to the incident room, Nick turned his attention to the death of Mrs Reid. Of his two suspects, Cathy had been considered the lesser likely of any wrong-doing, leaving Stuart in pole position. At this stage, no-one had been arrested, though Stuart, still protesting his innocence, had been warned not to leave the country.

Nick needed to refresh his memory of the bungalow, in the hope that something relevant would present itself. What had they missed? A fingerprint? A footprint? If Stuart was not the guilty one, then who was?

Half an hour later, he wandered down the cul-de-sac and turned into the front garden of the bungalow, admiring the tidy garden and the colourful cyclamen in pots that Mrs Reid would have enjoyed through the winter months. That was not to be.

An authoritarian voice brought his attention away from the garden.

'Can I help you?'

A bronzed elderly gentleman looked over the neighbouring hedge. He was wearing a rugby shirt and shorts, hardly appropriate for the temperature that had caused Nick to wear an overcoat. He had that distinguished appearance which comes with blindingly white hair contrasting with the deep, healthy tan of his skin. His piercing blue eyes bored into Nick as he spoke again.

'I don't think she's in, so you needn't hang about. She doesn't buy anything at the door anyway.'

Nick took out his warrant card and said 'I'm

Detective Inspector Nick Price and I'm here to investigate a murder. And your name is…?

The man spluttered, 'A murder? Who's been…? Not Mrs Reid?'

'I'm afraid so. I take it you are the neighbour who has been on holiday.'

'Yes. I'm Henry Roper. We've been to Australia. Six weeks. Got back late last night. How was she…?' He wafted a hand as if it would complete his question without actually mentioning anything distasteful, like murder.

'She was found dead here yesterday. The cause of death is still under investigation.'

'Stuart will be heart-broken. He doted on his mother. Visited her every day.'

'It's early days, so we don't know who the perpetrator might be. Investigation is difficult. We often have CCTV to help us in the city, but out here, low crime area, nobody has CCTV.'

'I have. My wife's going through it now. She said earlier that she was getting bored. Postmen. Bin men. Delivery drivers. Nothing ever happens here, she says.'

'I'd like a copy of it on a memory stick, please? It may throw up something to help the investigation.'

'Of course. Right away.' He rushed into his house, eager to tell his wife the tragic news about Mrs Reid. Something had happened here after all. Nick looked over the hedge and saw that the camera would have covered a corner of Mrs Reid's garden.

'Could be interesting,' he thought.

He then went into the bungalow and viewed the scene in the lounge.

The forensic team had done all they needed to and a commercial cleaner had then been employed to remove all the blood and vomit and coffee that had, unfortunately, stained the carpet. The combined smells of disinfectant and deodorant were overpowering. No doubt they would wear off in time. A new carpet would help. He walked through into the kitchen, noting that on everywhere he would have touched if he were a stranger arranging to poison Mrs Reid - door and drawer handles and cupboard doors - he found fingerprint powder; all the logical places to touch, plus a few The team knew their stuff.

'May I come in?'

Henry Roper had returned, now sensibly clothed in trousers and a thick jumper, offering Nick the memory stick.

Nick thanked him and tucked the stick into an evidence bag before he left, thanking Roper and securing the door as they went.

He handed the memory stick to Liz Marston as he arrived at his office.

'An afternoon's telly-watching for you,' he grinned. 'It's from Mrs Reid's neighbour, Henry Roper. There's six weeks recording on this. There may be something useful, you never know.'

'Righto, boss. I'll do my best.'

'I know you will. And while you do, I'll go to Bertrand's and have a few words with Stuart's colleagues.'

FIFTY ONE

Nick was surprised to find that the first person he met at the dealership was Caroline Paterson.

'I thought you would have left by now. The last time we spoke, you were looking forward to retirement.'

'That was just a dream, after all. Following Ryan and Ellie's deaths, then Janet's er...unfortunate departure, Mr Formstone asked me to stay on. We're trying to keep up our usual service, but our reputation has suffered. I attend as many shows as I can, sometimes with Daniel, sometimes alone, but I'm finding that we get more enquiries about our reliability than about the quality of our cars. People are so cautious. It's so depressing.'

'So Daniel doesn't always go with you to shows?'

'No. He's a bit erratic. He takes time off when he feels like it with no explanation and I have to go alone. It's not a problem. I've done it for years.'

Nick glanced towards the glass-fronted office at the end of the room and noted that Daniel was in there alone.

'Stuart not in today?'

'No,' Caroline said. 'He is shattered by what happened to his mother. As are we all. She was such a nice lady. He's taken the rest of the week off. So much to do at the bungalow.'

Nick thought back to his visit earlier. There had been

no sign of Stuart there then.

'Did Stuart have any money problems that you know of?' he asked.

'I wouldn't have thought so. He's a single man on a good salary here. Doesn't go out much. He went to a couple of pop concerts in Liverpool with Ellie last year, but nothing since Ryan appeared on the scene. He's not in any sports clubs as far as I know. His contribution to keeping fit is walking up the stairs here every morning.'

Nick smiled as he recalled that Caroline had been sceptical about Stuart's keep-fit efforts at their first interview. He looked across to where Daniel was gazing at a screen in Stuart's office.

'I wouldn't mind a word with Daniel while I'm here, so would you excuse me a minute?' he said,

'Not at all,' Caroline said and turned to her desk again.

'D'you mind if we have a word,' he said as he entered the office.

'No. OK. What can I do for you?'

Daniel had guessed that Nick would be wanting to speak to him and had prepared himself so that the request did not come as a surprise. Innocence was written on his face as he turned to face the detective.

'Stuart not in today?' Nick said.

'No. He's taken time off. You've heard about his mother, I suppose?'

'Yes. It's very sad. Any news about the hi-jacked car?'

'No. We've seen the last of that one, I think.'

'Do you think someone has it in for Bertrand's?

'Such as who? The BMW team enjoyed our embarrassment at the show, but I don't think another company would stoop that low. Competition is one thing. Sabotage is another.'

'Who knew the number of the transporter?'

'I'm not sure. John and Susan might have known it. They made all the travel arrangements. I don't think that I ever knew it. Still don't. It didn't matter to me, I was going by car. Caroline might have known as she oversaw all the paperwork. Is it important?'

'We're looking at all the possibilities. Stuart's going to inherit a nice bungalow, isn't he?'

'Is he? I've never seen it.'

'Yes. Very nice.'

Nick's plan to hop from topic to topic hadn't tripped Daniel into a mistake, but he still had his suspicions about the young man. He left to speak to John and Susan in the outer office.

John was positive that he had never known the registration number of Raybrook's transporter.

'It was their vehicle,' he said, 'so they booked passage on the ferry. We had nothing to do with it.'

Susan agreed. Raybrook's would have arranged accommodation for their drivers if it had been necessary, though she felt that they would probably have slept in the cab of the lorry.

Caroline said that she had checked out all the paperwork with no mention of the transporter, which was all Raybrook's responsibility.

Nick decided that a visit to Raybrook's was necessary.

'Hi, Shona,' he said as he walked into her office.

'To what do we owe the pleasure?' she smiled. 'Have you found the missing car?'

'No such luck,' he replied and went on to ask her who had known the number of their lorry.

'Why is that important?' she said, as the lorry was back on their yard.

'Someone needed to know the number before they made the false plates. Nobody at Bertrand's knew it, so it must have come from here.

She tried hard not to blush, though in fact, the effort was unnecessary as she had turned pale. She recalled a phone call that she had received before the trip, a call that she had tried hard to forget.

'Remember, keep this to yourself,' the voice had said. 'Tell me the number of the transporter, then forget you've told me. If you tell anyone, including the police, you'll find that accidents can happen at any time, driving home, out shopping, anywhere.'

What harm would come from someone else knowing the lorry number, she thought, so she had given him the number, When the hi-jack had taken place, she had relaxed, thinking that her caller had needed the number just to identify the lorry for the hi-jack. But now the police were interested. What should she do? Her mind was in turmoil. She twisted a paper-clip in her fingers until it was straight, then refolded it and flung it into the waste basket in frustration. Nick noticed the nervous behaviour.

'Has someone threatened you, Shona?' he asked gently. He needed to coax a reply from her. She nodded but said nothing.

'We can protect you, Shona.'

'Not all the time,' she said, remembering the caller's message. 'Look what happened to Ken. I'm saying nothing.'

She was adamant. Nick got nothing further from her and returned to Chester.

Back at the office, he gave Eamonn the task of trawling through Raybrook's telephone account to establish the caller's number. Raybrook's was a busy firm, with many enquiries from the local area, particularly Chester and Liverpool. Eamonn was heard muttering darkly about needles and haystacks as he set about the mammoth task. It would take him at least a day to isolate a number, starting at the date Raybrook's had been booked and finishing at the date of the hi-jack. He would need to isolate, and ignore, the firm's own mobile numbers and those of their user companies. Repeated numbers could also be ignored. The caller had rung just once. Most of the one-off callers would have been genuine enquiries which had not developed into a booking, one of the remainder would probably have been Shona's caller.

'Wish me luck,' was Eamonn's only other comment as he set about his task.

FIFTY TWO

Nick looked forward to his weekend visits to Pollard's with Helen. She was becoming physically fitter by the day; Gordonstoun Rambler, known as Flash, was learning fast and Helen had a target - to compete at the Cheshire Show in June. Nero would also be ready for the competitions by then.

The planning for the show was all new experience for Nick, which added both to his interest and Helen's excitement, as Flash was developing into a capable jumper. They had high hopes for him.

The death of Jamie Turner and the appearance of Ecstasy at Pollard's gave Nick a further reason to visit his favourite venue. Drug dealing is not done in the open. It would need constant watching of behaviour, noting who meets who. Any unlikely pairings would be noted for later investigation. To enable him to do this, he parked the horse-box conveniently to be able to sit in the cab and watch the entrance to the toilet block in the wing-mirrors without being observed himself. Drug dealers would be as wary as he was in this cat and mouse game.

Toilet-watching would not be his only occupation that day. Joe Hassall was there with his son and Tom was spending much of his time, once their horses had been prepared for competition, in company with Annabelle. They seemed happy together, laughing in agitated conversation, with linked arms as they walked. Their previous spat, when Tom had called Annabelle a stupid tart, had obviously been forgotten. Kids, eh?

To start the day, though, Nick's main duty was to help Helen with the horses, at which he was becoming more proficient as time went on. They both enjoyed this time together, working with a common purpose to get the horses looking their best. Although they often took her father's groom, Linda, with them, Nick's improving abilities allowed Linda some time off. He now felt part of a team. Oddly, as leader of a team for the rest of the week, he found his new role quite satisfying, especially when his horses (he regarded them as his own) looked so smart as they entered the ring with shining coats and well-oiled hooves. Helen was a sympathetic rider and the horses responded to her firm but gentle touch from hands and heels. She never took them out of their comfort zone until she thought they were ready for a challenge and the confidence they gained from their successes was invaluable. The trust was two-way.

There was always a good crowd at Pollard's on competition days; nothing in comparison with football matches or even county shows of course, but a sizeable group who found Pollard's a great venue for an afternoon out, given the variety of activities on offer.

'Hi, Josh.'

'Hi, Dan. Glad, you could make it'

The two men stood together in the queue at an ice-cream van, watching Nick as he walked off towards a stand-pipe, carrying a bucket for water for the horses.

'Yeah, that's him,' Daniel said, 'so where is she?'

'That horse-box, there,' Josh pointed out Helen as she folded travelling rugs and put them away in the box.

'Hmm. Tasty piece.' Daniel took a photo on his phone. 'She looks strong too. I don't think force will be any good. I'll have to think of something else. Good job I came.'

'OK. Now's your time to vanish. Don't let him see you here. Ta-ra'

Daniel returned to his car and drove away, his mind

plotting his next move. Detective Inspector Price would be putty in his hands and Kieran would be proud of him if, -no, when - he pulled it off. Second-in-command at Burke's would be within his grasp.

Nick's eyes narrowed as he saw Malcolm approaching. The black sheep had turned up again at Pollard's. This was becoming a habit and so suspicious, not in line with his family history at all, as told by Helen. He had no children entering in the pony classes. He was not a member of any riding group. He lived in Liverpool. So what on earth was he doing in this part of Cheshire? There was no satisfactory answer to his presence here. 'Just keeping an eye on things' was hardly informative. Was his nick-name Macca? It was a common enough nickname in Liverpool. Nick knew of others with the same nickname. Sir Paul McCartney for one.

'Morning, Malcolm.'

'Hi Nick. Having a good day?'

'Yes. You know how it is. Horses come first.'

'Tell me about it. I played second fiddle to horses all my young life,'

'And here you are again. Still keeping an eye on things?'

'You've got it. Where's Helen?'

'Walking the course. She'll be back any minute.'

They both looked at the ring where Helen was pacing out the distance between jumps.

'Meticulous, isn't she?' Malcolm said.

'Yes. Precision personified. But you have to be at this game. One fence down and you're out of contention.'

'Excuse me a moment,' Malcolm said as he rushed off towards the toilets. Nick glanced ahead of him and noticed Tom Hassall also going into the Gents. Was it a coincidence? As soon as Malcolm went in, Tom came back out looking black as thunder, too quickly to have done more than make a

U-turn. Malcolm took longer to reappear and when he did, he just waved across to Nick and walked off towards the ringside. Tom, meanwhile, had made his way to his horsebox, where Annabelle sat waiting on the tailboard. To say Tom looked frustrated would be an understatement. He flung himself down next to Annabelle, and an agitated conversation followed, culminating in both youngsters turning away from each other, like book-ends.

Annabelle had made up with Tom, though the 'Stupid tart' comment still stung. He was usually good company at horse shows and they enjoyed competing against each other. Added to which, he always had money which he lavished on her. Her father was an old-fashioned farmer with old-fashioned ideas, who never spent money unnecessarily. Whereas she normally wore a plain stock pin to hold her cravat in place for show-jumping, she now had a beautiful horse's head, jewelled pin which Tom had bought for her from the shop at Pollard's. They both felt very grown-up as they took lunch in the restaurant and the egg-and-cress sandwiches provided by Annabelle's mother were consigned to a waste-bin. She sat and waited, not entirely patiently, for him to return from the toilets, though she knew the real purpose of his visit. No sooner had he gone in than he reappeared. It had not gone well, it seemed, as his demeanour showed. He stamped his way back and flung himself down on the tailboard.

'What's wrong?' she asked.

'Couldn't do a deal. Someone came in. Macca wasn't very pleased.'

'Perhaps that's telling you something.'

The atmosphere turned frosty.

'Telling me what? And don't go on about me giving up. Just remember where that stock pin came from. And your posh lunch. And the silver chain for your birthday. You're in it as much as I am.'

'I'm not selling E to anybody. I enjoy being with you.

I don't need drugs to have a good time. And look what happened to Jamie.'

The atmosphere took a sudden dive, from frosty to arctic.

'Are you saying that was my fault? Just because he took too many.'

'You sold them to him!'

'Just keep your voice down. And next week you can eat your own crummy sandwiches out here.'

They turned their backs on each other, both regretting the words that had passed, both wanting to turn the clock back – just ten minutes would be enough.

FIFTY THREE

The echoes of 'Onward Christian Soldiers' died away in the ancient chapel as the congregation sat. The Pastor stood on the platform and began his sermon. He had no need of notes. His faith was part of his make-up, part of his DNA, or so he felt. He had discovered the teachings of St Oda, first penned by the revered saint when he was Archbishop of Canterbury during the first millennium. The words were as relevant now as they were then. He had not been named St Oda the Severe for nothing. Strict adherence to the rules, particularly the Ten Commandments, was necessary. Failure to comply would be followed by severe punishment. The Pastor felt that his flock needed constant reminders of the need to live according to the scriptures, backed up by the threat of whatever punishment he deemed appropriate. In his church he was judge and jury, and many a transgressing adherent had felt the sharp edge of The Pastor's tongue.

Cassie Morgan, for example. Hers was a childish misdemeanour which could have been dealt with much more simply. On the other hand, The Pastor would have said that his treatment worked. Cassie would never steal again. Would that have been the case if a gentle admonishment had been applied? He thought not.

Or the young man who was observed kissing a young lady, not his wife, in a dark corridor after a Tuesday night prayer meeting, who was publicly shamed before being expelled from the group altogether.

'Thou shalt not...' was at the centre of the beliefs of the Odonian Church.

'We live in difficult times,' he began quietly, a dramatic technique he often used to good effect, gaining his audience's agreement and their confidence, lulling them slowly, before hitting them with a stark truth at full volume later on.

'...difficult times when sinfulness becomes the norm. When evil actions are rewarded.'

'Like what?' A voice from the back row ventured a question, not previously heard of in the church.

There was no sign of irritation at this interruption. He continued in a conversational voice.

'You want an example? I'll give you one. A man murders a small child. His punishment is to be provided with four meals a day, with television entertainment and sporting activities for the rest of his life. And you are willing to foot the bill for all of this. How can you say that the punishment is just?'

Nods and murmurs from the bulk of the audience, with no response from the original enquirer showed that The Pastor had made his point. Buoyed by the general approval, he continued.

'Let us remind ourselves what the Bible says on the subject of dealing with sinners. Matthew, Chapter 18 suggests that sinners be treated as pagans, in other words, they should be excluded from the church.'

The last four words were delivered at full volume, before dropping down to conversational level again.

'Then St Paul, in his first letter to the Corinthians, tells us...' Again the walls shook as he repeated Paul's words. 'Expel the wicked person from among you.'

He felt that he had made his point as he concluded, 'These are the rules that St Oda expects us to cling to; to lead a sinless life; to avoid exclusion from the church. Which is why I continue in my efforts to bring you all into the fellowship of the church, pure and sinless, as St Oda meant us to be.'

FIFTY FOUR

Leaving Eamonn burrowing into phone records, Rob Davidson and Bridget Carson visited the Bertrand's building. They enjoyed a gentle stroll through the city. There was no rush. George Smith would be turning up for his night duty just before five o'clock and he'd be sure to have time to talk.

True to form, his face lit up as he recognised Bridget from his previous job, but she kept her thumbs well hooked into her belt to avoid the offered handshake. Her response to his welcome was pleasant enough, followed by the enquiries about her health (How are you?) and her job (Are you enjoying Chester?), to which she gave monosyllabic answers.

'We're still looking into the murders that occurred here,' Rob told him. 'What we know so far is that you were here in the building. The only person on the Bertrand's floor was Ellie Mason and nobody else had a key to the front door.'

'Well, except the CEO.' George said. 'He has always had a key, but he doesn't use it very often. He always lets me know if he's in, just in case there's an emergency. And he always says goodnight when he leaves, on his way out.'

'You didn't mention that before.' Rob said.

'Well, it was irrelevant. I didn't see him leave that night, therefore he wasn't in the building.'

'What if he was in the building and he left through the back door.'

'I'd have heard him. Your colleagues tested that theory when they were here before. You can't operate that back door quietly. There's a push bar. You can hear it from here. You can try it again if you like.'

'I'd like to look at it, later, perhaps,' Bridget murmured.

Rob was unsure about the information he was

hearing. Why would an ex-policeman withhold vital information? He would know that full information was necessary to solve crimes. He continued, 'Do you always do your rounds at the same time every night.'

'On the dot. I check the back doors as soon as I come in, then at seven thirty and midnight I check each floor. There's nothing to see. I look along each corridor to see that all the office doors are shut. Then, starting at the top floor I work my way down to the ground floor.'

Bridget had a thought.

'Do you use the lift or the stairs?' she asked.

'I use the lift. All the way up to the top floor and then one by one to the lower floors.'

Bridget saw a flaw in this system. George travelling in the lift did not provide the full-time security that his employers thought they were getting. They were impressed by the fact that he was an ex-police sergeant, but had not checked his routines. A major mistake, she thought, but she refrained from comment. He could have been by-passed by anyone who knew his system.

'Let's have a look at this back door again,' Bridget suggested. Rob wondered why, but decided to ask later, and followed her out to the back corridor.

As they stood near the lift, she pointed to the door away to her left.

'That's the door. Would you say it's locked from here?'

'Looks like it.' Rob was mystified, and when they walked up to it, sure enough, the door was locked and barred, as it should have been.

'Why are we looking at this again?' Rob asked.

'Before we came out, I looked at Dave's notes from the original interview. Smith said he only looked along the corridor to check the door. You did it yourself just now.'

'Yes. And it *was* locked.'

'But what if it only looked locked?'

'How do you mean?'

Stepping to the door, she shoved the push bar to open it. She ran her fingers down either side of the bolt.

'Still a little sticky,' she said.

'What's this all about? You've lost me.'

'Have you ever used duct tape, Rob?'

'Yes. Sticks like…'

She pressed on before he could complete his comparison.

'And when you remove it, it leaves a residue. Like this.'

She indicated two sticky patches, one on either side of the door. She had a triumphant look on her face.

'Dave's notes mentioned these patches and they set me thinking. The only reason there would be patches on both side of the door would be from a strip of duct tape applied to hold the bolt in. You could then open and close the door without a sound. And when the door was closed, George Smith would assume that all was well because it looked OK from a distance.'

'So what does that do to our list of suspects?'

'It weakens their cases because we now know they had a means of escape without passing George in reception. And there's one more suspect to add to the list.'

'Who's that?'

'The CEO. He had a key to get in and the means of escape. He's got to go on the list.'

'What about motive, means and opportunity?'

'In Ellie's case, the means was her hair, the opportunity – she was here, working late and everybody knew, or so they said…'

'And motive?'

'That's always the difficult one, but there's bound to be one.'

FIFTY FIVE

There was a relaxed atmosphere in the incident room.

'This is excellent work, you two,' Nick said, as he read Bridget's report on their visit to Bertrand's.

'All down to Bridget,' Rob said.

'I confess, I didn't spot the reason for the stickiness either,' Dave put in.

'In that case, well done, Bridget. What made you think of it?' Nick said.

'I thought of how I would disable the bolt. Your ordinary desk tape wouldn't hold it in, but heavy-duty duct tape would.'

'She's got a criminal mind; good thing for a detective,' Eamonn put in, with a smile and a wink to Bridget, who was, by now, blushing with all the unexpected adulation.

'So, now we have a new suspect to interview. Also, we haven't spoken to the parents of Ryan and Ellie. Perhaps there is something in their private lives that might help us find their killers. A shot in the dark, I know, but this case has gone on too long. It needs some new input. How have you got on with tracing that phone call, Eamonn?'

'I'm on the last page of ten. I should have a result by the end of the day.

'What about the CCTV, Liz?'

'Close to a finish. End of the day for me, too.'

'In that case, Rob and Bridget can visit Ryan's parents, Dave and I will see Ellie's parents. Let's hope this gets a result. Everybody back here by five.' He tidied up the papers on his desk and prepared to leave. There was a spring in everybody's step as they left on their separate errands.

Rob felt more relaxed. Bridget's acute assessment of the situation at the back door had convinced him that there was no further need to nurse-maid the new arrival. She had proved herself an able observer, with the makings of a good detective. Bridget was also relaxed, her confidence given a boost by the compliments of the whole team.

Nick and Dave walked together up to the front door of a detached house on an avenue off the Wrexham road. The well-trimmed lawn, edged by colourful flower beds matched those of the neighbours, making for a very pleasant outlook for the whole road.

A white-haired man answered the door to Nick's press of the doorbell and Nick introduced himself and Dave, having confirmed that the man was indeed Charles Mason.

They were conducted into a well-furnished lounge. Clean, tidy, with ornaments and photographs on display. Charles Mason introduced his wife, Mary, who looked on the verge of tears when Nick explained that they wanted to talk about Ellie. She offered them tea, which Nick accepted. He thought that the routine of making tea would calm down her nerves and would make their chat more of a conversation, less of an interrogation.

He asked whether the Family Welfare Team had helped them after Ellie's death and was glad to hear that they had. The conversation roved around Ellie's plans for the future, which Mary Mason found hard to ignore. She had been involved in planning for the wedding to Ryan, 'Such a lovely boy,' she called him. She had looked forward to being the mother of the bride. But it was not to be and her disappointment showed in her words and her body language.

Nick brought her round to talking about Stuart. He

had also been in favour in the Mason household. He had been welcomed here many times during the period that he and Ellie had been together. She was unclear about why Ellie had changed partners but she did not have any impression of jealousy on Stuart's part when the split occurred.

Tears finally flowed when Ellie's pregnancy was mentioned. The Masons had only deduced that she was pregnant a couple of days before she was killed; her mother's instinct had recognised morning sickness, though it was later, when the pathologist had told them that the baby was Stuart's, that they received a double blow. First, their hopes of becoming grandparents were shattered. Second, as a devoutly religious family, a pregnancy outside marriage was bad enough, but for the father not to be her intended partner was a major disappointment.

Conversation moved on to Ellie's history, which in turn, led to the production of the family photograph album. Charles had been a prolific photographer in the past. Ellie's life was recorded in black and white, then in colour as technology, and Charles's choice of camera, improved.

Inside the front cover of the album was a pocket containing personal documents, passports, birth certificates and such like. Charles carefully drew out a marriage certificate.

'One of the happiest days of my life,' he announced proudly, as he read 'The marriage of Charles Edward Mason to Mary Formstone...'

Nick interrupted him.

'Where have I heard that name before? Isn't that the CEO at Bertrand's?'

'Yes. He's my brother, Neville.' Mary said. 'He helped Ellie to get the job in the first place. Luckily, she was good at it so there was no need for embarrassing dismissals. Mind you, he was very cross when I told him she was pregnant. He hasn't spoken to us since. As if it was our fault. He's so unreasonable.'

Nick got to his feet.

'I think we've taken up enough of your time, now,' he said. 'Thank you for your co-operation. You've been very helpful.'

Dave added 'And thanks for the tea.' as they made for the door. As they walked down the path to the car, Dave commented 'That was a bit abrupt. What's the rush?'

'We have another suspect to interview. This time with a better result.'

FIFTY SIX

Neville Formstone sat in the interview room, whence he had been brought following his detention for the murder of Ellie Mason.

Nick Price had arrived at his office and he had agreed to talk about the night of Ellie's murder down at the station. He was not surprised. He knew that actions had consequences. His actions would bring the direst consequences. He had no regrets. What he had done was right. What she had done was wrong, sinfully wrong. Her actions had brought about the direst consequences for her as well.

Sitting waiting in the interview room, his mind went back to that evening. Following a brief interview in the afternoon, where he had sympathised with Ellie following the death of Ryan, she had said that she would be working late. He knew that there would be nobody in the building except George Smith, but his patrols were so predictable that it would be easy to avoid detection. George never rattled doors to check that they were locked. A perfunctory glance down the corridor would be his only check of the back doors. Interview with Ellie over, Neville took a roll of duct tape from his desk drawer and left, via the back door.

He then pictured the scene in the office, almost as if watching a film of what went on later.

Ellie was sitting at her desk, working. She looked up as the office door creaked and someone entered the room. She turned to see who would be here at this time of the evening. As far as she knew, nobody else was working late.

'Hello, Ellie. Working late are we?'

It was Neville Formstone.

'The work has to be done. I need to catch up after this morning's delays.' She was tight-lipped, almost curt with her replies as she turned back to her work.

'You told me this afternoon that you would work late tonight, so I thought it would be a good chance to have a chat without ringing phones and chatty colleagues interrupting.'

'Oh.'

'You'll be missing Ryan's input as well, I'm sure.'

'Yes.' *He's never spoken about Ryan before, she thought.*

'Stuart suggested that the new recruit could sit with you for a week to familiarise himself with what goes on here. He could then spend some time with John and Susan, to see what they do, then he could follow Caroline for a month before she leaves. What do you think?'

'Stuart knows what he's doing, I suppose.' *Stay non-committal. Don't get drawn into a conversation.*

'I also wondered about the Brussels Show. You can't do that on your own. Or perhaps Daniel could come with you to Belgium. Learn the ropes.'

Please God, no. It mustn't happen.

'I'm not sure that's a good idea. It's too soon for me to decide. I told you this afternoon that Ryan and I were to be married next year. I'm in no state to talk about the future at the moment. So please, let it rest. I have work to do.'

'Of course you do. There's one more thing.' He walked behind her chair and put his hands on her shoulders. She tried to shake them off, but he held her firmly.

'What are you doing?' she asked, her fear showing in the tremor in her voice.

'Just sit still. You told me this afternoon that you were doubtful about going to Belgium.'

'Yes. Without Ryan it wouldn't be the same.' Further squirming again failed to escape Neville's grip on her shoulders. The smooth voice, filled with menace, continued.

'But that is not the real reason, is it?'

'It's part of the reason. The rest doesn't concern you. It's personal'

'But it does concern me, Ellie.' His fingers dug into her shoulders as he tightened his grip.

'Let me go and I'll tell you,' she lied, thinking that once free she could, perhaps, escape.

'You can tell me from where you are. Be sensible. Tell me and I can let you go.' Now he was lying. His grip on her shoulders and the ominous tone of his voice told her so.

'It's to do with the office, nothing else.'

'Are you sure?'

'Yes.'

'I think you're lying. You can tell me, you know that!'

'No!'

'Are you sure?' By now, she was shaking with fear as his desperation to find answers held her tightly in her chair. There was no escape. 'Tell me!' he shouted.

'I'm pregnant Are you happy now?'

The grip slackened on her shoulders, but not slack enough for her to be released. His voice was calm, smooth, sympathetic. Inwardly, he was seething, his eyes blazed with temper, thoughts of punishment boiling up inside him.

'There you are. It wasn't difficult, was it? Silly girl, getting yourself into a state.'

As her head fell forward in relief, her long hair hung like curtains around her face.

'How did you know?' she asked. His voice became smooth and quiet again.

'You have been ill every morning this week. Your visits to the ladies' room have been noticeable. I checked with your mother and she confirmed it.'

'I asked her not to tell anyone, especially you.'

'But she had to, didn't she? She has no desire to burn in Hell with you.' His eyes blazed as red as the fires of Hell.

'Did Ryan know?'

'No. It's not his.'

The infidelity struck him like a blow between the

eyes. He lost complete control.

His left hand held a clump of her hair on her left, his right hand reached around the front and took a handful from the left to the right, then suddenly pulled with both hands, the hank of hair crossing her throat. He pulled, hard. She tried to scream, but the intake of breath never reached her lungs.

She heard his voice as though it was in the distance.

'Sinner! Fornicator! You shall be punished. You will burn in Hell'

Her head swam as the pressure on her throat increased, her limbs thrashed until, under the relentless pressure on her windpipe, her struggles ceased.

Neville looked up and noted, with a degree of satisfaction, that the setting sun shone fully on to the windows, its bright reflection preventing anyone from outside seeing what had happened within.

He replaced Ellie's hair in its normal place, made his way to the door and left the way he came, leaving her lifeless body slumped in her chair.

Neville had then made his way down the stairs to the back door, with its push bar to open it. When he left in the afternoon, he had stuck some duct tape across the bolt, preventing it from engaging when he closed the door. All was set for his return that evening. He removed the tape as he left, leaving no sign of his visit. Or so he thought.

Nick Price and Dave Martin arrived for the interview.

'Sorry to have kept you,' Nick said, then set up the tape recorder and offered Neville the opportunity for his solicitor to be present.

'I have no need for a solicitor,' he said.

Dave thought, 'Here we go. Another one claiming innocence. No need for a solicitor indeed. We'll see.'

'And why are you so sure of that?' Nick asked.

'Because I am guilty of the crime. Furthermore, I am guilty of breaking God's laws and he will be my judge.'

'Well, I can only investigate crimes against the law

of the land, so what can you tell me about Ellie Mason's death.'

'Simple. She was guilty of the crimes of fornication and of adultery. The father of her unborn child was not even her intended husband.'

'But what gave you the right to exact this punishment?'

'Because I am God's representative here in Chester. I am the Pastor of the Odonian Church, responsible for the behaviour of my flock. I am judge and jury over these people.'

'But Ellie was your niece.'

'All the more reason for her to set an example to the rest of our congregation. She let me down. She let her family down.'

'There is a law that is common to both religious and civil codes,' Mr Formstone.

'What's that?'

'Thou shalt not kill.'

'Exactly. I am guilty to both.'

FIFTY SEVEN

Back in the incident room, Nick announced the arrest and confession of Neville Formstone as a result of his visit to Ellie's parents.

'You pounced on him pretty quickly, boss. How come?' Eamonn asked.

'Of our other suspects, George Smith was an unlikely option, in that he was alone in the building with no alibi. Stuart was unlikely to have killed his ex-girlfriend, especially after a successful reunion, so when Bridget and Rob came back with the news that the CEO could also have been in the building, plus the tampering with the back door, it left only one possible person who could have done it. Finding out that they were related was a bonus.'

He looked across to the newcomer.

'Bridget, find out what you can about the Odonian church. Neville was the Pastor at the Chester branch. We still need to know all about it for when he goes to court. He seems keen to take his punishment at the moment, but he may change his mind after a few weeks in our version of purgatory. Next, Rob, what did you find out from Ryan's parents?'

Rob stood up, notebook in hand.

'Nice, ordinary couple. Mr Palmer. He's recently retired and volunteers at St Joseph's school as a minibus driver. Mrs Palmer volunteers at a charity shop. They lead a quiet life. Proud of their son's achievements. The one important thing we found out – Ryan suffered from vertigo. They were surprised that he even went up to the roof, let alone walked near the edge. Which casts doubt on Daniel's statement.'

Nick brightened.

'It certainly does. We'll have that young man in again. Let's see if his story still holds water.'

Liz joined the conversation.

'He does tell lies.'

Nick spun round.

'Why do you say that?' he asked.

'Because he said he'd never been to Mrs Reid's home.'

'And?'

A triumphant grin crossed her face.

'The CCTV shows him walking up the path that morning, before the carer arrived. He was there for about quarter of an hour, then left, walking casually as if nothing had happened. Of course, at that stage, nothing had.'

'Any sign of his car?'

'No. It was outside the range of the neighbour's camera.'

'Bridget, find out the make and number of his car, then knock on doors and find out if anybody saw it parked nearby at that time.'

'I'm on it,' she said, eager to do well.

'He's a cool customer and no mistake,' Nick said. 'Looking back, he was unruffled on that first morning. There was no sign of guilt, and if he had anything to do with Ryan falling off the roof you would expect something to show up in his demeanour or body language. Cool was the word I used. Cool he was. We'll have him in.'

Eamonn spoke up.

'Before you do, my trawl through these phone numbers threw up just one question mark. There were three calls from one number, the timing of which struck me as odd. Two calls were before the hi-jack took place and one just before the transporter arrived back.'

'Could be a coincidence,' Rob suggested.

'Could be. But when you find out that the caller was Burke's of Anfield…'

'Well they're moving cars all the time. Coincidence.'

Eamonn was frustrated by Rob's playing down of his discovery.

'They have their own transporter. I've checked. So why hire another? Also, is it another coincidence that Daniel Thompson worked there before applying for the job at Bertrand's? I'm not sure what his motive is in all this, but it's worth looking into.'

Whether Eamonn was feeling let down by his old partner seeming to turn against him or jealous of the congratulations previously showered on Bridget, Nick was not sure, but a pat on the back was in order.

'Good work, Eamonn,' he said. 'Now, Dave and Rob, you go and arrest Daniel. He should still be in the office at Bertrand's. Liz and Bridget, It's 4.30. Time you went home. Let's have you here bright and early tomorrow. It's going to be a busy day. Eamonn, just run me through the figures you've been sorting out then you can go as well.'

The office cleared as quickly as if Nick had pulled the pin out of a hand grenade, leaving a sullen Eamonn alone with Nick.

'I didn't need to see what you've been doing, but you seemed put out with Rob's objections. Or is there something else bothering you?'

'Take no notice, boss.'

Nick realised that he was on the right track.

'But I do. Perhaps you would have preferred to go out with Bridget yesterday and you think I made the wrong decision.'

'There's something in that.'

'Well look at it my way. We needed a fresh pair of eyes on the scene and she needed to go out with an experienced officer. She came up with the conclusions about the tape on the door, solving the case of Ellie Mason and resulting in the arrest of Neville Formstone. You stayed here and used your experience to come up with a possible sequence of events connecting Daniel Thompson with the hi-jack and with his previous employer. So tell me which of my decisions was wrong.'

'Well, if you put it that way…'

'Exactly. We're a team, Eamonn. Now go home and get a good night's sleep. Tomorrow will be a busy day.

FIFTY EIGHT

Dave and Rob made their way into Bertrand's building, with the intention of interviewing Daniel Thompson before arresting him. They faced him across the table and went through the same questions he had answered before. It was familiar territory and he felt confident that he could remember his replies from the previous occasion.

Dave looked at his notes.

'In our first interview you said you stayed in the waiting room until you were called for interview.'

Dave flicked a few pages over.

'Then, in our next interview you told us you had a conducted tour of the building. You looked into other offices. Is that right?'

'Yes.' He wondered where this was going. A simple 'yes' would be enough.

'Did you or Ryan speak to anyone in the accounts office?'

'Not that I recall. They all had their heads down. You know what accounts clerks are like. Beavering away over a column of figures. They didn't even look up.'

'Mr Thompson. I am arresting you...' As Dave repeated the arrest speech Daniel realised that he had made a mistake by embellishing his evidence. He needed to get to his boss. Kieran would help him out. As they walked into the foyer, he asked whether he could pop into the toilet in the back corridor.

Dave looked at him and reluctantly agreed. Daniel indicated the handcuffs behind his back.

'It'll be difficult with these on,' he said.

At the toilet door, Rob removed the cuffs.

Immediately, Daniel took off at speed, sprinting down the corridor, towards the back exit. He crashed his way through the door, slamming it behind him and dragging a wheelie bin against it, making it impossible to open quickly. By the time Dave and Rob found their way to the car park, Daniel was speeding out of the city towards Liverpool.

* * *

Next morning, Helen was riding Nero along the leafy lanes. It was her favourite time of day. Very little traffic came this way. Occasional riders found this a peaceful place to ride, though the early morning was too much for many. They preferred to exercise their horses in the evening. The only sounds were country sounds; birds sang, dogs barked, milking machines hummed, horses clip-clopped. She was in a kind of dreamland, enjoying her surroundings, until she rounded a bend to find a stationary car, a man waving his arms to stop her and another man lying prostrate on the ground.

'Can you help us,' the man said. 'My mate wasn't feeling well and we decided to swap, but he collapsed when he got out of the car. I don't know where we are to tell the ambulance where to find us.'

Helen quickly dismounted and looped a lead rope over a gatepost, then crossed the lane to look at the prostrate man. As she bent over him, her world went black as a hood was slipped over her head. The man behind her held her wrists together as the other tied them with a cable tie.

She screamed and struggled, to no avail.

'If you stop struggling, you won't get hurt,' one of them said as they pulled her to her feet. She gauged where he was from the direction of his voice and she lifted her right knee sharply, connecting with his left thigh.

'Close,' he said 'but don't try that again,' punctuating his reply with a punch to her stomach. 'You'll travel in the boot for that.'

'Why are you doing this?' she screamed.

'You'll find out.'

They bundled her into the boot and closed the lid.

'What about my horse?'

'It'll be fine. Somebody will find it.'

They were in a rush to go and scrambled into the car, driving off at speed.

Helen wept tears of frustration as she lay in complete darkness. What is happening to me? Is Nero ok? I wish I could ring Nick. I wish I could move.

She screamed at every pothole that caused her to bump her head. Her wrists were painful from her struggles to free herself from the tight grip of the cable tie. She sensed rather than felt the blood which moistened her hands in the darkness. She guessed from the change in traffic noise and road surface that they had left the lanes and were on a motorway. To where?

* * *

Nick left Tom Cameron's office knowing that all that his boss had said to him had been deserved. It was almost word for word what he had said to Dave and Rob when they told him that they had lost a prisoner. It was largely the same that the two experienced officers had said to each other in their frustration when they were unable to open the back door of the building, giving Daniel time to make his getaway.

'It was a childish excuse.'

'We know, boss,' a crestfallen Dave said. 'Just an excuse and we fell for it. You must know how we felt.'

'I know exactly how you feel, because I feel the same, and I didn't lose him – you did. Which way did he go?'

'We don't know,' Rob replied, 'we were inside the building. By the time we'd run out of the front doors and round to the car park at the back, he'd gone. And it's a one-way street, so it doesn't give us a clue.'

'What about CCTV?'

'There isn't any. Remember? Old man Bertrand wouldn't have it, either inside or out.'

'Ok, Dave. Don't rub it in. I remember now. Let's start at the beginning. Where does he live?'

'Bootle. North Liverpool. I rang Stuart Reid to ask him when you were in with Cameron.'

'At last, a bit of initiative. What's the number of his car?'

'I got that as well.'

'Right. Let me ring Diane Coleman in Liverpool. It's her patch. We've worked together before. She may be able to track him down via ANPR. He's likely to have gone up the M53.'

Before he could make the call, his phone rang.

'Are you Nick Price?' a voice said.

'I am. How can I help? Who are you?'

'You needn't know who I am, but you can do me a very big favour.'

'Oh. And what's that?'

'I'd like you to lay off looking for Daniel Thompson.'

Nick almost laughed.

'I'm sure you would, but as he is wanted for murder, the answer is 'no'.'

'Don't be hasty. Perhaps you'd like to reconsider. I have a friend of yours here. I'll hand the phone over…'

'Nick…It's Helen… I've been…'

The phone was snatched away

'Now if you are ready to reconsider, she will be returned to you unharmed. If not, she will be handed over to my boys. They have some imaginative games to play with pretty girls, and it would be a pity to …but I think you get my drift.'

Nick's blood had run cold the moment he heard

Helen's voice, and it turned to icy as his caller described her possible fate if he failed to agree to the demands. Daniel would be free and blameless. Ryan's death would be written off as suicide. The caller's future operations in Cheshire would be facilitated by information which Nick would provide. He would be well-recompensed, of course, and would need time to consider.

'...and if you take too long to decide, I will return her to you – piece by piece.' The phone went dead.

'You all right, boss?' Dave asked as Nick went pale.

Nick nodded as he took in the ultimatum.

Nick Price – a bent copper? It was the furthest thing from his mind. He knew how policemen everywhere viewed a bent copper. The most disgusting thing on earth. But he was a servant of the public who knew where his duty lay. He must uphold the law. But at what expense? Helen's life was in danger. He could not allow a hair of her head to be damaged. But in the hands of a dangerous criminal?

His phone rang again. It was Helen's mother. There was panic in her voice.

'Nick. What has happened to Helen? A neighbour found Nero tied to a gate but no sign of Helen. I'm so worried. Where is she?'

The normally strong, capable woman, who had supported Helen through the agony of her broken back, was breaking up as she spoke, imagining the worst about her daughter. And Nick could only offer the worst of news at a time when his heart was in a struggle with his head over a way out of their predicament.

'I've just heard,' he said. 'She's been abducted. We're working on it. That's all we know at the moment. We'll get her back, whatever it takes. I'll keep you informed. Try not to worry. Must go.'

'Try not to worry' indeed! The poor woman was bound to be distraught and would be until this matter was over. He turned to Dave and Rob who had listened, open-mouthed, to the conversations.

'Somebody, I don't know who, has kidnapped Helen. He will return her unharmed if we lay off Daniel and say that Ryan's death was suicide.' He felt unable, at this stage, to tell them of the remainder of his caller's demands. His determination was focussed entirely on getting Helen back safely.

Nick's phone rang again.

'Hi, Nick. It's Malcolm.'

'Helen's brother?'

'Yes. I've heard you're looking for Helen.'

'Has your mother told you?'

'No. Does she know?'

'Yes, someone found Nero in the lanes but no Helen, so she rang me. I've since heard that she's been kidnapped. I had a call from her kidnapper, but I don't know who he is. How did you find out so soon?'

'Don't ask. You need to speak to DI Coleman in Liverpool. Can't stop. Bye.' The line went dead.

It was becoming a morning of mysteries.

Where was Daniel?'

Where was Helen?

Who is the kidnapper?

Where does Diane Coleman fit in?

He had intended to ring Diane anyway, so that must be his next task. She answered on the first ring.

He didn't wait for a greeting.

'Diane. It's Nick Price.'

'I've been expecting your call. I believe your girlfriend's been abducted.'

'Yes, but I don't know who has Helen, or where she is being held.'

'I know both of those things but before I tell you, let me explain. I already have plans for making arrests this morning of a gang leader plus some of his hierarchy. This is the person who has your Helen. We'll be an armed unit, with a well-practiced plan of action, so I can't have another unarmed group complicating matters.'

Nick could see the logic.

'But I need to be there,' he protested. 'It's Helen we're talking about.'

'I know, Nick. It's difficult. It's just our two cases coming to a conclusion at the same time. However, I can agree to just you coming along with us, but no-one else. But be warned. We will be armed. So will our targets. You must hang back and only make a move when it is safe to do so.

Nick was relieved to hear that he could go along. He would have agreed to any conditions as long as he could rescue Helen. He could never have sat in his office waiting for news.

'Agreed. Where do I meet you?

She told him and half an hour later he was on the car park at Rose Hill, Liverpool's police headquarters. Kitted out in a bullet-proof vest and a helmet, he joined Diane's group in their response vehicles. A new experience for Nick, with a group of grim-faced men, fully armed with H&K carbines and Glock pistols. He would never forget the smell of gun oil which filled his nostrils. As they travelled, Diane briefed him on the operation. His instructions were brief.

'Keep back. Head down. Don't move until told.'

Diane's men spread out when they arrived at Burke's of Anfield, a name familiar to Nick from his own investigations. With their accustomed stealth, they surrounded the showroom area.

Kieran Donovan was in his office, holding forth to a group of eight or nine men, hard men, some with shaved heads and garish tattoos, others small with weasel-like features, all, no doubt, with experience of life behind bars. He was explaining his plans for expansion into Cheshire. Suddenly, the door burst open and Diane's men filled the room. One of Donovan's men reached into his jacket for a pistol, but the barrel of a police carbine in his chest changed his mind.

'Don't do it!' was the command.

He didn't do it.

Diane's objective had been achieved – almost.

She rushed out and explained to Nick that, despite the success of multiple arrests, the leader, Kieran Donovan, had escaped in the confusion.

During all the noise and movement, Nick had seen a man, he thought he looked like Daniel, slipping out of the back of the showroom and into a workshop area at the rear.

Now that it was safe to move, he ran to the workshop. Inside, all was quiet. The ground floor was tidy, a mechanic's workshop with neatly laid out tools near the benches. He heard voices coming from the floor above

'Let me go!' It was Helen's voice.

Donovan's voice cut in.

'Dan, she's got to go. The police are here.'

'What are we going to do?'

'Price is not having it all his own way!'

'What do you mean?'

'We'll let her go. But I want him to remember me for ever.'

'How does that happen?'

'I'll keep one of her fingers.'

Helen screamed at the thought.

He smiled, grimly.

'Her ring finger will do nicely.'

Donovan dragged the struggling, protesting Helen across to the bench and cut the cable tie on her wrists. She swung her arm to give him a backhand swipe across the face.

'Bitch,' he growled and slapped her face, the heel of his hand splitting her lip and drawing blood. He took hold of her right arm and twisted it up her back, bending her face-down over the bench. He took her left hand and held it outstretched on to the bench ahead of her. His weight on her body held her right arm painfully in place, her hip bones grinding on the edge of the bench. He turned his head to Daniel.

'Right. Cut it off,' he commanded.

He was finding Helen's struggles too much to handle. Daniel watched helplessly.

'What with?'

'Anything. There's tools about. A hammer and chisel over there.'

The screaming and kicking went on, unsettling Daniel.

'Just put the chisel in the joint and whack it with the hammer.' Donovan shouted, his desperation starting to show.

Daniel leaned forward, hesitantly.

Wide-eyed, Helen watched as he placed the sharp blade of the chisel in her knuckle joint and raised the hammer.

'HIT IT!' Donovan roared.

Blood flowed from Helen's split lip and, in desperation, she spat blood forward, the bulk of it smearing her exposed hand.

Daniel yelled and dropped the tools. He backed off.

'I can't stand blood. Never could.'

Donovan stood up, releasing Helen, just as Nick rushed up the stairs, followed by one of Diane's men.

Between them, they overpowered Donovan and stretched him out, face down on the floor, his hands cable-tied behind his back. Nick ran to the weeping Helen and took her in his arms. As he led her towards the stairs, they passed the prostrate Donovan on the floor, and Helen delivered a swift kick to his ribs.

Of Daniel, there was no sign.

FIFTY NINE

Tom Cameron was furious.

'If this gets into the papers, we'll be the laughing-stock of the force. Of the nation, in fact,' he shouted.

'I know, sir.'

'Well, what are you going to do about it?'

'So far, our colleague at Liverpool has agreed to keeping Thompson's house under surveillance...'

'And what good will that do? I can just see him now, saying 'I've escaped from the police twice. I think I'll go home and have a cup of tea. They'll never find me there.' Come on, Inspector Price, (he emphasised the word *Inspector* as though it might be temporary) let's have something proactive. This lad is not daft. He's dodged us twice. Get ahead of him. Rattle his cage. Go on. Get after him before I say something we'll both regret.'

'Very good, sir,' was the best Nick could manage before he left Tom Cameron's office.

The Chief was right. They will be looking extremely stupid. He gathered his team in the incident room. They looked as glum as he felt. They knew the situation and how ineffective they appeared.

'I have just had a rollocking from the boss which I would like to pass on to you, but you can guess the gist of it.'

'We heard. The door wasn't closed. It echoed up and down the corridor,' Eamonn said.

'In which case, I'm expecting you all to come up with something that will restore our reputation. Put your criminal minds to work. What would you do in this situation?'

'Besides go home for cup of tea, you mean?' Eamonn's paraphrasing of Tom Cameron's comment brought laughter into the room. The team spirit was still there. Nick was sure they would come up with something.

* * *

'A gin and tonic will work wonders, darling.'
'Not too strong, Mummy. I've still got a headache.'

Ruth Fletcher was well known for her generosity, some would say, heavy-handedness, when pouring drinks, and Helen really wanted to relax, not get bladdered at the start of her new-found freedom.

Nick had delivered her to her mother's house after her rescue, partly to assuage Ruth's doubts about her daughter's well-being and partly to make sure that Helen would actually get some rest after her ordeal, which she would not have done if he had taken her home. He had to return to work, of course, so Helen would have taken herself off to see to the horses and one job would lead to another. And, for once, she had settled for relaxation with her mother.

'You know, dear,' you could be enjoying a life of comfort and luxury,' Ruth began.

Helen's heart sank. '*Here we go,*' she thought. '*Not the old lecture again.*'

'Mummy. Please let's not go over this ground again.'
'I'll keep going over this ground until you see sense.'

Helen put her case once more.

'From what I can see, you married Daddy because he could offer you a life of luxury. You never needed a job. You had the best of everything; cars, clothes, horses, dogs, holidays, you name it, all provided by Daddy's money.'

'Exactly, 'Ruth said. 'And you could do the same. Gerald Wingfield is still available.'

'Mother! It's not an auction!'
'He's exceedingly wealthy.'
'I don't care!'
'And very handsome.'
'I don't care!'

'We would have beautiful grandchildren.'

'Now you are treating me like a prize mare.'

'It has to be thought about, dear. What kind of life will you have on a police pension?'

'I don't know and I don't care. Nick and I are happy together. We'll take what comes.'

Voices had reached a crescendo. Then, in the silence that followed, Helen asked quietly 'One question. Do you love Daddy?'

'I think I do, dear.'

'Well, I know I love Nick.' She emphasised the *know*. 'So let that be an end to it. I'll have a proper G and T this time.' She handed her glass to her mother, who, for once, was unsure of her next comment.

With glasses refilled, with a stronger balance between the gin and the tonic, the two women sat in an uneasy silence. Finally, Ruth spoke, in a little voice in complete contrast to the volume of their earlier conversation.

'But I was so worried about you this morning. You could have been killed, all because of Nick's work.'

'I'm sorry I told you that bit. But it doesn't happen all the time. And he came to rescue me. My knight in shining armour. I know you were worried and I'm sorry it happened. I could be injured riding a horse, though. I was. Remember? I was in a wheelchair for over a year. Gerald Wingfield didn't want a disabled wife then, did he? He wouldn't even look at me. Who took me out and was proud to be seen with me? Whose face lit up every time he saw me? It was Nick. He cared, and he's the man for me.'

SIXTY

Daniel had made his way to Chester, following his narrow escape from the police. He felt on top of the world. Even an armed group had been unable to arrest him. As a result of forward planning, or due to a sense of survival, he had left his car two streets away, already packed with his sleeping bag and necessities for a prolonged stay. Having slipped out of Burke's compound unseen through a hole in the back fence, he ran down an overgrown lane to the road, then walked inconspicuously to his car. Nobody would remember a businessman strolling along the road. Running in panic would be a dead give-away. He was in Chester in half an hour, patting himself on the back for his skill and forethought. He parked in a back street near the canal, having changed his number plates for a pair taken off a scrap car weeks ago in readiness for any eventuality.

City streets were well covered by CCTV and ANPR these days, so it was as well to be prepared. It was also difficult to find a place that was not supervised by the technology to change the plates and he had driven in circles until he found a country lane quiet enough for him to make the change.

He walked to an all-night store a mile away for provisions, wearing a hoodie purchased from a charity shop on the way. He didn't fancy sleeping under bridges with the regular rough-sleepers. He decided to sleep in the car, but was on the look-out for a squat or other unoccupied building for a more substantial, less obvious, hiding place. When the dust settled, he would move on. He had spotted a narrowboat moored on the canal. It looked as though it had been there for some time from the cobwebs on the tiller. The owner seemed to have little regard for security – the padlock was held by a cheap hasp and staple, incorrectly fitted with the screws exposed. It was a simple job to unscrew the device and gain entry. He transferred his sleeping bag and provisions from the car. This would be his home for a short time while the police were running in circles looking for him. In time, his appearance would change. Longer hair and a beard would disguise the previously well-groomed business man. The boat was appropriately named *Hideaway*.

We were meant to be together, Daniel thought.

* * *

Mrs Millicent Bertrand and her daughter, Louise, sat behind what had been Neville Formstone's desk. Facing them were her senior staff; Caroline Paterson, a long-time employee and Show Team manager, Stuart Reid the Office Manager and Roberta Nicholls, the Accounts Team Leader. The meeting had been called at short notice, with no clue as to the agenda. Whether she had good or bad news to impart, nobody knew. They had grounds for remaining optimistic, since she had already spoken to them individually, though without any indication of her future plans.

'You must all be wondering why I have called this meeting. I don't blame you. Past weeks have been an ordeal for you all. You may know that my potential buyer has been arrested and will probably spend many years behind bars. There will therefore be no sale. The bad apples have been removed from the barrel, though I believe Daniel Thompson is still free and on the run. He is no longer an employee of Bertrand's. I would, however, like to make some staff changes. Our new CEO will be Caroline. She knows more about this company than anyone and I am sure you will give her your full support. Stuart will continue as Office Manager and we will open interviews for a Show Team Leader in due course. We will give shows a miss for twelve months, to let the dust settle and to rejuvenate our reputation. I hope Roberta will continue as Accounts manager. We will come back stronger next year. Finally, Louise and I will take a deeper interest in the company than we have done in the past, but do not worry ...' she smiled, 'we do not intend to interfere!'

She turned to her daughter.

'Louise!'

The younger director turned to a cupboard and produced a tray loaded with a bottle of champagne and five glasses, her mother passing out the glasses as Louise filled them.

'To the future,' Millicent said, to which the others replied with enthusiasm, adding congratulations to Caroline on her promotion. There was an atmosphere of optimism in the office once more.

SIXTY ONE

That evening, Caroline walked up to a two-up-two-down cottage near the canal. It had been a lengthman's cottage in its day, now let as a residence, having avoided demolition due to its Grade 2 status. She knocked the door, using the shining brass fox head knocker.

Janet Bagley answered the door.

'Oh, hello.' Janet was surprised.

'Hello, Janet. How are you?'

'Much better, thanks. I miss coming to the office, though.'

She invited Caroline into the living room and switched off the television set.

'Don't switch off on my account,' Caroline said.

'It's only the news. Doom and gloom again,' Janet smiled. Caroline looked about her.

'This is a beautiful cottage, Janet. Old and beautiful.'

'It was a lengthman's cottage in the old days.'

'Pardon my ignorance, but what is a lengthman?'

'He would be employed to look after a length of the canal, probably a mile in each direction, so you would find these cottages about two miles apart along the canal. He would report problems, clear weeds, just to keep a clear passage for boats – and horses, in those days.'

'I've learned something new tonight,' Caroline said, then continued. 'We've had some changes at Bertrand's. I'm the new CEO.'

'Congratulations. What happened to Neville?'

'It was sad. He's been arrested. It seems that he was

the one who killed Ellie. She was his niece, you know.'

'That makes it really sad,' Janet agreed.

'I've come to see if you would like to come back to work with us. We need someone like you.'

A look of doubt crossed Janet's face.

'Is …he…still there?'

'Daniel, you mean?'

'Yes.'

'No. He's gone too. He escaped from the police and he's on the run.'

'I thought I saw him last night. On a boat, further down towards the city.'

'On a boat?'

'Yes. It's been moored up there for weeks but I don't think it's his. It's called *Hideaway*. It's blue.'

Janet was surprised at Caroline's reaction.

'Excuse me, but I must dash. I'll call to see you again.'

And dash, she did, leaving Janet wondering about the purpose of Caroline's visit.

It was sometime later that Caroline drove into the city and up to the Bertrand building. Leaving her car illegally parked on double yellows, she ran up to the door. There was no sign of George inside. She looked at her watch. Seven thirty! Damn! George would be on his rounds. She waited impatiently, hopping from foot to foot and banging on the windows with her hands until, finally, George appeared.

'Come in, Mrs P,' he said. 'What's the rush?'

'Tell you later,' she flung over her shoulder as she headed for the lift.

In her desk, she found the card that DI Price had left with her. She rang the number on her mobile.

'Hello. DI Price,' Nick said.

'Hello, Mr Price. It's Caroline Paterson.' she said. 'I may be barking up the wrong tree, but I believe you are still looking for Daniel Thompson.'

'We are indeed.'

'I think I know where he is. One of our girls thinks she saw him on a narrowboat on the canal. Only 'thinks' mind you, but I thought you ought to know.'

'We do. He's been quite elusive. Which boat and whereabouts is it?'

'It's a blue boat called *Hideaway* and it's near the University residences. I hope it's not a wild goose chase.'

'I agree, but I'll get down there right away. Thank you for the tip.' He hung up and immediately rang his sergeant. Dave agreed to meet him at the canal side, near a popular pub called Telford's Warehouse. They agreed to arrive without sirens which would only alert their quarry. Surprise was the watchword.

Darkness was falling as they arrived. They walked upstream but found nothing. Downstream was more successful. *Hideaway* was thirty yards below the locks. All was quiet. No lights showed, but they didn't expect any. Daniel would have had no wish to advertise his presence on board. Silently, Nick and Dave stepped aboard. The boat rocked gently. Then Nick suddenly opened the door and both men shone their torches into the gloom. Daniel was lying on the single bed and made no effort to respond to his visitors. As Nick drew closer, he could see why.

Daniel was dead.

The long knitting needle protruding from his left eye socket had been driven up into his brain.

'I'll ring Anu,' he said as he dialled their forensic pathologist.

Dave made notes of the state of the boat and rang round the team.

Daniel's few provisions were on the kitchen surface. The owner of the boat had left it empty and moderately tidy. Bread, butter, tea bags, milk and cornflakes and a six-pack of pork pies with two missing. There was no sign of a struggle. Daniel was enclosed in his sleeping bag, zipped up to his chin, which had made it difficult, if not impossible, to fight back against his attacker, whoever that might have been. Nick touched his cheek. He was still warm.

First to arrive was Rob Davidson, a highly efficient Scene of Crime officer. He set up floodlights and a tape around an exclusion area to keep back gawpers who drifted out from the pub, then drifted back when they found there was nothing to see. A cable from a portable generator led to a floodlight inside the boat to enable Anu and her team to work on the body.

A couple of constables arrived, and Nick set them the task of visiting the neighbouring boats, a new slant on their usual door-to-door enquiries.

Nick and Dave chose to visit the pub, where they hoped to find out who owned the boat and perhaps find the owner. They enquired as to whether any suspicious activity had been noticed in the area. They drew blanks on all counts. It was a quiet area, with its car park used by students living in the accommodation block and customers of the pub.

A PCSO came up to Nick.

'Anything I can do to help?' he asked.

'You could stand out here to stop people coming across to the canal.'

'What's happened here, then? We don't see much crime in this area. Noise late at night is about the only complaint I get, but that's students for you' he said.

'We have a problem on a boat,' Nick told him, without going into details.

'And I have a problem with a car. Parked two days ago and nobody's been near it. Mercedes, so I don't think it's been abandoned. Number plate doesn't help. I checked online and it says it's a Ford Fiesta.'

Bells started ringing. Mercedes? Burke's? Daniel? Runaway? Must be worth a look.

'I might be able to help you,' Nick said to the PCSO. 'Give me a few minutes, but don't touch the car. Just keep an eye on it and make sure no-one else touches it, unless it's one of my constables.'

Filled with the importance of being what could be a crucial part of an investigation, the PCSO strutted back to the Mercedes. With his thumbs tucked into the shoulder straps of his yellow jacket, he stood guard, the look on his face daring any passer-by to even look at the car.

When Nick arrived back at the boat, he found that Bridget had answered his emergency call.

'Glad you could make it,' he said. 'I thought you had a hot date tonight.'

'Not so hot, unfortunately. Fish and chips on a bench by the river. I was glad of the excuse to leave. What can I do?'

He brought her up to date with the situation in the boat, then asked her to check with Rob to see if Daniel's car keys were on the boat. 'If so, take them round the corner to where you'll find a PCSO guarding a car. Wear some gloves and see if the keys match the car. If they do, drive it round to our compound and lock it up. I'll send a DC along to bring you back.'

Rob ticked his list to confirm that Bridget had taken the keys. She in turn set off around the corner to find the car. As she approached it, the PCSO stepped forward.

'What are you doing, miss?'

'I'm checking this car.'

'Oh no, you're not. It's part of an investigation.'

'So am I.' She showed him her warrant card.

'Pull the other one. You students can forge anything on a computer. That's a fake.'

'I'm a detective constable.'

'What, made up to the eyeballs?'

Bridget regretted coming out directly from the riverside. Blue eyeshadow, long eyelashes and glossy lipstick were not normal on duty. Luckily, Nick came around the corner.

'Problems?'

The PCSO realised his mistake. 'Sorry, miss. We get a lot of this round here. Students, you know. Let me help you with the door.'

'Don't touch it!' she almost screamed, adding to his embarrassment. 'Fingerprints,' she explained. 'I'm wearing gloves.' She found that the key fob worked with a welcoming bleep. She sat in the driver's seat, started the engine and drove away.

The PCSO's account of the encounter in the pub later was that he helped a pretty police lady to check a getaway car as part of an investigation. 'I didn't touch it, of course. Fingerprints, you know,' he said, knowledgably tapping the side of his nose to impress his mates.

Nick's first job next morning was to ring Caroline Paterson to ask her the name of the girl she said had seen Daniel.

'Janet Bagley,' she said. 'She lives in an old lengthman's cottage near the student block by the canal. She used to work here and was suspended when there was a problem with unpaid invoices. Daniel was thought to be the cause of the missing invoices and therefore of her suspension. She has hated him ever since. She even tried to drown herself in the canal.'

'So how did you find out that she had seen Daniel?'

'I've just been promoted to CEO of the company, and I wanted to ask her to rejoin us. I called to see her last evening. When I asked her to come back, her first concern was whether Daniel would be there. It was clear that if he was, then she would turn me down. It was then that she told me she thought she had seen him by the canal.'

Nick congratulated her on the promotion.

'Is that when you rang me?' Nick asked.

'Not immediately. I went round to see if it was him. I asked how he was, and he said he was OK. I asked him why he was hiding away. He said that someone from Liverpool was threatening him over something that happened when he worked there - I think he called him Macca – and he wanted to lie low for a while. I was only there for about ten minutes, and I thought it best to let you know.'

'I'm glad you did. Thank you for the information. You've been very helpful. We'll be in touch. Bye for now.'

He closed the call. She didn't know how helpful she had been, putting herself in the frame. As one of the last people to see him alive she made herself a strong suspect for his murder.

'Rob and Eamonn. Go to Bertrand's and bring Caroline Paterson in for interview. Dave, get your coat. We're going out.'

On the way, Nick explained to Dave all that had happened and that they were going to bring in Janet Bagley, a name that was new to Dave. She knew where Daniel was and she had a grudge against him. She had attempted suicide on his account. Motive – hate. Method - A knitting needle. A lady's weapon. Opportunity - they're living quite close to each other.'

'What about the other suspect, the one that Rob and Eamonn are bringing in? Same method, same opportunity,' And she is unlikely to have rung you if she was guilty.

'Yes, but no clear motive - yet.'

SIXTY TWO

Nick and Dave sat opposite a tearstained Janet Bagley in the interview room. With the recorder set and Janet's refusal of professional help on the grounds that she had done nothing wrong duly noted, Nick asked her some basic questions.

They established that she knew Daniel Thompson, not very well as he was in a different department. She did not like him because he had caused her a lot of trouble. Yes, she had attempted to take her own life, but that was because of the shame of being accused unfairly. No, she would not have wanted him dead.

She had caught a glimpse of his face one night. He was wearing a hoodie and was carrying a bag from the all-night store up the road. It was dark, when she had bumped into him on the corner of the building and saw his face in the glow from a street lamp. She would recognise those eyes anywhere after he had taunted her at the office.

Yes, she had followed him to the boat, but only to find out where he lived.

Dave tried to shake her story, but she was adamant. It was a brief glimpse, but she was sure it was him. She had not planned revenge when she found out where he lived. She felt uncomfortable, knowing he was living so close to her, but there was nothing she could do; she couldn't leave her cottage, perhaps he would move on, if he was living on a boat. They can only stay in one place for so long, she thought.

Nick asked about Caroline's visit.

'What time did Mrs Paterson call on you?'

'Six o'clock.'

'You seem certain.'

'The six o'clock news was just coming on telly.'

'And how long did she stay with you?'

'Ten minutes, quarter of an hour at the most. We chatted about the cottage. She asked me to go back to Bertrand's; she told me Daniel had escaped from the police, then she rushed off when I told her I thought he was living nearby. That seemed bit odd.'

'Odd?'

'Well, one minute we were chatting, the next minute she couldn't wait to get away.'

'Did you go out afterwards?'

'No. I looked out later when I heard a crowd outside. I think it was because the police were there, but there was nothing to see, just people walking about.'

'One last question, Miss Bagley. Do you knit?'

Janet could not suppress a giggle. It was such an incongruous question.

'No, my mother tried to teach me, but she failed, miserably. It's been a family joke ever since.'

'Thank you for talking to us. We'll be in touch if we need any more information. You are free to go now.'

Nick turned to Dave when she had left.

'I think she's in the clear, don't you?'

'Yes. She didn't seem the devious sort at all. Honest answers. No bodily give-aways. Let's see what a chat with Mrs Paterson brings.'

Caroline was brought in and sat opposite the two detectives. Nick asked if she required her solicitor to be present, but she declined on the same grounds as Janet Bagley.

'I've nothing to hide, so fire away,' she said.

Dave reset the recorder and Nick began.

'How did you discover that Daniel was living on a boat?'

'Janet told me she had seen him.'

'Why had you visited Janet that evening?'

'I had recently been appointed as CEO of Bertrand's'

(she relished repeating the title) 'and I knew that she was keen to return to her old job, so I went round to ask her to come back right away. Her suspension was over.'

'This was after work that evening?'

'Yes. CEO is a twenty-four-hour job, Mr Price, and I couldn't wait to get Janet back into the office.'

'She's obviously impressed you. Were you equally impressed with Daniel's work.'

'Yes. I could have easily seen him managing the Show Team when it eventually gets re-instated - if this hadn't happened, of course.'

'Of course. What did you do when Janet told you where Daniel was living?'

'I had to check it out. I knew that you were looking for him. It would be better if he stopped running away and owned up to whatever he had been doing. If it was anything criminal, I'd be looking for a new Show Team Leader in the future anyway.'

Dave joined in the questioning.

'You are very protective of Bertrand's reputation, aren't you, Mrs Paterson?'

'Indeed I am. I have been part of the company since its inception, when Roger Bertrand was alive. A wonderful man. Just the two of us at a little filling station. It's a pity he didn't live to see the success it became.' She took a handkerchief from her pocket and dabbed her nose.

'Are you all right, Mrs Paterson?' Nick asked as he pushed a glass of water towards her.

'Thank you. I'll be fine,' she said and took a sip.

'So from manning the pumps to CEO is a big step?'

'Indeed.'

'You must be very proud.'

'I have always been proud of our company, our cars, our staff and now myself.'

'How long did you spend with Daniel when you found him?'

'Just ten minutes. I didn't want to scare him off before you came along.'

'Very commendable. What did you say to him?'

'I wanted to keep him there, so I offered to go and do some grocery shopping for him. 'Wait there' was the last thing I said to him. Then I went to the shop.'

'Which one?'

'It was the Classic Mahal, open till midnight. When I got back I rang you from the office.'

'The office?'

'Yes. I had to find your number from your card in my desk.'

Nick thought hard about what he had learned so far. There was a something that didn't register. He would need to check.

'I think we'll take a rest there,' he said and Caroline was left alone in the interview room.

Back in the office, Nick appointed Bridget to carry out the next task. She was puzzled, but she checked her watch and left quickly. An hour later, Nick and Dave were back in the interview room with Caroline. She sat nervously. She was unsure of what Nick had in store. Why had he needed a pause? Dave switched on the recorder.

'Well, Mrs Paterson, We have a problem. Your story adds up, it seems. Let's follow the timeline. You arrived at Janet's cottage at 6pm, she told me, and you left at, say 6.15.'

'Correct,' she said.

'You would have arrived at Daniel's boat by 6.20 and you were there for ten minutes, you said, so you would have left by 6.30.'

'Correct again,' she said. feeling more confident. So far, so good.

'I have checked that it was approximately a 20 minute walk to the shop, 20 minutes to walk back, add 5 minutes for filling your basket and paying, that's 45 minutes there and back, taking us to 7.15.

'Correct.'

'Then 10 minutes in which you drove round to Bertrand's, leaves you banging on the doors because George was on his rounds at 7.30.'

'Exactly. I told you I had nothing to hide.'

'But, and it's a big but, you didn't go to the shop, did you?'

'But I did…'

'The shopkeeper doesn't remember you. He has very few customers between 6 and 7pm. We checked his CCTV and you were not on it.'

'Perhaps it was the wrong shop. I gave you the wrong name…' She was desperate, clutching at straws.

'And there is no sign of the groceries you said you bought. I think that you fabricated a story to account for the time lapse. I think that, in that period between 6.20 and 7.15, you killed Daniel as he was trapped in his sleeping bag. I am arresting you for the murder of Daniel Thompson. Anything you do say…' She hardly heard the rest of the statement. Her blood thundered in her ears. Her head swam. Where did she go wrong? Her lifetime's ambition crumbled beneath her.

She was heard to mutter, 'I was so proud…' as she was led to the cells, where she had time to contemplate her situation.

She leaned against the brick walls of her cell. Blue had been her favourite colour and here she was in a blue-painted cell. At least it was cool and the colour helped her to calm down. At least she hadn't told them how Roger Bertrand had died. It was branded on her brain.

As she saw it, the choice back then, had been between her and Millicent, who was pregnant with his child.

'Who do you love? Me or Millicent?' she had shouted as he worked under a car.

'We had our fun, Caroline, but I'm married to Millicent now. So it's her I choose.'

Famous last words. Deadly famous. The trolley jack

holding up the car suddenly clicked as if released by an unseen hand. The car dropped, killing Roger outright.

'If I can't have you, I'll have your company,' she thought.

She became a diligent worker, helping Millicent to run the company, making herself indispensable in the process. Millicent had no interest in cars or business and was content to let Caroline run things while she dealt with her new baby and lived the high life off her director's fees..

Over the years, Caroline had made many contacts in the trade, including Kieran Donovan, and between them, they had hatched a scheme whereby the value of Bertrand's would be reduced for him to make an offer. He needed to find a legitimate home for the money that was amassing from his drug dealing and this was his opportunity. He had a keen employee who had no scruples. He would be ideal for the task. Enter Daniel Thompson.

On the morning that interviews for her job were being held, she suggested to Ryan that it would be charitable if he were to give the other interviewee a conducted tour of the building. Ryan was not keen on going on to the roof, but agreed reluctantly and had a reassuring thumbs-up from Caroline as he left the office. 'You'll be fine,' was the message it conveyed, completely the opposite of the intended outcome.

But Daniel had let Kieran down through his fear of blood. He had escaped when Kieran and his gang were arrested and was now on the run.

By luck, she had found him. He had to be silenced.

She had looked around the boat. The name painted on the side showed the owner was a Delia Graham. How long it had been unoccupied was not clear. Perhaps Delia has found a warmer home for the winter and would not be returning until the spring. She had not taken her knitting with her. There was an unfinished garment on the worktop of the kitchen, alongside Daniel's meagre groceries. Caroline's eyes lit up as an idea came to her. She pulled a long needle out of Delia's handiwork.

'What are you doing? Go away and leave me alone.' Daniel was struggling to unzip his sleeping bag, still prostrate on the narrow bed like a stranded caterpillar. Caroline turned and dropped on to him, her knee grinding into his midriff, winding him.

'Lie still,' she commanded.

'What are you going to do?' he spluttered, still failing to operate the zip.

'You'll see,' was the reply, then he gasped for air as she fell on top of him, pinning him to the bed. Her left hand gripped the top of the sleeping bag under his chin, making it impossible for Daniel to unzip it. Her right hand held the long knitting needle. They lay, face to face, inches apart.

'You have let us down, Daniel.'

'Us?'

'Me and Kieran.'

'I pushed Ryan off the roof for you. I poisoned Stuart's mother. I planned the hi-jack. What more could I do?'

'You could have helped Kieran instead of being a wimp.'

'I can't stand the sight of blood. It's not my fault.'

'I cannot allow you to run around loose,' she said.

He was screaming in fear as he saw the needle moving towards his face. Caroline lodged the tip into his eye socket, then pushed, hard. Twelve inches of steel crashed its way through bone and tissue and brain. Daniel's body felt as though it had been connected to the mains electricity. Shocks ran here and there as the needle was pushed upwards. His arms and legs thrashed as best they could, within the confines of the sleeping bag, then stopped. Permanently.

A trickle of blood ran down his cheek and Caroline straightened her skirt and jacket before she left as quietly as she had arrived.

She looked at her watch and cooked up a story to

cover the time it had taken. She would need to be convincing when she spoke to the police.

Unfortunately, her alibi turned out to be unconfirmed. How silly to have made up a story that could be so easily disproved, It was the end of a life filled with lies.

SIXTY THREE

Saturday morning, and Nick and Helen were at Pollard's. Their early arrival had given them time, when all the preparations of the horses were done, to enjoy a coffee in the restaurant. There had been some silences as they drove to the venue, silences which were only broken by talk about horses and the competitions ahead. Seated at the table, both fiddled with the spoons, trying to decide who would break the silence.

Nick reached across the table and took Helen's hand.
'I think you were very brave...'
She halted him in mid-sentence.
'We went through it together You were my knight in shining armour.'
'I wouldn't say that. We both reacted to the situation. But that's not what bothers me. It's not every copper's wife who gets kidnapped. I'm so afraid that the experience will make you decide not to become one. I know there's pressure from your mother.'
'How?'
'I see the way she looks at me. The things she says. I know it's not because she dislikes me. She dislikes my job and the possible threat to you. She's your mother. She loves you. She's bound to worry. It's what mums do. And I can't promise that it can't happen again.'
'No. But we can worry about it if it does. And if it does, we'll deal with it – together. The copper and his wife. And if that was the most cock-eyed proposal of marriage, the answer's 'Yes' while I still have a ring finger!'
They laughed, kissed and walked out into the sunshine.
'Hello, Mr Price.'

'Hello, Annabelle'

'How are things with you?'

'Absolutely perfect, Annabelle. How about you?'

'I'm ok, thanks.'

'How's Tom?'

'He's much better, now that his friend Macca has been arrested. It's helping to keep him off the tablets now the supply has dried up.'

'Macca's been arrested? How did you know?'

'It was in the Daily Post the other day. They printed the names of that gang that were arrested. Josh McArdle was amongst them.'

'And he was Macca? That's good.' He decided to change the subject. 'Are you riding today?'

'Yes, Just one class.'

'Well, good luck, then. See you later.'

They walked on to their horse-box. Helen changed into her riding kit and went to walk the course when a familiar face appeared.

'Hi Nick.'

'Hello again, Malcolm. This is becoming a habit.'

'It's the last time, I'm afraid.'

'How come?'

'What's the saying? My work here is done.'

'And what work was that?'

'This and that. Looking after the good guys. Taking out the bad ones.'

'Just like me, then.'

They said their farewells and shook hands. Malcolm turned to leave.

'It takes one to know one,' he said as he walked away.

Nick's eyes followed him as his statement formed a meaning in Nick's head. Of course! It now made sense.

* * *

ABOUT THE AUTHOR

Hilton Jones has had a varied experience of life, having worked as a tax-man and a teacher before running an award-winning canal boat firm. His leisure activity was amateur dramatics with an interest in various equestrian sports. His pen has rarely been idle; plays, sketches, pantomimes and novels have flowed over the years or, in recent years, appeared on his monitor screen.

Printed in Dunstable, United Kingdom